Who Blowed Up the Church House?

AND OTHER OZARK FOLK TALES

AND OTHER Ozark Folk Tales

ILLUSTRATIONS BY GLEN ROUNDS

Who Blowed Up the Church House?

COLLECTED BY Vance Randolph

WITH NOTES BY HERBERT HALPERT

GREENWOOD PRESS, PUBLISHERS
WESTPORT, CONNECTICUT

0825631

Library of Congress Cataloging in Publication Data

Randolph, Vance, 1892–   ed.
    Who   blowed up the church house?

    Reprint of the ed. published by Columbia University
Press, New York.
    Bibliography: p.
    1. Tales, American—Ozark Mountains.
I. Title.
[GR110.M77R3 1975]   398.2'09767'1   75-31424
ISBN 0-8371-8497-5

Originally published in 1952 by Columbia University Press,
New York

Reprinted with the permission of Columbia University Press

Reprinted in 1975 by Greenwood Press,
a division of Williamhouse-Regency Inc.

Library of Congress Catalog Card Number 75-31424

ISBN 0-8371-8497-5

Printed in the United States of America

TO JEAN LIGHTFOOT KAPPELL

PREFACE

PARTS of this collection were published in *Hoosier Folklore*, the *Southern Folklore Quarterly*, and *Western Folklore*. A few items are reprinted from my books *The Ozarks* and *Ozark Mountain Folks*, issued by the Vanguard Press in 1931 and 1932, long out of print. Others appeared in two pamphlets, *Funny Stories from Arkansas* and *Funny Stories about Hillbillies*, published by E. Haldeman-Julius in 1943 and 1944. I thank the owners of these copyrights for permission to use the material here.

V.R.

Eureka Springs, Ark.
June, 1952

CONTENTS

CHANGE comes slowly in the Ozarks, and the hill folk are still close to the pioneer way of life. When I first visited this region, in 1899, there were no highways, no automobiles, no juke-boxes, no movies. People spent their evenings at home, without any radio. They did not read much, but entertained themselves and their children with songs, riddles, games, and stories. These were part of an oral tradition, handed down from one generation to the next, passed from one isolated hilltop to another. The early settlers had little of our modern enthusiasm for novelty. They did not feel, as we do, that a new song or a new story is better than an old one.

The telling of tales was a social accomplishment, not a profession. Fiddlers who played the country dances were generally paid, but nobody made any money out of storytelling. Farmers swapped stories in their own homes and at small neighborhood gatherings. The finest yarns were spun by the flicker of log fires and seem less effective in lighted rooms. The men and women who told me these stories did not read them in any book. Many of the items here presented are not considered fit for children's ears today, but they were common household stories fifty years ago, and most rural youngsters heard them. These people are old now, but they have not forgotten. The tales are still told occasionally, when old-timers get together.

As I have pointed out elsewhere,[1] the Ozark country is full of men who delight in telling whoppers to our summer visitors. So long as tourists are ignorant and credulous, tall tales will be abundant. But the stories in this book are not regarded as

[1] *We Always Lie to Strangers,* 1951, p. 271.

tall tales, and the casual tourist never hears them. They belong to an older generation, people whom I knew only in their latter years. I lived in the Ozarks for a long time, and gathered hundreds of stories. It is much easier to collect these items than certain other types of folk material, such as family ballads and superstitions. When my elderly neighbors learned that I was interested in old tales they talked freely, although some of them were a little disturbed by the mechanical difficulties of recording. At one period I had an assistant who took down every word in shorthand. Sometimes I used a phonographic recorder and transcribed the story from the play-back. More often I made notes in pencil as the storyteller spoke, and typed the material a few hours later, while the details were still fresh. Whatever the method, my purpose was to record each tale as it was told to me. The stories were not rewritten in the Grimm tradition. I did not combine different versions, or use material from more than one informant in the same story, or try to improve the storyteller's style. I just set down the tales as accurately as I could, and let it go at that.

In preparing the manuscript for publication I added titles, changed a few proper names, and sometimes revised sentence structure in the interest of clarity. I tried to keep the Ozark idiom intact, but made little effort to reproduce the peculiarities of pronunciation. Many of my neighbors say "skeer" for scare, "sass" for sauce, "bile" for boil, and so forth. They make "yonder" rhyme with gander, and pronounce "onion" so that it sounds like "ing-urn." Most old hunters use a very long *a* in panther, and a *t* sound instead of *th,* but I do not believe anything is gained by spelling it "painter" as the local-color novelists do.

Even educated hill folk, under the spell of an old story, often revert to the dialect of their childhood. Senator Lon Kelley of Pineville, Mo., in ordinary conversation, used better English than most college professors. But in telling me how "Jay Caught the Devil" he shifted smoothly into the old-time pitch and cadence, said *throwed* instead of threw, and scattered double negatives all over the place. Lon Kelley was not acting, or consciously imitating anybody. He was speaking his native language, repeating the tale as he heard it from his elders long ago.

In a few cases it seemed best to translate dialect terms. One storyteller told me that a character was "kind of *durgen*." The word durgen is common in the Ozark backwoods, but readers elsewere wouldn't understand it, so I wrote "kind of old-fashioned" instead. For the same reason I changed *chinch* to bedbug, *grub hyson* to sassafras tea, *ramp* to garlic, *mommix* to mess, *stinging-lizard* to scorpion, *tomfuller* to hominy, and *woodscolt* to bastard. Some old hillmen say *skeleton* when they mean skull, and *crane* when they mean heron, and I took it upon myself to correct these errors.

When an informant became too profane, I used the blue pencil freely. Cusswords are easily disregarded in conversation, but they grow monotonous in print, and clutter up the page to no useful purpose. I once persuaded an aged hillman to spin a yarn into my recorder, and played the record back without noticing any excessive profanity. But that night, when the typist got it transcribed, we found that *God damn* appeared twenty-seven times in a 900-word script. I left four attributive *goddams* in the text to preserve the flavor of the old gentleman's speech, and deleted the other twenty-three.

Some of our finest Ozark anecdotes deal with sex in terms which offend squeamish readers. My feeling is that these forthright tales cannot be cleaned up without spoiling them, so I omitted many such stories from this book. In one case, however, I tried my hand at expurgation. The man who told me about "Hogeye and the Blacksnake" used a four-letter verb meaning copulate. Believing that this word could be eliminated without weakening the narrative, I cut it out. Probably I did wrong, but that's what happened.

Many thoughtful hill folk believe that the best stories are told by illiterates. They feel that "something goes out of a man" when he learns to read and write, just as a good fiddler is ruined if he learns to play by note. "In a place where the art of storytelling has still survived," says Charlie May Simon,[1] "the art of letter writing has never begun." Of the fifty-six men and women who told me these tales, only twelve admitted that they could not read, but forty-three said that the stories derived from illiterate old settlers. This may well be true, because book-learning is not important in a frontier culture, and our pioneers had very little of it. Jesse L. Russell, who has lived in Carroll county, Arkansas, for eighty-one years, declares that "ninety per cent of the people here during the 1870's would be classed as wholly illiterate. To be able to sign one's name was quite an accomplishment. Practically all the veterans of the Civil War signed their pension vouchers by mark."[2] Even today, a surprising number of mature, intelligent citizens are unable to read or write.

A small-town schoolteacher, graduate of a denominational college, tells me that she heard dozens of these stories as a child. "They aren't really folktales," she says, "but just vulgar old jokes." Well, I admit that few of them are comparable to the carefully selected fairy stories she read in the college library. Many of the items in this book are scraps of local tradition and humorous anecdote, the sort of thing that German folklorists call *Sagen und Schwänke*. These are the tales that my informants liked best, and I string along with the old-timers.

It was a lot of fun, gathering this material. The people who

[1] *Straw in the Sun*, 1945, p. 219.
[2] *Behind These Ozark Hills*, 1947, p. 61.

told me these tales were all personal friends. Some of them have grown dim with the years, but I remember Weed Marshall, innkeeper and Confederate veteran, just as vividly as ever. And I shall never forget Ed Wall, the trapper who said seriously that "a half-growed otter has got more sense than any man in Pineville." Nor Farwell Gould, who told me that he rode into battle at Pea Ridge with a jug in his hand, because "there wasn't no safe place to set it down." Lon Jordon swapped stories and played for dances, all over Arkansas, but he dropped everything to help me record fiddle tunes for the Library of Congress. And there was John Turner White, shocked by the smell of dead Yankees at Wilson's Creek, who became a Justice of the Missouri Supreme Court. It is pleasant to recall Ethel Barnes, and how she introduced me to the talent around Hot Springs. There are sportsmen in many states who remember Hawk Gentry, shot to death by a peddler near Galena, Missouri. Nobody could forget such storytellers as Lew Beardon, and Mary Burke, and Elbert Short, and Elizabeth Maddocks, and Frank Payne, and Marie Wilbur, and Rose Spaulding, and Pete Woolsey.

Many of these people are dead now, but I remember them all, and several others who must be nameless here. They were real men and women. I wish that the readers of this book could have known them.

V.R.

Eureka Springs, Ark.
May 15, 1952

Who Blowed Up the Church House?

AND OTHER OZARK FOLK TALES

WHO BLOWED UP
THE CHURCH HOUSE?

ONE TIME there was an old bachelor named Longstreet and he did not do no work, because he drawed a big pension every month. After while he got so fat he wouldn't even chop his own kindling, and he hired some fellow to haul wood into

3

town and rick it up right by the back door. The old man kept a fishpole in the house, and it was just eight feet long, with a notch cut in the middle. He used to bring out the fishpole and measure the wood careful, and if the woodpile was eight foot long and four foot high, he would give the fellow seventy-five cents. But if it measured even one inch short, old man Longstreet says it ain't a full rick, and he would not pay nothing till the fellow put on some more wood.

The fellows that cut wood and sold it did not like old man Longstreet much. He did not get along very good with his neighbors, neither. Every time a little cold spell come along, old man Longstreet would be up town grumbling how somebody was stealing his wood in the night. "There's folks in this town that ain't got no woodpile at all," says he, "but there's smoke coming out of their chimney just the same, and you can smell meat a-frying." Finally he put up KEEP OUT signs in his back yard, and he says he is going to shoot anybody that come around there of a night. The sheriff told him he better get a big dog to watch the woodpile. But old man Longstreet says it would cost too much to feed the critter, and the goddam neighbors is mean enough to poison a dog anyhow.

The Baptist church set right across the lane from old man Longstreet's place, and one Sunday they had got a new preacher down from Springfield. It was pretty cold, and the preacher wanted to build a little fire to take the chill off the pews. Old man Longstreet was not home, as he had went fishing somewheres, so the new preacher went into the back yard and got an armload of wood. He says surely nobody will begrudge a few little sticks for the worship of God, but he didn't know old man Longstreet. The preacher got the fire going good, and then he walked out to the door of the church, a-thinking about his sermon.

All of a sudden the stove blowed up KER-WHAM! It knocked

4

the pulpit down, and broke most of the windows, and scattered live coals all over the church house. The whole place was full of smoke, and the preacher was hollering like a scalded bird dog. He wasn't hurt none, but he was scared witless. Some folks come along and pumped water, and carried it round in their hats, or else the church house would have burnt plumb down. And if that stove had blowed up after the meeting got started, it might have killed half the Baptists in the settlement.

The folks thought old man Longstreet had fixed a stick of wood with powder to blast out the scoundrels he claimed was stealing his wood in the night. But the old man swore he never done it, and he figured the neighbors must have loaded up a stick and put it in the woodpile to murder him, as they are a low-down thieving lot and he would not put anything past them. The neighbors says they never done no such a thing, and who would want to kill a crazy old fool like that, which he has got one foot in the grave already? One fellow says old man Longstreet is always having trouble with the woodcutters because he claims they don't give him a full rick for his money, and maybe the woodcutters put the powder in to get even with old man Longstreet. The fellows that hauled the wood says it is a outrageous lie, and people better be goddam careful who they are accusing of things like that. And one woodcutter says everybody would like to get rid of old man Longstreet and the neighbors too, but he can't afford to buy powder so long as them tightwads only pay seventy-five cents a rick. "If they will give me a dollar and a quarter," says he, "I'll put free dynamite in every woodpile, and them damn fools can blow each other up all over town for all I care."

We never did find out which one done it, or who they was trying to blow up. Some says one thing, and some says another. There was a piece in the Durgenville paper about how the folks down our way is against religion, but the home folks all knowed

5

better. There ain't nobody in this county would blow up a church house on purpose, and run the risk of killing a lot of good Christian people. It was just one of these here unfortunate accidents, and you can't make nothing else out of it.

SHE ALWAYS ANSWERED NO

ONE TIME there was a pretty girl with red hair, and she kept house for her daddy because her mother had run off with a peddler. And there was a boy named Jack that wanted to go with her, but the old man told her to say "No" every time a boy asked her a question. So when Jack says, "Can I come to see you Sunday night?" the pretty girl answered "No." And when he says, "Will you go buggy riding with me?" she says "No." So then he says, "Well, do you want to get married?" but the pretty girl says "No" again. Jack seen he was not getting nowheres, but he didn't know what to do about it.

Jack thought about this awhile, and then he went to see old Gram French and give her two boxes of snuff. Gram listened while Jack told all about his troubles, and then she says, "Well, you better go marry one of them girls at Gizzard Springs, and let the redhead go." But Jack says to hell with Gizzard Springs, and if he can't get the pretty girl with the red hair he don't want no woman at all. And then he begun to talk like he is going to hang himself in the barn, or else maybe he will run off and join the army. Gram just set there until Jack quietened down, and then she told him to go and ask the redhead three questions. She made him say the questions over till he learned all three of them by heart, to make sure there wouldn't be no mistake.

When Jack got to the house he seen the old man was not

at home, and the pretty girl was out in the barn looking for eggs. So he says, "Do you want to live single all your life?" and the pretty girl with the red hair says "No." Then Jack spoke up again and he says, "Do you want to marry anybody else except me?" The pretty girl looked kind of funny when she heard this one, but finally she says "No." When it come to the third question, Jack took a big breath and then he whispered in the pretty girl's ear. She jumped like she was shot, and hollered "No!" at the top of her voice. Then she looked at Jack, and they both busted out laughing. So Jack just grabbed the pretty girl with the red hair and throwed her right down in the hay. They was as good as married right then and there.

When the girl's daddy come home, she told him all about what happened and how she answered "No" every time, but Jack had got the best of her just the same. The old man grumbled considerable, but after while he says, "Well, if a boy is smart enough to figure out them three questions, he ought to make a fair-to-middling husband anyhow." And so Jack and the pretty girl with the red hair went to town and got married, and they lived happy ever after.

SLOW TRAIN THROUGH ARKANSAS

ONE TIME there was a fellow named Jackson that lived over in Missouri somewhere. He was knowed as Three-Finger Jackson, because one of his hands got crippled up when he used to be a brakeman on the railroad. This fellow Jackson was always cracking funny jokes, and the folks all said he ought to go on the stage or something, because they didn't have no radio in them days. Jackson couldn't hardly write his own name, but he married a girl that was plenty smart, and she wrote down a lot of jokes just like he told 'em. After while they got this stuff printed in a little yellow book, and the name on the cover was *A Slow Train through Arkansaw*, by Thos. W. Jackson.

It was all about how the trains in Arkansas was no good, or the roadbed neither, and the passengers have to get out and push when they come to a steep grade. One time the cars run mighty smooth for a while, so everybody knowed they had run off the track. The train whistled at every house, and if it was a double house they had to whistle twice. When the train stopped away out in the woods a drummer says "Conductor, what is the matter now?" and the trainman answered "There is some cows on the track." So after while the train stopped at another place, and the fellow says "Well, we must have caught up with them cattle again." And then they took the cowcatcher off the engine and put it on the hind end, to keep bulls from jumping on the caboose. A woman kept hollering how the cars was slower than cold sorghum, so the brakeman says "Well, why don't you get off and walk?" The woman says she would, only her folks was not expecting her till the train got there. And one of the passengers wanted to commit suicide, so he run half a mile ahead and laid down on the track, but the train was so slow he couldn't wait, as he had to get up and find something to eat. Also there was a man with whiskers three foot long a-riding on a half fare ticket, because he was a little boy when he got on the train. The whole book was full of stories like that, and some of 'em worse yet.

The folks that live in Arkansas didn't have no use for such foolishness, but people up in Missouri thought it was very funny, and so did the damn fools in Oklahoma. And them windbags down in Texas just laughed theirself sick. The goddam

8

book only cost a quarter, and the first thing we knowed it was selling like hotcakes all over the country. The Yankees went plumb hog wild about it, and all the way from New York to California everybody was laughing about the slow train through Arkansas. The truth is that the railroad in Arkansas wasn't no different from anywhere else, but them people didn't care nothing about the truth. They would rather believe the jokes in that book Three-Finger Jackson wrote.

Finally it got so bad that our citizens couldn't go out of the state hardly, because if a man says he is from Arkansas the people would laugh right in his face. And then they ask him how does it happen he ain't barefooted, and does he wear his cow-catcher on behind? So pretty soon they would get to fighting, and the foreigners mostly ganged up and put the Arkansawyer in jail. And sometimes a Yankee come down here and started shooting off his mouth about slow trains, so naturally the home folks would run him out of town, and lucky they didn't ride him on a rail besides. If Three-Finger Jackson ever showed up in Arkansas he would have got killed, just as sure as God made little apples.

You wouldn't hardly believe that folks would stay mad for fifty years over a two-bit joke book, but that's what they done, right here in Arkansas. Even now an outsider better be careful how he mentions slow trains, but it's all right for us Arkansawyers to joke about it. Just the other day there was a piece in the Little Rock paper about how the Governor of Texas says his state is so big you can get on a train and travel two days and nights, but when you wake up you're still in Texas. The Governor of Arkansas just grinned at him. "Yeah," he says, "we've got trains like that in Arkansas, too." Everybody laughed, and it was all took good natured.

It just goes to show that people has come a long way since Three-Finger Jackson's time. A few years back, no gentleman in his right mind would have made such a crack as that, let alone the Governor of Arkansas.

THE COOKSTOVE AND
THE CIRCUS

ONE TIME there was a family lived away back in the hills, and they bought a fine new cookstove. Stoves was kind of new then in that neighborhood. Most folks had pots and kettles and Dutch ovens fixed so they could cook their victuals right in the chimney. Cookstoves was mighty handy, and didn't burn so much wood. But wood was free for the cutting in them days, and a stove cost a lot of money. Some of the old-timers figured cookstoves was dangerous, because they give off gas and was liable to explode. Folks used to tell a story about a preacher's wife that put her cornbread in the firebox and then built a big fire in the oven. And lots of people thought that victuals cooked on a stove didn't taste very good, anyhow. One old man got sick, and when the doctor wanted to know how was his appetite, he says "I ain't et much since we got the stove."

Well, anyhow, this family bought the cookstove, and they liked it fine. Folks from away up the creek come down to see how the contraption worked and taste the victuals that was cooked on it. They used the stove all winter, and was mighty proud to have it. But along in the spring the word got around that a circus was coming to town. The folks seen them big colored posters, with elephants and lions and trapeze performers on them. Everybody was crazy to go, but it cost a lot for a big family to get in, and cash money was mighty scarce.

When circus day finally rolled around, the whole family

10

was in town before daylight. It took two wagons to fetch them, because there was so many kids. They brought the cookstove too, with three joints of pipe, all polished up like new. The old man says as soon as he sells the stove, he'll have money enough to buy tickets all round and ride on the circle-swing besides, with red lemonade for everybody. One of the older merchants, a friend of the family from away back, spoke up and says, "Don't you think it's kind of foolish to sell your stove just for one day's entertainment?" The old man looked at him, kind of surprised. "Why, no, I reckon not," he says. "Circuses is educational, and I wouldn't want none of my children to miss it. As for the stove, hell's bells! We can cook in the fireplace!"

THE DEPUTY'S WIFE

ONE TIME there was a patch farmer, and he got to be a deputy sheriff. Sometimes he would have to be away from home two or three days. He thought maybe his wife was trifling on him, so he used to sneak back at night and hide in the orchard. He never did catch nobody, but he still figured maybe she was trifling on him.

He thought about it a long time, and finally he fixed up a way to find out for sure. He got a crock of cream out of the springhouse and set it under the bed. Then he took a big turnip and tied it on a string. He fastened the string to the springs, just long enough so the turnip would not touch the cream if one person was laying in the bed. But if two people got in the bed, the springs would sag enough to let the turnip down into the cream. Then he told his wife that he would be gone until noon the next day, and rode off down the trail. He figured that if a man come to see his wife in the night there would be cream on the turnip, and he would have her dead to rights.

When he got to town the sheriff told him to go and arrest a fellow way down in the south end of the county, and off the road at that. So he did have to be away all night sure enough, and part of the next day too. And that night the sheriff sneaked out to the deputy's house. The sheriff was a big stout man, and he weighed pretty near two hundred pounds. He put his gun under the bed, and when he went to get it in the morning he seen the turnip and the crock of cream. "What's this contraption under your bed?" says he.

The woman she looked under the bed and seen how things was. "I told you my husband was a smart fellow," she says. "He must have set this here trap to catch me." And then she jumped on the bed by herself, and the turnip did not touch the cream. But when her and the sheriff both got on the bed, the springs sagged down till the turnip was pretty near out of sight. "It's lucky you seen that thing," she says to the sheriff. So then she took a towel and wiped the turnip dry. "That would-be Edison won't find no cream on his plumb-bob," she says, "and I'll give him hell for even suspicioning such a thing." And then they laughed some more, and the sheriff he sneaked out the back way, same as he always done.

Well, when the deputy come home it was about two o'clock, and he was pretty tired, because he had been up all night. The first thing he done was to yank the covers off the bed, so he could look at the turnip. The woman follered him into the bedroom. "For goodness sake," she says, "what are you up to now?" The deputy give her a sour look. "I invented this here machine," says he, "to find out who's been sleeping in our bed while I was gone." The woman laughed mighty scornful. "There wasn't nobody in that bed but me," says she. The deputy shook his head. "You don't weigh no three hundred pounds all by yourself," he says, "and you couldn't flounce around enough to register on this here invention." The woman come up close, so as to take a good look. "Register, my foot!" she says. "I don't see no cream on the turnip."

The deputy went out in the yard, and cut him a good stout hickory. "No, you don't see no cream on the turnip," says he. "But how come two pounds of butter in that there crock?"

THE CHAMPION

ONCE UPON A TIME there was a fellow who was always telling big stories. Folks used to say he was the champion liar of the whole country. But them tales of his wasn't really lies, and everybody knowed it. They was just windy stories, and folks used to come for miles around to hear him tell 'em, when he got to going good.

One day a bunch of the boys was setting in front of the store at the crossroads, when this here windy fellow come riding up on a mule. "Howdy, Emmett," says the postmaster. "Light down, and tell us one of them big lies of your'n." But the fellow didn't stop only a minute, and he looked mighty serious. "No time for foolishness today, boys," says he. "Old man Slinkard has fell off'n the barn, and it looks like his back's broke. I'm a-going after Doc Holton."

After Emmett went down the road toward town the boys just set there and looked at one another. They all knowed old man Slinkard, and most of them was kin to him. Pretty soon they all got on their horses and rode over to the Slinkard place, to see if they could do anything to help out. It was pretty near four miles, through some mighty rough country. They was all hot and sweaty and tired before they come in sight of the house. And the first thing they seen, when they finally got there, was old man Slinkard out a-hoeing his corn.

"Well, I'll be damned!" says the postmaster. "He never fell off'n the barn at all! That goddam Emmett lied to us!" The other boys was all pretty sore too, but they couldn't pass up a chance to pour it on the postmaster. "I don't see where you got any kick a-coming," says one fellow. "Didn't you ask him to tell us one of them big lies?" The postmaster he says yes, but he didn't figure on riding no four miles in this heat just for some fool idea of a joke. "Well, I don't see how you can blame poor Emmett," the fellow says, "because he done just what you told him." And then they all laughed like fools, and that's all there is to the story.

SNAKE IN THE BED

ONE TIME there was a fellow that had the name of drinking too much popskull, and one morning his wife sent for the doctor. The boy that rode in says the fellow had went plumb crazy, and kept hollering that there was snakes on him. When the doctor got there the fellow was yelling loud as he could, and it took three big men to hold him in the bed. Soon as he seen the doctor he says, "For God's sake, Doc, make these damn fools turn me loose! There's a big snake wroppin' round my legs!"

The doctor figured on giving the crazy man some morphine to quieten him down, so he got out his syringe and told the woman to fetch some hot water. And he says to the fellow, "You just take it easy now, because everything is going to be all right." The fellow kept on fighting worse than ever, and it was all them three men could do to hold him. "You listen to me," says the doctor, "I am going to take all the covers off this bed, so you can see there ain't no snake on your legs." Then he pulled the quilts off one at a time, till he come to the blanket that was right next to the fellow's hide. "Hold his head up, boys, so he can see there ain't no snake," says the doctor, and then he pulled off the blanket. And there laid a blacksnake, six foot long if it was a inch!

When Doc seen that snake he just throwed himself backwards, plumb to the other side of the house. And when them three big men seen it, they dropped the fellow like a hot potater, and took out. And no sooner did the crazy man get loose, till he was off like a turpentined cat, and never stopped till he got to the barn. There was a jug hid in the hay, and he took three or four big snorts right quick. He set down and rested awhile, and then he went back to the house. The three big men was gone, but the doctor was still there, and the old woman was a-fanning herself with a turkey wing. The fellow walked right in and picked up his pants and put them on. And then he put on his shoes, and then he stuffed the tail of his shirt inside the pants. "I've had kind of a hard day," says he, "and I need a little something to steady my nerves," and so he took another big drink. Then he handed the jug to the doctor, and Doc took a pretty good snort himself.

After while Doc he laughed a little, and put the syringe back in the little tin box. "The folks told me you was plumb out of your head," says he, "and I thought so too, the way you was carrying on." The fellow just grinned, and looked sideways at the old woman. "I maybe got a little drunk," he says, "but I ain't no more crazy than anybody else," and so he took another drink. "I bet you'd holler and kick too, if three men was holding you down in bed, and there was a big snake wroppin' round your legs." And the doctor he says "Yes, I reckon I would."

15

THE STRANGER AND
THE BEANS

ONE TIME a fellow was a-traveling, and he stopped at a log house to stay all night. There was a man and a woman in the cabin, but they didn't have no children. They set down to supper, and the main dish was green beans seasoned with sowbelly. It was mighty good, too, but the man and the woman was both light eaters. The stranger only got about half as much as he wanted, because he was minding his manners and didn't want to look like he was greedy. When supper was over there was a lot of beans left, and the woman put the platter in her kitchen safe. The doors of the safe was made of tin with nail-holes punched in it. The stranger could smell them beans, and he got mighty hungry.

The folks only had one bed, so the stranger layed down on one side, and the woman on the other. The man, he slept in the middle of the bed, of course. Away in the night, there come a hell of a racket out by the barn somewheres. "It's them damn chicken thieves again," says the man. He jumped up and grabbed the shotgun, and then he made a run for the chicken house, without even stopping to put on his shoes. Soon as he was gone the woman nudged the traveler and whispered, "Stranger, now's your chance!" So the fellow got up, opened the kitchen safe, and et the rest of them green beans.

FILL, BOWL, FILL!

ONE TIME there was a king, and he had a daughter. The hired man's name was Jimmy, and he got to sparking the king's daughter, till the king seen he would have to do something about it. They had a pet rabbit that always come to the king's house at night, so he says if Jimmy kept the rabbit for a week he could marry the king's daughter. Jimmy took the rabbit over to where he lived, and trained it so it would come when he rung a bell.

The king told his pretty servant girl if she would fetch the rabbit he'd give her five pounds, as money went by the pound in them days. Jimmy got the best of her, and she give him half the money besides. She picked up the rabbit and started off, but Jimmy rung the bell and the rabbit broke loose and come

17

back. So she went home and told the king she couldn't get the rabbit.

Well, the king told his daughter if she would fetch the rabbit he'd give her two hundred pounds. The king's daughter went over and says to Jimmy, "We are going to get married anyhow, and two hundred pounds would be nice for us to have." Jimmy got the best of her too, and she give him half the money besides. She picked up the rabbit and started off, but Jimmy rung the bell and the rabbit broke loose and come back. So she went home and told the king she couldn't get the rabbit.

Next the king told his wife if she would fetch the rabbit he'd give her three hundred pounds. The king's wife done her damnedest, but Jimmy got the best of her too, and she give him half the money besides. She picked up the rabbit and started off, but Jimmy rung the bell and the rabbit broke loose and come back. So she went home and told the king she couldn't get the rabbit.

Late in the night, here come the king himself and says he would give five hundred pounds for the rabbit, but Jimmy got the best of him too, and the king give him half the money besides. Then he picked up the rabbit, and he told Jimmy to come along. When they got to the king's house there was a great big bowl setting in the middle of the floor. The king says, "Jimmy, are you a good singer?" and Jimmy allowed he was pretty good. "Well, if you can sing that bowl full, you can marry my daughter," says the king, "and if you don't sing it full, I am going to cut your head off." So Jimmy done the best he could, and this is what he sung:

> The first come over was the king's own servant,
> To steal away my skill,
> I took and got the best of her,
> Fill, bowl, fill!

The next come over was the king's own daughter,
To steal away my skill,
I took and got the best of her,
Fill, bowl, fill!

The next come over was the king's own wife,
To steal away my skill,
I took and got the best of her,
Fill, bowl, fill!

The last come over was the king himself,
To steal away my skill,
I took and————

"Hold on, Jimmy," says the king, "that's enough! Don't sing another word! The bowl's plumb full, and you can have my daughter!"

HOW KATE GOT A HUSBAND

ONE TIME there was a fellow going with a girl named Kate, and he promised to marry her before the baby was borned. But then one day he seen a rich girl in town, so then he thought maybe it would be better to marry the rich girl. When Kate heard about this she dressed up in a cowhide with the hairy side out, and a black mask over her head, and two gravels under her tongue. When the fellow come down the lane Kate riz up out of the brush, and groaned. The fellow was scared something terrible. She says she is Old Scratch redhot from home, come to carry him off to Hell because he has broke his promise to marry Kate. He got down on his knees and begun to beg and blubber how he will marry Kate before the moon changes if they will give him another chance.

So next morning he come to Kate's house hollering for Christ's sake hurry up, we must go to town and get married. So that is what they done, and Kate never did tell how she fooled him until after the baby come. The fellow says he knowed it was Kate all the time, and the rich girl says good riddance and it serves the damn fool right. And Kate says maybe she can't be tablecloth, but she sure don't aim to be dishrag. So they lived happy ever after, just like other married folks.

THE HERON AND THE EEL

ONE TIME there was a big old heron standing in shallow water, trying to catch a fish for his dinner. He didn't see no regular fish, but there was a little eel come swimming along. So pretty soon the heron grabbed the little eel and swallowed him quick as a wink. The trouble with a heron is, he's only got one gut and it runs straight through. In less than a minute the old heron heard a splash in the water behind him. He looked around, and there was the little eel swimming along just like he done before.

20

"There's another one!" says the old heron, and he grabbed the little eel and swallowed him quick as a wink. In less than a minute the old heron heard a splash in the water behind him. So he looked around, and there was the little eel swimming along just like he done before. "Well, by God!" says the old heron, "the creek's full of 'em!" and he grabbed the little eel and swallowed him quick as a wink. In less than a minute the old heron heard a splash in the water behind him. So he looked around, and there was the little eel swimming along just like he done before. The same thing happened twice more, and it seemed like the little eel knowed every inch of the trail by this time. All he had to do was follow his nose, and it was surprising how quick he could run through that old heron and splash out in the water again.

The old heron finally figured out that he had been a-swallowing the same little eel every time, but he never let on. He just backed up to a old stob of dead sycamore that was sticking out of the riffle. He braced himself right good, so his hind end was jammed tight against the stob. "Now, you little varmint," says the old heron, "I've got the deadwood on you!" And with that he grabbed the little eel and swallowed him quick as a wink. And this time he didn't hear no splash in the water behind him, because the little eel could not get out no-how. So the old heron he just stood there with his tail up against the sycamore stob till the little eel was plumb digested, and that's the end of the story.

But ever since that day, when one fellow has got another one over a barrel, he says "I've got the deadwood on you," just like the old heron says to the little eel when he backed up against the sycamore stob.

THE DUMB SUPPER

ONE TIME the old folks went to town and left three girls alone in the house, and the girls set a dumb supper to see who they was going to marry. To set a dumb supper you got to do everything backwards and not make no noise. So the girls never said a word while they baked three little pones of bread, and set three plates on the table, and drawed up three chairs. Still walking backwards, they opened the door and both windows, and then all three of them set down to wait for the change of the hour.

It was a plumb dark night, and the wind was a-rising. Just at midnight a regular gale tore through the house and blowed out the light. A minute later there come a flash of lightning, and the girls all seen a tall man standing by the table. The least girl she hollered "Oh my God!" and of course that broke the spell. They got the door and windows shut, and lit the lamp, but the stranger was gone.

The girls was all talking at once now, but nobody could tell much about the stranger except that he was tall, with a long coat, and he wore cowboy boots outside his pants. All of a sudden the oldest girl pointed to her place at the table. The plate was still there with the little pone on it, and the fork and spoon was there, but the knife was gone. There couldn't be no mistake about that knife, because it wasn't a common case-knife like the others. It was a sharp steel knife that Pappy had the blacksmith make out of a file, with a fine deerhorn handle riveted on.

The old man missed his knife next morning, so the girls had to tell about the dumb supper. Pappy just grumbled about the knife, but the old woman give the girls hell. She says dumb suppers ain't Christian, and no better than prayers to the Devil. She says all conjuring is wicked and terrible dangerous besides, and she made the girls promise they would never do nothing like that again.

By and by the oldest girl she married a man who was on the public works and made pretty good money, so they moved into town. Then she got to working in a boardinghouse and going to dances of a night. The next thing anybody knowed, she left her husband and run off with a fellow from the Indian Territory. He was a big tall fellow, and he wore cowboy boots outside his pants. Finally him and her got to fighting in a hotel somewheres, and the hotel people found her laying dead, with a knife stuck in her belly. It was a homemade knife with a deerhorn handle, the sheriff said. Looked like some blacksmith made it out of a old file.

THE BOY THAT FOOLED
HIS FOLKS

ONE TIME there was a man and his wife lived beside the river, and so they run a ferry. Sometimes travelers would stay at their house all night. They never had no children except one boy, and he run off when he was ten years old, and that was a long time ago.

So then one evening a young fellow come through town, and he stopped at a store. He was riding a good horse, and he wore good clothes and a white hat. He had a gold watch and chain, and rings on his fingers. He says to the storekeeper, "Don't you know me?" The storekeeper says no; so then the young fellow told who he was, and asked about his paw and maw. The storekeeper says they are all right, and they are still running the ferry same as ever. Well, the young fellow says he is going down there and stay all night. He says he will not tell the folks who he is till tomorrow, and he will give his paw and maw a lot of money out of the saddlebags. So then the young fellow went off down the river road. A couple days after this the old man that run the ferry come over to get him some tobacco, and the storekeeper says, "Well, you must be having a big time at your house now that your boy is home." Then the storekeeper told how the young fellow had been there, and how he was aiming to pass himself off for a stranger, so he could fool his paw and maw and give them a lot of money out of the saddlebags. The old man he did not say nothing, and pretty soon he went home.

Next day the old woman killed herself, and they found her hanging to a rafter in the barn. The old man never amounted to much after that. Sometimes he would just lay under a tree all day. People come along and blowed the horn and wanted to be set across the river, but he did not pay them no mind. Just before the old man died he told the storekeeper how it happened. "It was my boy come to our place that night," says he, "but me and maw didn't know him. There was gold and silver in them saddlebags. So maw she cut his throat, and we buried him under the chickenhouse."

HOOT-OWL JESSUP

ONE TIME there was a prominent citizen who lived in a big town, and he was trying to get elected to be a Congressman. He kept a-campaigning round, but the country people wouldn't vote for him. So he bought a farm, and when people would come along the road, they could see him out in the field, with overalls on like a regular farmer. Sometimes he would put on boots, and have his picture took with dogs and guns, to make out he was a great hunter.

A bunch of jokers took him out coon hunting one night, and they hid in the brush so he thought he was all by himself. Just then a big hoot owl lit in a tree right beside him. "Whoo, whoo, whoo-oo are you?" says the big owl. The fellow didn't know what it was, and he was kind of scared, but he answered right up: "I am Joseph K. Jessup, and I am an Attorney-at-Law, and I am running for Congress in the Third Congressional District!" The boys all heard what he said, and they just rolled on the ground and laughed themselves sick. Next day Jessup denied the whole story. He says it was a lie made up by his political enemies. But the tale got into the newspapers, and people in the Third Congressional District laughed about it for twenty years. Jessup was beat in the election, but after while he got to be a Federal Judge, and they say he done pretty good at it. But folks never did forget the coon-hunting story, and he was knowed as Hoot-Owl Jessup to the end of his days.

THE DEVIL IN THE GRAVEYARD

ONE TIME there was a rich man crippled pretty bad with the rheumatism; also he had two grown sons, and somebody had stole seven of his best sheep. It was a widow woman and her boys that done it. The old woman used to wait in the graveyard, and the boys would sneak through the pasture and carry out a nice fat sheep. If the sheep was not fat enough, the old woman made them turn it loose and fetch out another one.

The old rich man wanted his sons to hide and watch the sheep, but there was no place to hide only in the graveyard, and they did not like to go there of a night. The old man says it seems like young fellows nowadays are afraid of their own shadow, and he kept telling how he could catch them thieves easy, only the rheumatism was so bad he couldn't walk to the graveyard. The rich man's sons got pretty tired of hearing about it, so one night they just picked the old man up and carried him over there.

The widow woman was setting on a tombstone, but there wasn't no moon, and she couldn't see very good anyhow. She thought it was her boys coming out of the pasture with a sheep. So she says, "Is he fat?" and reached out to feel the old man's leg. The rich man's sons was scared bad, so they dropped their pappy and took out for home. But when they got there the old man was right at their heels, hollering loud as anybody. He says there ain't no doubt who was waiting for him in the grave-yard, because he seen the Devil plain as day, with brimstone all round his head, and smelled like a old goat besides.

And from that time on the rich man used to tell everybody how the Old Boy himself riz up out of Hell to cure the rheumatism, after the best doctors in the country had done give up the case.

HOW BOOGER DONE HIS WIFE

ONE TIME there was a fellow named Booger. He was scared of his wife, but he used to run after the women anyhow. One day he went out buggy riding with a pretty school-marm. They tied the horse to a fencepost, and set down on the ground beside the spring branch. Him and her stayed there a long time, a-romping around on the grass. They was having a high old time, laughing and squealing so loud you could hear it plumb to the big road.

Just about that time an old woman come along, and she just stood there a-watching them. Booger seen the old woman, and he knowed she would spread the news and make trouble. So he dropped the schoolmarm like a hot potater, and told her to walk through the woods to the schoolhouse. Then he drove straight home and said to his wife, "Let's you and me go for a ride, like we used to." She says all right, and so they went. When they come to the spring Booger says, "Let's you and me light down and rest a while, beside this here spring branch." She says all right, and it wasn't no time at all till Booger was doing his wife just like he done the schoolmarm. And she giggled and squealed just like the schoolmarm, too.

Next morning, when the old woman begun to tell how he had been carrying on with the schoolmarm, Booger's wife just laughed. "Shucks," she says, "I don't believe a word of it." The old woman went right on a-talking. "I tell you I seen that schoolmarm plain, and I heard her a-squealing like a pig!" Booger's wife, she just laughed some more. "Well, if you must know," she says, "that was *me* you seen out there yesterday. As for squealing, ain't a woman got a right to squeal a little, when she's laying out in the grass with her own husband?"

THE PORTER AND THE SQUIRE

ONE TIME there was a rich man named Squire. He was not a Justice of the Peace, but everybody called him Squire anyhow. He had a pretty daughter, and she wanted to marry a fellow that was a porter, but the Squire would not let her do it, because the porter was too ornery. So one day they figured out a way to fool the Squire. The girl she hid in a old barrel they kept down cellar. Then the porter come along and says, "Squire, I want to buy a barrel to make beer in." The Squire he just laughed, as he thought the porter didn't have no money. "Go on, boy," he says, "you couldn't buy a green cob to stop the bung."

So then the porter pulled two silver dollars out of his pocket. Well, says the Squire, barrels is high now, and you can't get much of a barrel for two dollars. The porter he says most any barrel is good enough for the beer I am going to make, and so they went down cellar. The Squire drug out a pretty good little barrel, and there was some sour beer in it. And he says here is a fine barrel that you can have for a dollar and a half. But the porter says it ain't big enough for the beer I am going to make, and how much do you want for the big barrel on the end of the row? The Squire says, "Well now, I've had that big one several years, and maybe there is some good wine left in it." That was a lie, because he knowed it was full of holes and wouldn't hold stump water.

Well, after they talked awhile the Squire says, "You can have this big barrel just as it stands for two dollars, and if there is any wine in it you can have the wine too, but remember I don't guarantee nothing." The porter says the barrel has maybe got vinegar in it by this time, as the wine has turned sour. "Well, maybe it is full of grit, chips and whetstones for all I know," says the Squire. "Just give me the two dollars, and you can have the barrel and whatever is in it."

So the porter give the Squire his two dollars, and then he kicked the barrel and it fell all to staves, and there was the Squire's daughter inside. "Thank you, Squire, that's just what I was looking for," says the porter, "all I need now is a green cob to stop the bung." And then the porter and the girl just laughed like fools, and off they went to find the parson so they could get married.

The Squire was pretty mad at first. But after while he cooled off and says, "Well, it looks like that porter is smarter than he has been give credit for. Any fellow that can get the best of me is a pretty good trader, and my daughter is a fool anyhow, so maybe it is horse-and-horse at that." Next day the Squire he give them a little house to live in, and four good cows, so everything turned out all right after all.

THE JENKINS BOYS

ONE TIME the two Jenkins boys was benighted on a lonesome road, and they come to a house. The folks that lived there had a pretty daughter. There was two big beds, so the old man slept in one with his wife, and the Jenkins boys in the other. The pretty girl she slept in a trundle-bed by herself, on the other side of the fire. Away in the night the fire died down, so Bob Jenkins crawled over and got in bed with the pretty girl. He stayed there a long time, and finally him and the girl both went to sleep.

The old woman woke up after while, and she went outdoors to see how high the moon was. Bob opened one eye and seen her go out. While she was gone Bob started back where he belonged, but he got turned round some way and went to bed with the old man. When the woman come back she seen a bed with two men in it, so she went and got in the other bed where there was only one man. She thought it was her husband she was getting in bed with, but she soon found out different. She stayed there a long time, and finally her and Tom Jenkins both went to sleep.

Bob figured he was in bed with his brother, so he begun to laugh, and he says, "Tom, I sure had a good time while you was asleep!" The old man just kind of mumbled something, and Bob says, "I crawled over and topped that pretty girl, that's what I done!" The old man started to get up, and when Bob seen who it was, he hit the old man on the jaw and pushed him down under the covers. Then he run quick and pulled the old woman out, and got in bed with Tom. The woman was smart, so she jumped in bed with her husband before he could get out from under the quilt. The old man he begun to cuss and holler. "Hush up, John," says the woman, "what will the company think?" And the old man says, "To hell with the company! One of them boys was in my bed, bragging how he slept with our daughter!" But the old woman says, "For God's sake hush up, there is nobody in your bed but me, and you must have been dreaming." The old man looked around and seen the old woman in bed beside him. He seen his daughter in the trundle-bed, and looked like she was sound asleep with her mouth open. He seen the two Jenkins boys in their bed, and looked like they was sound asleep too. So he says to himself, "Maybe it was a dream sure enough, because it don't make sense no other way. If one of them boys *did* sleep with my daughter, what for would he wake me up in the night to brag about it, and then knock me senseless besides?"

Next morning the Jenkins boys went on down the road. Bob was carrying a jar of honey the pretty girl give him, and Tom had a nice lunch the old woman give him. The old man didn't have much to say, and he only eat one egg for breakfast. When the boys was plumb out of sight he says to his wife, "How do you figure I got this here big lump on my jaw?" The woman-folks just looked at each other, and all of a sudden they both busted out laughing. "You was thrashing around pretty bad in the night," says the old woman. "I reckon you must have knocked your head against the bedpost!"

HOGEYE AND THE BLACKSNAKE

ONE TIME there was a fellow named Rockett, but everybody called him Hogeye. He was a tall, slim gambler, and he could play the fiddle too. Hogeye and his wife lived right at the edge of the big timber. Mostly in the winter time he just layed around and slept, but in the spring he used to sneak out of a night. His wife would see him go sometimes, but she never let on. And when she woke up in the morning there was Hogeye back in the bed. Hogeye and his wife got along all right, and he was good to her, but they never did have no children. She says to her folks that Hogeye was not like any other man in the world. And she was a little bit afraid of him sometimes, because she could not tell what he was thinking about.

One time Hogeye sneaked out of the house on a moonlight night, and the woman peeked through a crack to see where he was going. She seen him stop at the pasture gate a minute, and then he was gone. So she slipped down to the gate, and there was all Hogeye's clothes laying on the ground, and his shoes was there too. She was scared to go any further, so she run back to the house and got in bed. When she woke up next morning, there was Hogeye sound asleep, and he had dust all over him. And she thought what for would a man take his clothes off and waller in the dust? But she did not say nothing about it, and neither did Hogeye.

About a month after that Hogeye's woman seen him sneak out again, and it was a moonlight night, so she followed him. And when she got to the pasture gate there was all Hogeye's clothes laying on the ground, and his shoes was there too. She slipped along by the fence, and pretty soon she come to a kind of clearing where the ground was all dry and dusty, like a place

31

where chickens go to dust theirself and rest in the sunshine. She seen two or three snakes, but they was just blacksnakes and not poison, so she was not scared of them.

When she got to the fence-corner, she could see pretty near all of the big dusty place, and there was her man laying on the ground stark naked, and he looked longer and slimmer than he ever done before. And right up against him was the biggest blacksnake in the world, as big around the middle as a full-growed woman. Hogeye and the big snake was a-wiggling around so, she thought at first they was fighting. But they wasn't.

Hogeye kept opening his mouth and sticking out his tongue, but his eyes was kind of dead-looking, like a blind man. There was little blacksnakes a-crawling around, and it come in the woman's mind that maybe these young ones was Hogeye's children. And she seen that this big dusty place was Hogeye's home by rights, and he just come in the house to sleep and rest up.

Lots of women would have made some kind of trouble right then and there, but Hogeye's wife was smarter than most. She just went back to the cabin and crawled in bed. When she woke up next morning Hogeye was sound asleep, same as always. And that same day she took her good clothes and some money they kept in a fruit jar under the smokehouse, and went over to her folks' place. Her pappy give her a ride down to the crossroads, and then she went on the bus to a big town where she had some kinfolks. She got a job in a lunch-counter place, and done fine there, and had a pretty good time.

Hogeye sent word for her to come back home, but she never done it. "Every man to his own taste," she says. "If it was a sheep or a heifer, maybe I'd have put up with it. But I sure don't aim to play second fiddle to no blacksnake!"

32

THE BOOT THAT
KILLED PEOPLE

ONE TIME there was a little old man a-riding along, and he seen a big rattlesnake. He got down off his pony and killed the snake. The hell of it was, there was two of them rattlers, and while he was stomping the big snake to death, the other one bit him unbeknownst. The little old man rode home and went to bed. Next morning he was dead as a doornail, and his left leg all swelled up.

Soon as the burying was over, the folks divided up the little old man's stuff. One of the brothers didn't get nothing but a pair of boots. They was pretty near new, so he shined them up good and kept them for Sunday. The first time he wore them boots he got to drinking pretty heavy, so the boys put him to bed in the hotel. Next morning he was dead as a doornail, and his left leg all swelled up.

Well sir, they buried that fellow in the town graveyard, and the undertaker got most of his money. But they sent the pony back home, with his boots and six-shooter tied to the saddle. The Indian woman that kept house for him sold the pony and saddle, and she give the gun to her boy friend that was studying to be a road agent. She would have give him the boots too, but they was not near big enough, and she set them up on a shelf. One rainy day the woman had to go out in the hills on some Indian business, so she wore the boots herself, and they fit pretty good. She got kind of sick that night, after she went to bed. Next morning she was dead as a doornail, and her left leg all swelled up.

33

The neighbors figured there was something fishy about it, so they called the sheriff, and he got a town doctor to see if the woman had maybe been poisoned. But the doctor says it looks to him like she was snake-bit. The Indians come and took the woman out to bury her somewheres, and they left the house with the door open for good luck. One of the neighbor's little boys come into the house, and he found the boots and put them on. So he went a-stomping around all day, and he was mighty proud of them boots. But along in the night the little boy got awful sick. Next morning he was dead as a doornail, and his left leg all swelled up.

The town folks come out there again, and the sheriff says God damn it, here is four people dead with their left leg swelled up, and something has got to be done about it. The doctor he says the woman and the little boy was both snake-bit, and he don't know what was the matter with them two men, because he did not examine them two men. But this Indian talk about boots killing people is just superstition, he says, and not to be took serious.

The sheriff was a smart man who had heard it thunder a good many times, and he knowed Indians are not such fools as lots of people think. He took his knife and cut them boots open, and then he put on his specs and looked mighty careful. And pretty soon he found the rattlesnake teeth in the left boot-top. Them fangs was no bigger than a needle, and they was stuck in the leather a-pointing down. So when anybody would put the boot on, there wasn't no harm done, but when they went to pull the boot off, one of them fangs would stick in their leg. And that is how it come that the boot did not kill nobody in the day time, but when they took their boots off at night, it sure would kill them.

The town doctor seen the rattlesnake teeth in that boot-top, and he did not have nothing more to say. The sheriff cut off the

34

leather with the fangs in it, and built a fire in the chimney, and burnt the whole business plumb to ashes. Then he made a sign with his hand like the Indians do, and he looked at the town doctor to see if he was laughing or not. But the doctor was not laughing, so they got on their horses and rode back to town.

THIRTY PIECES OF SILVER

ONE TIME there was a fellow name of Seth Burgess, and the railroad run right by his farm, and he says the train killed some of his stock. And then the sparks come out of the engine and burnt his house. So then he says, "I will sue the railroad people and make 'em give me ten thousand dollars, or maybe fifteen." Old Colonel Stone was Seth's lawyer, and the Colonel says, "We will win this case easy, because the jury is all home folks and they sure ain't going to favor the goddam railroad."

Colonel Stone was a fine upstanding man, and he dressed better than anybody in town. But when the railroad lawyer got there, he was a shabby little fellow, and you could see where his pants has been mended. People was expecting he would hang around the tavern to bribe the witnesses or something, but he never done it. He just set in his little room at the hotel, and did not bother nobody.

It just happened that our preacher was holding a revival that week, trying to pay off the mortgage on the church house. One man would give a dollar, and another man maybe would give two dollars, but it was coming in mighty slow. And then the little lawyer stood up and he says, "How much is the balance on that mortgage?" The preacher he says it is still three hundred

35

and sixty dollars. "I'm with the railroad company," says the lawyer, "and the railroad company is mighty strong for religion. We know that without God there ain't no law and order, nor no honest dealings anywhere. We want to see good Christian towns all along the road, and we aim to do our part." And with that he give the preacher a check for the whole three hundred and sixty dollars.

Most of the jurymen was at the church house that night, and so was their wives. One old sister asked how much Colonel Stone put in the plate, and a man says, "The Colonel was here one night, and he give us fifty cents." And she asked how much did Seth Burgess put in, and the man says, "Nothing, because Seth don't never come to church." When the folks went home they passed by the hotel, and there was a light in the little lawyer's room. The woman that run the hotel says he is in there now, a-reading the Bible.

When the trial come up, Colonel Stone he made a long

36

speech about how the railroad capitalists is carrying off the world in chunks, and we got to look out for the rights of our citizens. The little railroad lawyer he says it is a fine speech, but maybe the jury would be more interested to know who set Mister Burgess's shack on fire. The train only comes through once a day, but there is people lighting matches and smoking cigarets every minute from sun-up till way after midnight. Let the jury think that over, he says, because it is between them and their own conscience in the sight of God. So then the little lawyer he set down.

Soon as they got in the jury room, one fellow says, "That house Seth Burgess is hollering about was just one room and a tar-paper roof, and didn't cost more than fifty dollars." And another fellow says he could have bought the whole farm for two hundred dollars, with the house on it and a barn full of Johnson-grass. And another fellow says he thinks poor folks ought to stick together, but Colonel Stone ain't got no mended place on his pants, and neither has Seth Burgess. Nobody mentioned how the Colonel only give fifty cents to the church, while this railroad lawyer give three hundred and sixty dollars, but they all knowed about it, and maybe some of them was thinking what their wives would say when they got home.

So pretty soon the jury turned in a verdict for the railroad company, and they didn't give Seth Burgess nothing. The little lawyer shook hands with everybody, and then he got on the train and went back to Little Rock. Colonel Stone went a-roaring off to the tavern, and he says them goddam jurymen has sold out for three hundred and sixty dollars, which is only thirty dollars a head. Thirty pieces of silver, he says, and them psalm-singing hypocrites ought to go out and hang theirself. But after supper the Colonel says, "Well, I always heard that little shrimp with the patch on his pants is the smartest lawyer in Arkansas. And maybe he is, at that."

37

THE TOURIST THAT
WENT TOO FAR

ONE TIME there was a big fellow from Chicago come down to Taney county to go fishing. He got pretty drunk every day, and acted kind of foolish, but the home folks just let it pass. They knowed he didn't mean no harm. When a fellow works hard all year in one of them big towns, and only gets a week off to go fishing, we figure it's all right for him to cut up a little if he feels like it. Some tourists are worse than others, though. To tell you the truth, damn near all of 'em are. But they bring a lot of money into the country, so we just try to show 'em a good time and not have no hard feelings.

When this big fellow from Chicago set the privy afire, the folks that run the boardinghouse didn't say a word; they knowed he wasn't used to privies, and it was maybe a accident, anyhow. And when he took up pinching people's legs in the diningroom, the girls just laughed and kind of kept out of his way. And the time he busted into the Bear Creek dance-set, folks figured maybe he didn't understand about square dancing, so they passed it off for a joke. Even when he tried to shoot our sheriff, there wasn't no real harm done, because Tommy grabbed the gun out of his hand and throwed it in the river. But there ain't no denying he was a mighty unconvenient fellow to have around, and everybody watched him pretty close after that, for fear he would get in some kind of trouble.

The constable told him not to go in the beer tavern at Kimmerling's Ferry, because it was full of boys from way up the creek, and the Sowcoon Mountain bunch is liable to come along any minute. But the big fellow says he lived all his life in Chicago, and it is the toughest town in the world. There is men in Chicago which could eat all these hillbillies for breakfast and then holler for more oysters, he says. So then he ordered a drink for everybody in the house, and the barkeeper set out glasses of beer, but nobody touched the beer only a couple of floozies from Springfield. All them country boys just let the beer set there, and went right on drinking whiskey out of their own bottles. The big fellow begun to get pretty mad, and he says people better look out who they are insulting. "I'm the best fighter in the world!" he says. The boys just kept on drinking their whiskey, and talking quiet amongst themselves. "I'm the best damn fighter in the United States!" says the big fellow, but them up-the-creek boys just looked at him kind of contemptuous. "I can lick any man in Missouri!" says he. Nobody didn't return no answer, but the barkeeper begun to get restless. "Well, by God!" says the big fellow, and with that he jumped four foot high and cracked his heels together twice. "I can lick any son-of-a-bitch in Taney county!" he yells. This time the leader of the Sowcoon Mountain bunch was a-standing in the doorway, and he was one of them thin-and-ready boys. "Stranger," says he, "you have went too far." So then he jumped on the big fellow and beat him pretty near to death before he could fall down even. And soon as he did hit the floor, somebody kicked most of his teeth out.

And then the constable come and dragged the big fellow from Chicago outside, and it took three men to load him in a wagon so they could haul him back to the boardinghouse. "When that there tourist wakes up," says the boy from Sowcoon Mountain, "you tell him there ain't no son-of-a-bitches *in* Taney county." And all them up-the-creek fellows nodded their heads like billygoats. "If a man is a-looking for son-of-a-bitches," says the boy from Sowcoon Mountain, "I reckon he better go to Chicago, or some of them other big towns."

OLD KITTY ROLLINS

ONE TIME a traveler was a-riding down the road, and he seen a house that was chuck full of cats. There was cats running all over the place, and setting on the gallery, and some had even got up on the roof. One great big tomcat walked over to the traveler and says, "When you get to the next house, stop and tell 'em that old Kitty Rollins is dead." He could talk just like a human, with a big loud coarse voice at that.

So the traveler rode on, and the next house he come to looked like it was plumb deserted. But the traveler got down and went in anyhow, and there was just one old bedraggled looking cat a-setting in the corner by the fireplace. "I come to tell you that old Kitty Rollins is dead," says the traveler. The old bedraggled looking cat jumped up and says, "By God, I'll be king yet!" and out of the door he run.

THE SNIPE HUNTERS

ONE TIME there was a fat man come to the boarding-house, and the folks said he was from New York. He used to set around of an evening, and listen to the boys a-talking. One night they asked him would he like to go snipe hunting, and he says yes. The boys figured it would be fun for them, and a educational experience for the fat man from New York.

The whole crowd went out in the timber, pretty near to

Reeds Spring, and they lit a candle about two inches long, and set it on a stump. Then they give the fat man a little tin whistle. They give him a tow sack, too, and showed him how to prop it open with a willow stick. "That there whistle is the best snipe-caller in this country," they told him. "Just keep a-tooting good and loud. That will fetch them snipes to the light, just like moth millers. And when they see that black shadow where you got the sack propped open, they'll fly right into it every time. All you got to do is wring their necks."

The fat man he set down and got ready to catch the snipes. "Where are you fellows going?" he says. "We're going out to beat the brush for half a mile each way," says young Jim Henson. "That kind of stirs up the snipes, and gets them to circulating around good." So the fat man he begun to toot his whistle, and the boys scattered out in the brush. They figured on stirring round and hollering for awhile, and then they would all go home and leave the fat man to get back the best he could. Everybody thought it was a great joke to play on a fellow from a big city like New York.

The boys whooped and hollered up and down them hills till they was pretty tired, and then walked all the way back to town. When they got to the boardinghouse they heard a funny little noise, and they seen a light in the fat man's room. And there he was, setting in a big easy chair and tooting on his tin whistle. When he seen them fellows all dusty and briar-scratched, the fat man laughed so hard he mighty near strangled. "You boys will be the death of me," says he. "That's the first time I've been snipe hunting in forty years. I didn't know they *had* snipe hunts any more." Finally one of them fellows wanted to know how he come to beat everybody home. The fat man laughed some more. "I got Bob Applegate to follow along with the buggy," says he. "You wise guys were still hollering and tromping down brush when we left."

That fat fellow stayed around town pretty near all summer, and every night he would set out on the gallery and toot his little tin whistle. The folks in town all knowed about the snipe hunt, and them fool boys never did hear the last of it.

UNCLE ADAM'S COW

ONE TIME there was two old men lived up Magnetic Holler, right close to a little branch that they call Mystic Spring nowadays. One of these fellows was Uncle Adam, and he had a wife. The other one was knowed as Uncle Dick, and he didn't have no wife, but he had two cows. They got to trading jackknives and shotguns, and finally Uncle Adam swapped his wife for one of Uncle Dick's cows. Folks used to trade wives pretty free in them days, and nobody said much about it. Lots of them wasn't really married anyhow, so there wasn't no great harm done.

But it wasn't long till word got around that Uncle Adam's

woman had up and left him, and moved all her stuff over to Uncle Dick's cabin. The next time Uncle Adam come into town, somebody asked him if Uncle Dick had stole his wife. "Hell no," says Uncle Adam, "it was a fair swap, all open and above board. Dick give me his best cow for the old woman, and two dollars boot."

Folks got to laughing about it, and one day the sheriff stopped Uncle Adam in the street. "This here trading wives is against the law nowadays," says he. "And everybody knows a woman is worth more than a cow, anyhow." Uncle Adam laughed right in the sheriff's face. "Don't you believe it, Sheriff," he says, "don't you believe it! Why, that there cow of mine is three-fourths Jersey!"

DEACON SPURLOCK AND
THE LEGISLATURE

ONE TIME old Deacon Spurlock took the notion he wanted to be Representative, and finally the people got together and elected him. The deacon was getting pretty old, and listening to long windy speeches in the Legislature made him sleepy, so some smart-aleck newspapers called him "the Snoring Solon." But he was a good honest man, and not afraid to speak up when them slick Representatives from big towns was trying to put something over on the home folks.

Some fool from Kansas City introduced a bill to put farmers in jail for catching fish with seines. Deacon Spurlock was against it, because most of his neighbors used seines, and hauled the fish into town, and sold them. But while the city folks was debating, old Spurlock dropped off to sleep. The fish bill was beat anyhow, and by the time the deacon woke up the Representatives was talking about a new law to stop people from running whorehouses. Deacon Spurlock thought the bill against seining fish was still before the House, so he jumped up and says "This here bill is an outrage, gentlemen! Such a law would spread untold hardship and privation among my constituents! Why, lots of the folks down in my district don't have no other way to make a living! They've always done it, and so did their parents and grandparents before them!"

All them legislators just stared at the deacon for a minute, and some thought he must have went crazy. And then they seen how it was, and everybody laughed and yelled and clapped as loud as they could. A lot of people come over to shake Deacon Spurlock's hand, and pound him on the back, and brag about what a great speech he made. One fellow says he liked to see a man stand up for the folks that elected him, no matter what kind of business they are in. Everybody knowed there wasn't no whorehouses in the deacon's county, because they didn't have no town big enough to support a whorehouse. But all them city people pretended like they thought Deacon Spurlock was working for the red-light district. And a fellow from Jackson county, which is full of sporting houses, made out like he was terrible shocked. "Can it be that this pious old man, a deacon in our own church, has sold out to commercialized vice?" he says. And them smart alecks hurrahed louder than ever.

The folks all knowed that Deacon Spurlock never had no truck with whoremasters, and he could have been re-elected easy. But when he got home the deacon says he is done with politics, and they better send somebody else to be Representative. He says them fellows up at Jefferson City is a scatter-brained lot that don't do nothing but play jokes on one another, and he don't want no part in such foolishness.

44

GRAVELS FOR A GOOSE

ONE TIME there was a farmer a-plowing in his field, when along come two smart-aleck town boys, and they says to him, "Where can we get some gravels for our goose?" They meant that they was looking for some fancy women, like them that stays at the sporting houses in big towns. The farmer pointed to his cabin down the road. "Yonder's where I always go," says he. "She might fight you off a little at first, but you'll get it all right." The two smart alecks started for the house at a right fast lope, and the farmer follered along through the brush to see what happened.

He seen the smart alecks go in the door, and everything was quiet for about half a minute. Then come the God-awfullest hullabaloo you ever heard, with people cavorting round like they would bust the house down. Them two town boys come a-tearing out and made for the road. Their hats was gone, and their clothes was tore, and one of 'em had a bloody nose. The farmer's wife run right after them, hollering fit to wake the dead. She had the shotgun, and fired it off twice, but she didn't hit nobody. Soon as the smart alecks was out of sight the farmer come a-running up, and he says, "For God's sake, what is the matter?"

Well, she sure told him what was the matter, and she says, "Do you aim to stand there like a fool, while your wife is throwed down and ravished by criminals from the city?" So the farmer says, "No, I reckon not," and with that he grabbed the shotgun and run off through the woods. After while he come back, and he says, "I chased them fellers pretty near a mile, but they got plumb away." The old woman kept on a-grumbling how things has come to a pretty pass, and it looks like decent people ain't safe in their own home nowadays. The farmer talked some about riding to town and getting the sheriff to fetch bloodhounds, but he was afraid it wouldn't be no use. "I figure they must be fifty miles off by this time," he says, "they was the fast-runningest fellers I ever seen."

The farmer's wife was still a-grumbling, but finally she says maybe them boys was just carried away by their passions, when they seen a pretty woman away out here in the woods. And they didn't actually *do* nothing anyhow, but just scared the hell out of her, and made her mad. Maybe it is better to hush the whole thing up, so as not to have no scandal, she says. The farmer he stomped and argued awhile, and then he says, "Well, have it your own way, and we will do whatever you think best." And so they et supper and went to bed.

The farmer didn't say no more, but he laughed about it a good deal, specially when he heard her telling the kinfolks what a terrible experience she had went through. And all the rest of his life he figured it was a great secret joke on the old woman.

THE GREAT BADGER FIGHT

ONE TIME the old soldiers was trying to raise money for the G.A.R. hall, and so they give a dance. But the dance did not do much good, because the G.A.R. fellows had all been in the Federal army. The best people in town was mostly Confederate sympathizers, and they would not help build no hall for them damn Yankees to set around in, bragging how they won the War. They can hold their reunions out at the Fair Grounds, and it is good enough for them, the people says.

Some of the G.A.R. fellows had a white bulldog named Ben Butler, and he was the biggest bulldog ever come to this country, and licked all the other dogs easy. So the old soldiers spread the word that they was going to have a badger fight in Braden's Livery Barn. They told everybody they got a giant wild badger from up North that could kill any common dog, but Old Ben could maybe lick the badger. The day the pensions come there was old soldiers flashing their money around town, and some was betting on the badger, but mostly they was betting on Old Ben. So pretty soon all the people was talking about the badger fight. The Methodist minister was a Southerner, so he preached a sermon against badger fighting. Such bloody spectacles was brutal and degrading, he says, and good Christian people ought to put a stop to it.

At first the old soldiers was not going to let anybody in only members of the G.A.R., but then they decided to sell tickets to a few prominent citizens. The tickets cost two dollars, and two dollars was a lot of money in them days. But it was surprising how many people bought tickets anyhow, and some folks drove in from twenty miles out in the country to see the badger fight.

When the big night come, Braden's Livery Barn was jam full of people setting on the benches, and they borrowed all the undertaker's chairs besides. The boys had the badger in a big box with iron corners, and two men standing there with pitchforks to protect the crowd if anything went wrong. Old Ben Butler was a-raring to go, but when they opened the door of the box it looked like the badger would not come out. Everybody was excited and hollering by this time, and finally the G.A.R. boys says somebody will have to pull the badger out with a iron chain, but all them fellows kind of hung back. Old Colonel Ledbetter says he seen Yankees run like rabbits during the War, when he was a-riding with General Bedford

Forrest. But he didn't know they was afraid of badgers, he says. And pretty soon he says, "Damned if the badger don't act like a Republican too, and I will go down there and pull him out myself." So the old Colonel hobbled out in the ring and grabbed hold of the chain. He pulled kind of easy at first, but still the badger didn't show up. Then the Colonel throwed all his weight on the chain, and out come a big old china chamber-pot. The G.A.R. boys had filled it up with lead to make it heavy, and fastened a old coonskin cap on top, with the tail hanging down behind.

When Colonel Ledbetter seen how he had been sold, he just throwed back his shoulders and marched out of Braden's Livery Barn. He says it is a dirty Yankee trick, but he would not lower himself to talk about chamber-pots with the G.A.R. Some of the people was pretty mad on account of the two dollars, specially the folks that had drove in from way out in the country. But mostly they just laughed and went on home, and that is the end of the badger fight story.

THE BIG OLD GIANT

ONE TIME there was a boy found a dead crow, and the crow had a funny looking grain of corn in his mouth. It was big as a walnut, and blue instead of yellow. So the boy planted it down by the big bluff and poured a hatful of stump water on it. Next time he come that way, the corn had growed up big as a tree, with regular bark on it, and blade-fodder hanging down forty foot long. The boy couldn't see no tassel, on account of the trees on top of the bluff, and he couldn't see no ears on the stalk, neither. He went home and told the folks, but they just laughed and didn't pay no attention. So finally he

48

says to himself, "I'll go back and climb that there cornstalk, if I *never* see the back of my neck!"

Well, he clumb and he clumb and he kept on a-climbing, right on up past the top of the bluff, but there wasn't no ears on the stalk yet. He got so high up he couldn't see nothing but clouds. After while he come to a big pasture, so he got off the cornstalk to look around and stretch his legs. The grass in that pasture was ten foot high, and there was buckbrush in it bigger than apple trees. Pretty soon he seen some monstrous big sheep. There was one old sheep had a fine brass bell on it, about the size of a molasses barrel.

"The folks won't never believe this," says he to himself, "without I take something back to show 'em." So he out with his knife and started to cut the bell off'n the big sheep's neck. It took a long time to saw through the leather strap, pretty near a foot thick, but he finally done it. The bell was too heavy for him to lift, so he rolled it along on the ground, and it kept a-ringing. Just as he got to the edge of the big pasture, the boy heard a terrible loud hollering, and here come the big old giant that owned them sheep. He was maybe thirty foot high, and he was a-waving a club big as a saw-log.

Well, when the boy seen this here giant a-coming, he just rolled the bell over the edge, and then he jumped onto the big cornstalk and slid down. The big old giant throwed the club, but it missed him. The boy was pretty near to the bottom, when the old giant jumped on the cornstalk and started down after him. Just as the boy lit on the ground the cornstalk broke off, and the big old giant come a-roaring down the mountain and busted open like a rotten apple. By the time the boy's folks got there the big old giant was dead, and that was the end of him.

The folks got the neighbors to help, and they went out and buried the big old giant in the night, and never did tell no outsiders, so as to keep down scandal. But next winter every family for miles around showed up with quilts and laprobes and saddle blankets made out of some mighty funny looking wool. Nobody in the country ever seen cloth like that before, and the old-timers all say them things was made out of the big old giant's pants.

Some berry pickers found the big sheep bell four miles up the creek. The boy's pappy wanted to put it in the new church-house, but the preacher says a bell like that was not made with human hands, and maybe it was the Devil's work. And he says good Christian people better not ring that bell, because who knows what might come a-running? So they just left the big sheep bell there in the brush where it fell. And it's still a-laying there to this day.

NO RESPECT FOR THE DEAD

ONE TIME there was an old man lived way up the creek, and all of a sudden his wife died. He had a passel of children to be took care of, and he didn't fool away no time a-courting. Before the wagon tracks was out of the yard, he married a widow woman that lived down the road a piece. Some say he married her just one day after his wife's funeral. Most of the neighbors thought the old man ought to have waited a week or two, just for the looks of the thing. But folks didn't blame him much, because they all knowed he had to get somebody to see after them children.

People was hell on shivarees in them days, and if a fresh-married couple wasn't shivareed it meant that they didn't have no standing in the community, and was kind of looked down on. Everybody wanted to do the right thing by this here family, so they all come over to the house right after dark. Some was ringing bells, and some was shooting off guns, and some was just hollering loud as they could. One fellow had brought an old circle saw, and he was hammering on it with a cold chisel.

Everybody knows that when folks are being shivareed, they are supposed to set up something for the crowd. Mostly they invite the people into the house and feed them cake or pie or whatever they've got. Lots of new-married couples have chicken and fixings cooked up, and a fine table all set for the shivaree party. And sometimes the husband has got a jug of corn-squeezings hid somewhere outside, where the menfolks can take a little snort, just for luck. And maybe there is a fiddler in the crowd, so they can have a regular square dance right then and there. Anyhow, the least a couple can do is to pass out candy and cigars, or something like that.

This old fellow was pretty well-to-do, but he was terrible close with his money. And he was not in no mood for jollification anyhow, because of one thing and another. Pretty soon he come out on the porch in his nightshirt, looking mighty sour. "What's the matter with you folks?" says he. "Ain't you got no respect for the dead?"

Well sir, that shivaree party was so set back, they didn't know what to do. You could have heard a pin drop. Finally they took their guns and cow bells and walked out of the old man's yard. The fellow that fetched the circle saw just left it a-laying there and shuffled on after the other folks with his mouth open and the cold chisel still in his hand. There wasn't a word spoke till they got away down the road. Then somebody begun to giggle, and a minute later they was all laughing like fools. Some folks say you could hear them a-whooping and a-hollering clear over to the new highway.

It all happened a long time ago, but there's still a few old-timers around here that ain't forgot that shivaree. And they will bust out laughing to this day, when something happens to put them in mind of it.

LITTLE AB AND THE SCALDING-BARREL

ONE TIME there was a fellow they called Little Ab, and he used to go see other men's wives while their husband was not home. One night he heard somebody open the gate, and the woman says, "Oh God, that's my old man!" Ab knowed he could not get out of the house, so he hid in the scalding-barrel. When the man come in it was not the woman's husband, but just another fellow tom-catting around, and his name was Big Jim. Ab set in the barrel still as a mouse. He could not see nothing, but he sure heard a plenty.

After while the gate slammed again, and this time it was the

woman's husband sure enough, and he walked right in. Big Jim spoke up and says, "Howdy, neighbor! I just come over to borrow your scalding-barrel." The woman's husband did not like the look of things, but he says "All right, Jim. There it is, over in the corner."

When Big Jim picked up the barrel he took note it was mighty heavy, but he figured this wasn't no time to argue about the heft of a scalding-barrel. So he just took off with it, and never did stop till he was pretty near a mile down the road. "My God," says he, when he finally had to set down and rest a minute, "I sure did get out of that mess mighty slick." About that time Little Ab come a-crawling out of the barrel. "You sure did, Jim," he says, "and I didn't do so *terrible* bad, myself!"

PENNYWINKLE! PENNYWINKLE!

ONE TIME there was a woman who got mad at her husband about something, so she killed their baby with the fire-shovel. Then she skinned the baby just like a rabbit, and cut it up just like a rabbit, and cooked it just like a rabbit. When her man come home that night she set the meat on the table. Him and her was not speaking, so he didn't ask nobody what kind of meat it was. He set down and et every scrap of the meat, and the woman sent her daughter to put the bones under a marble stone down by the springhouse.

Nobody said a word all evening, so pretty soon they went to bed, but they could not get no sleep. It seemed like something was a-crawling around in the house, and crying. After while the man he says, "Who's there? What do you want?" And then the little ghost hollered back "Pennywinkle! Pennywinkle! My maw killed me, my paw et me, my sister buried my bones under a marble stone! I want my liver and lights and wi-i-i-ney pipes! Pennywinkle! Pennywinkle!" And when the fellow heard this, he got to thinking about what it meant. So after while he got out of bed and went down to the springhouse, and found the baby's bones under the marble stone.

Well, the man set there awhile and whetted up his knife. Then he went back to the house and cut his wife's head off. The step-daughter she run away through the woods, and nobody ever did find out what become of her. The folks took the baby's head and skin and bones out from under the marble stone, and put them in a regular little coffin, and buried them in the graveyard. And that is the end of the "Pennywinkle" story.

JAY CAUGHT THE DEVIL

ONE TIME there was a boy named Jay, and he went to see a pretty girl name of Jenny, but the girl was sick, and it looked like she was a-dying. Jay says, "I will fix everything all right," and then he got a big towsack and hid behind the bed. Pretty soon the Devil come a-walking in, and he says to the girl, "Come with me." Just then Jay jumped out and throwed the sack over the Devil's head, and they done a lot of rassling around on the floor. Finally Jay got the Devil in the sack, and tied the sack shut with rope. The Devil kept a-hollering, but Jay didn't pay no mind. Jay knowed you can't kill the Devil, but he figured on putting him where he couldn't do no harm. So he just stuck the Devil into a holler tree, and plugged up the hole.

When Jay got back to the house Jenny was just as peart and lively as ever, and him and her sure did have a good time.

They raised three fine boys, and every one of them done mighty well. When the youngest boy growed up and left home Jay got to feeling pretty old, and it seemed like he didn't have no fun any more. Every time he would go any place he seen lots of other old folks a-crippling round, and they all says they didn't have no fun neither.

So Jay went back home, and he just set there a-looking at Jenny. She had kept her hair black with soot off the griddle, and smeared some red stuff on her mouth, and got herself a lot of fine clothes. Jay knowed in reason she was slipping out of a night with some young fellows, but it seemed like he didn't care much. No fool like a old fool, he says, and to hell with it. But then Jay kept on a-thinking, and finally one morning he took his axe and went over to the old home place, where him and Jenny used to live when they first got married. There was a lot of saplings around the old holler tree now, but he found it all right. The hole in the tree was pretty near growed shut, but Jay chopped it open and pulled out the sack. Then he cut the rope, and up jumped the Devil just as spry as ever.

Some of the neighbors found Jenny dead in her bed that night, but it was several days before anybody run onto Jay. He was setting there with his back against the tree, cold as a wagon tire. There was a kind of foolish grin on his face. The axe was laying beside him, with a few big chips.

The doctor come out to look, and he says Jay's heart must have went back on him. A man his age didn't have no business trying to chop down trees, anyhow. "A lot of old folks is a-dying off this week," says the doctor. "Right in the middle of the deer season, too. I never get to go a-hunting any more. All I do is ride around looking at corpses, and sign these goddam death certificates." And then the doctor got in his buggy and drove back to town.

TALKING RIVER

ONE TIME there was two brothers, and their name was Barstow. Charley was poison mean, but Bud he was a fine fellow, only he couldn't talk. Bud he'd just mumble and make signs to Charley, and Charley would speak up and tell whatever it was Bud wanted to say. The Shaw family lived neighbor to the Barstows, and them three big Shaw girls would go swimming. Charley used to set in the bushes where he could watch, and he heard 'em talking about how their pap hid his money in Lummis Cave. So Charley and Bud started out a-hunting for the money, but Charley never told Bud it was old man Shaw's. Bud he thought it was maybe Spanish gold that had been laying there a hundred years anyhow and didn't rightly belong to nobody.

Bud done most of the digging, and pretty soon he struck a

56

old-fashioned skillet, plumb full of gold money. Charley was so tickled he like to went crazy, but Bud was studying the dates on them gold pieces, and he could tell the stuff wasn't very old. Bud was just as honest as the day is long, and Charley knowed that if he figured the money belonged to old man Shaw, he'd go right over and give it back to him. And just that minute the idea come in Charley's head to kill Bud and keep the gold money himself.

All of a sudden come a squeaky noise like somebody laughing, and there was a little dried-up old fellow smoking his pipe. Both boys was scared, because he didn't look like no common man, but Charley he spoke up: "Who are you, and what the hell you doing here?" The little man just laughed some more. "I'm king of these parts, and this here cave is where I live. And furthermore," says he, "I don't like a boy that sneaks around peeking at girls in swimming, and stealing folks' money, and figuring on killing his own brother."

Charley was scared pretty bad, but he knowed poor Bud couldn't say nothing, so he begun to tell how it was Bud that was trying to steal old man Shaw's money. But the little dried up old fellow just laughed, and Charley hollered out, "You ain't no king nohow, you damn little toad-frog!" and with that he reached for his pistol. The old king stopped laughing mighty sudden. "Toad-frog! Toad-frog yourself!" says he, and pointed his skinny old finger at Charley. Then he made a little *pop* with his mouth, like spitting out a persimmon seed. And with that little *pop* Charley dropped his gun and fell right down on the ground. He begun to kick and holler and wiggle and grunt; it seemed like he was shrinking up till his jeans was thousands big for him. Bud he just stood there plumb flabbergasted; Charley kept on a-getting less and leaster, turning green round the gills. "Toad-frog yourself!" hollered the old king, and in less'n a minute poor Charley *was* a toad-frog. "Git for the creek, toad-frog!" says the king, and there went Charley a-hopping along like the rocks hurt his feet.

Then the little dried-up old fellow asked Bud what he had to say for himself, and Bud started in a-talking just as good as anybody. "Well, you got to bury that money just like you found it," says the king. "And then you can go on home. But if you ever tell a living soul what you've saw here today, you'll *never stop talking again!*" And with that the old king was gone. He run down a hole, same as a groundhog.

When Bud got home the folks was so tickled at him a-talking that they never paid no mind to Charley being gone, but when he never showed up next morning they begun to ask questions. Bud told 'em he didn't have no idea what went with Charley. There was a good deal of talk, and the sheriff come out there wanting to know where Charley was saw last, and all like that.

Bud stuck to it that he didn't know nothing about Charley. But twenty years later, when he was a-dying, he called in the kinfolks and told them the whole story. Most of them thought he was out of his head. But right away after Bud died here come a big spring branch down the dry holler, so there was ten inches of water right in the road. Well, everybody knows a new spring does bust out all of a sudden thataway sometimes. But when they had the burying next day, everybody could see that the corpse didn't look natural. It didn't look like Bud, anyhow, and some folks went so far as to say that it *warn't* Bud.

The spring branch is still a-running, strong as ever. The tourist people named it Talking River, because it makes such a clatter, but the old-timers always called it Bud's Creek. And some folks still think Bud Barstow ain't what you might call dead, and that corpse we buried was maybe something else again. Anyhow, Bud's Creek is still a-talking, just like the old king said.

THE LITTLE BLUE BALL

ONE TIME there was three girls in a cabin, and the biggest one went out to sweep the front yard. A little blue ball rolled off the roof and down the hill. So the biggest girl follered it, and come to a great big house with a stranger setting on the porch. He told her to sweep the whole house except one room, and he says for her not to look in that room. But of course she done it anyhow, while the stranger was gone, and she got some blood on her leg. It wouldn't wash off, neither, no matter how hard she rubbed it. There was a little dog come along just then, and the little dog asked her to give him some bread and butter. But she says get out, I will not give you no bread and butter. Pretty soon the stranger come home. He seen the blood on her leg, and he knowed where she had been. So he cut her head off and throwed her in the room.

Next day the middle-sized girl went out to sweep the front yard, and she seen the little blue ball, and follered it to the big house, and got blood on her leg, and wouldn't give the little dog no bread and butter. And when the stranger come home, he knowed where she had been, so he cut her head off and throwed her in the room.

On the third day the least girl went out to sweep the front yard, and she seen the little blue ball, and follered it to the big house, and got blood on her leg just like the other girls. But when the little dog come along she give him all the bread and butter he could eat, and so he licked the blood off. And when the stranger come home, he didn't see no blood on her leg. So he married the least girl right away, and everything turned out fine after all.

59

JACK COULDN'T MAKE
NO CHANGE

ONE TIME there was a fellow named Jack, and he heired a lot of money when his folks died off. But he didn't have much sense, so he went into town and bought him a saloon. The first day he run the saloon there was a town fellow come in, and he says, "Give me some whiskey." Jack set him out a glass of whiskey and says, "That will be fifteen cents." But the town fellow says fifteen cents is too much, and he will take three beers instead, because beers only cost a nickel. So Jack poured the whiskey back in the bottle, and give him three beers. The town fellow drunk the beers and then he started out. Jack says, "You owe me fifteen cents for them three beers." And the town fellow says, "How do you figure that? Didn't I trade you the whiskey for them beers?" Jack he says, "Yes, but you never paid for the whiskey." The town fellow says, "Of course not, because I never drunk the whiskey. You poured it back in the bottle! I seen you with my own eyes, and I will swear to it in court!" And then the town fellow went out the door. Jack he set there a long time studying about it, and counting his money. He knowed he was fifteen cents short, but he couldn't figure out how the town fellow done it so slick.

Next day there was two town fellows come in, and one of them bought a glass of beer. He throwed a dollar bill on the bar, and Jack give him ninety-five cents change. Just then the other fellow says, "Here, I want a beer too, and both of 'em is on me. Give my friend his dollar back, and take 'em out of this," and he throwed a silver dollar down on the bar. So Jack give the first fellow his dollar bill back, and he give the second fellow a glass of beer and ninety cents change. So then the two fellows went on a-talking and laughing, but Jack was counting his money, and he seen something was wrong. So he says, "Boys, I made a little mistake in your change." The town fellows thought about it a minute, and then one of them says, "Yes, you took a nickel out of my friend's dollar, and you took a dime out of my dollar. That makes fifteen cents for the two beers, and two beers is only ten cents, so you owe us a nickel." Jack he begun to scratch his head again, and the town fellow says, "Oh, never mind, what's a nickel between friends? You can keep the change," he says. And then the two fellows went out the door, and he could hear them laughing away down the street. Poor Jack he set there a long time studying about it, and counting his money. He knowed he was ninety-five cents short, but he couldn't figure out how them town fellows done it so slick.

On the third day a town girl come in, and she says, "I am in a big hurry, and my father is very sick, and he sent me after a pint of Razorback Wine, and it costs seventy-five cents," and she throwed a twenty-dollar bill on the bar. Jack handed down

the bottle, and give her nineteen dollars and twenty-five cents change. "There must be some mistake," she says, "I only give you a one-dollar bill." Jack looked in the drawer right quick. "No ma'am, it's a twenty," says he. The pretty girl opened her little pocketbook again. "My goodness," she says, "I must have pulled out pappy's twenty-dollar bill by accident! Give me the twenty back, and take the wine out of this," and she throwed a one-dollar bill on the bar. Jack give her back the twenty-dollar bill, and out of the door she went. She was in such a hurry she forgot her twenty-five cents change. Jack stood there a minute with the quarter in his hand, and he says to himself, "Well, it is a shame to short-change a pretty girl like that, but I am twenty-five cents ahead, anyhow." And then he got to thinking, and counted the money in the drawer again. By God, he was nineteen dollars short! And this time Jack seen just how the town girl done it, so he run out in the street to catch her, but she was plumb out of sight.

On the fourth day Jack sold the saloon back to the fellow he bought it from. Three days of saloon-keeping is all I could stand, says he. Them town people is nimble as a weasel, and crooked as a barrel of snakes, and the women is worse'n the men. In a couple days more they would have got the gold filling out of my teeth, he says. So then Jack went back to the farm, where he ought to have stayed in the first place. And that is the end of the story.

THE WOMAN AND THE ROBBER

ONCE UPON A TIME, maybe it was in the War between the States, a woman was carrying gold and greenbacks under her clothes. She was taking it to some of her kinfolks up north, where things was not so disorderly. She had a good buggy at home, but it was better to keep off the main traveled road, so she come through on horseback, a-riding side-saddle. She rode up to a house, and the man said he would show her a short-cut where she wanted to go. When they come out on a high bluff he pulled her off the horse and says, "Give me your money." She says the money is sewed under her dress and he must look the other way, as she is a decent woman. He kind of started to turn, and in that minute she out with a derringer and shot him in the guts, before he could throw down on her. Soon as he was dead, the woman took his wallet and pushed him over the edge, and then she went on down the road.

When she got to her kinfolks' place, she told them what happened. After the trouble blowed over they all come South again, and camped with their wagons on top of the big bluff. And next morning the boys went around by the path and found a lot of dead people at the bottom of the holler. They was folks that this man had robbed, and then throwed off the bluff so they couldn't tell nobody.

THEM NEWCOMERS
RUINED THE MEAT

ONE TIME there was a well-to-do family, and they had a nice piece of home-cured bacon. It was the only bacon for miles around, because times was hard and most people didn't have no meat except rabbits. Well, the folks that owned the bacon never thought of eating it; they just used it to season up their beans. The neighbors would borrow the meat once in a while, if they was going to have company, or a wedding in the family, or something like that.

The meat lasted through the winter fine, but along about the middle of March it got pretty weak. You had to boil it in a pot of beans all day, to flavor them up right. But it still smelled like bacon, and the folks figured there was a lot of good wear in that meat yet. Then a gang of newcomers moved into the neighborhood, and nothing would do but they must borrow the meat on Easter Sunday. They was kind of dirty-looking people, but the old lady didn't want to hurt nobody's feelings, so she let them have it.

Well sir, when them foreigners fetched the meat back, you wouldn't have knowed it! The stuff had turned plumb yellow, and smelled like green cordwood. The old lady didn't let on, though. She just says, "Well, I hope you enjoyed your beans." The newcomer's woman she giggled kind of foolish. "We didn't have no beans, ma'am. There ain't been a bean in our house since Christmas. But my boy he picked us some fence-corner greens, and that bacon sure did make 'em taste wonderful."

When the old lady told the folks about it, they got pretty mad. There was some talk of running the newcomers out, but the old lady was against it. "Them poor people don't know any better," she says. "We'll just cut the meat up and throw it to the chickens, and not say nothing to nobody." So that's what they done.

THE BANJO-PICKING GIRL

ONE TIME there was a nam named Joe Keene, and he was a carpenter, and after while he got to be kind of a jackleg preacher, too. He had a wife and four children, and they all belonged to the New Ground Church, which is something like the Holy Rollers. There was a pretty girl come along from down South somewheres, and she could play the banjo besides. The New Ground folks used to have big meetings out in the woods, and then they built a brush-arbor just about where the Playmore Tavern is now. Them people used to pray and holler and roll on the ground pretty near all night, with the pretty girl picking her banjo and the elders a-preaching fit to bust their guts. They preached mostly in the unknown tongue, and you couldn't tell what it was about.

But everybody could tell that the banjo-picking girl was going to have a baby, and one night old Joe Keene throwed a fit, and then he says the Lord God come to him in a vision. Joe says the Lord told him to leave his wife and kids, as they was living sinful anyhow. And then Joe says it is revealed to him that he must marry the banjo-picking girl, because she has never been with a man but she is going to have a child by the Holy Ghost. Joe says he would never have believed such a

65

thing, only the Lord God told him about it with His own mouth.

Well sir, them New Ground folks had swallered a lot of mighty peculiar doctrine, but this here revelation kind of took their breath away. And Joe Keene's woman says she didn't have no idea who's been laying up with the banjo-picker, but she knowed it warn't no ghost. Most of the folks figured maybe Joe Keene did have some kind of a revelation, and he better do what God told him, because it's plumb dangerous to go against the will of the Lord God. And it is best not to take no chances in these latter days, when everybody knows the end of the world ain't far off, anyhow.

And so all the preachers and elders got together, and they voted to give Joe Keene a divorce. Him and his wife had been married in the church without no papers, so the law didn't have nothing to do with it. The New Ground folks done all their marrying that way. They says paper weddings is all right for rich infidels in town, but genuine Christian people must be joined in holy wedlock by God Almighty, and they don't need no papers from the courthouse. The New Ground saints don't believe in taxes, neither, and they never buy no dog-license because there ain't no Scripture for it.

Soon as they give Joe his divorce, he begun to holler "Praise God! Blessed be His holy name!" and he shook hands with everybody in the arbor. And him and the banjo-picking girl got married right then and there. After the service was over they started out afoot for Oklahoma, and you could hear them singing hymns all the way up Gander Mountain.

Along about New Year's there was a letter come from over in the Osage Nation, all about how the baby was borned in a barn somewheres; it was a fine boy, and they was expecting great things of him. There wasn't no more letters after that, but we heard that Joe Keene was arrested for selling whiskey to the Indians, and the girl run off with a trout-mouthed parson

66

from Sallisaw. But it all happened a long time back, and no-body don't rightly know what ever did become of them people.

LITTLE WEED MARSHALL

ONE TIME there was a fellow named Weed Marshall. He only stood five foot three, but he had been a fighter in his day and served under General Joe Shelby in the War between the States. After the War was over he come to Mayview, Mo., and he run the Mayview Hotel. It was a good hotel, too, and Weed knowed all the drummers in that part of Missouri. Them fellows thought the world of Weed, and everybody liked him, but they used to play jokes on him sometimes.

The drummers was mostly Democrats in them days, but they pretended like they was all Republicans, just to get a rise out of Weed Marshall. In the winter of 1891 a bunch of them come in one night, and pretty soon they begun to cuss the Democrat party something terrible. Weed stood it as long as he could, and then he run them all out and throwed their grips after them. "This is a public hotel, and I'm broad-minded," says he. "Yankees can eat at my table and sleep in my beds, if they keep their mouth shut. But you got to draw the line somewhere. If a man ain't got no more sense than to cuss the Democrat party I will throw him out, whether it's a-raining or not."

One day them drummers got hold of a big old man pretty near seven foot tall. They told him all about Weed, and coached him up just what to say, and they put a G.A.R. button on his coat. Weed didn't like tall fellows much, and he seen that little copper button soon as the big Yankee come in, but he never let on.

After supper the big fellow did not pay no attention to

67

Weed, but he begun talking loud to the drummers. "I'm seventy-two years old, but still strong as a bull," says he. "I can lick any man in Missouri. I come from Maine, where everybody eats codfish and potaters. You can't raise full-sized men on hot biscuits and Southern fried chicken," he says. Little Weed Marshall was getting pretty mad, because hot biscuits and fried chicken was his specialty. But he did not say nothing.

So then the drummers asked the big Yankee about what he done in the War. "Well, I never done much," he says. "I served with the Third Illinois Cavalry in south Missouri and Arkansas. But we had hard luck, and never got to see no real Confederates at all, just a bunch of ragged-tailed bushwhackers. They was led by a old chicken-thief name of Joe Shelby." Weed Marshall swelled up like a poisoned pup when he heard that, and he was breathing mighty heavy. But the drummers never paid him no mind. "Did you ever kill any of Shelby's men?" they asked the big fellow. "No, I guess not," he says, "they always run like turkeys, before we could get a shot at 'em. I did capture one, though. Caught him a-stealing corn out of my horse's nose-bag. Poor little devil was hungry, and scared pretty near to death. I just kicked his behind and sent him home to his mammy. He run off down the road, a-crying like a baby." The big man laughed, loud and nasty. "I never will forget that poor little ragamuffin, he was so comical," says the big fellow. "He was just about the size of this here hotel clerk."

The drummers all turned round to look at Weed Marshall, and they was all a-laughing. Weed knowed by this time that it was a joke, but he figured on playing his hand out, anyhow. "Listen, Yank," says he, "it was *me* you captured that day, and I been looking for you ever since!" With that he jumped plumb over the desk, and he had a dragoon six-shooter in his hand. The old gun roared like a Christmas anvil, and that big Yankee tore the screen door all to flinders. *Wham!* says the old gun again, and them smart-aleck drummers was all out in the street, falling down in the mud and hollering "Don't shoot!" at the top of their voice. Weed Marshall give the rebel yell just once, and then he set down in his chair behind the desk.

After while the drummers come a-sneaking back, because there wasn't no other place for them to sleep. They had mud on their clothes, and they was a-singing mighty small. Weed he just set there cleaning his six-shooter. Pretty soon the big man come back, too. "Them fellows put me up to it, Mr. Marshall," says he. "They told me it was a joke. I was in the Navy all through the War, and never even saw Missouri till a year ago." Weed was polishing his gun with a greasy rag, and putting little copper caps on the nipples. "Well, it'll cost you two dollars for that screen," he says, "and ten cents for putty, to fix them bullet-holes in the floor." And so the big fellow counted out two dollars and ten cents, and that was the end of it.

But nobody had much to say at breakfast next morning. The

big Yankee et seven hot biscuits, and liked them. And them drummers walked mighty wide of Weed Marshall for a long time after that.

THE VINEGAR JUG

ONE TIME there was a law in Polk county that people could not make whiskey and sell it, or else they would go to the penitentiary. Farmers was not allowed to make whiskey for their own families even. And so they did not plant no corn, and lots of folks just let their farms go and moved plumb out of Polk county. It looked like things was getting worse all the time, and most of the stores was boarded up, and the best houses was all empty, and people could not pay their taxes. And pretty soon there was nobody left in Polk county only the bootleggers, and they had to make their living by selling whiskey to each other. The hotel was full of foreigners, which they was mostly revenuers and snoopers from the Government, and these fellows was arresting everybody right and left.

One day there was a drummer come to town, but he could not sell nothing because most of the merchants was gone out of business. And his buggy broke down besides, so he had to stay there while they was fixing the buggy. The drummer he run all over the place with his tongue hanging out, but he could not get a drink nowhere. So finally he seen a farmer coming out of the grocery store with a glass jug of vinegar. And he says to the farmer, "For God's sake, take me somewhere I can buy a drink, as I am spitting cotton all day and I got to stay here while they are fixing my buggy." And the farmer says, "Too bad, stranger, but you can't buy no whiskey here for love nor money, as there is a law against liquor. Why, it's got so the sheriff himself can't

70

get a drink hardly." The drummer pulled out his wallet and showed the farmer some little cards, all about how he is a Odd Fellow and a Elk and a Mason, and he belongs to the Commercial Club and the Anti-Horse-Thief Association and the First Baptist Church besides. And he says, "Oh Lord my God, ain't there no help for the widow's son, and what is this country a-coming to, anyhow?" And so the farmer he says, "Well, brother, give me ten dollars and I will see what I can do. It's just round the corner, and you hold this here vinegar till I get back." So the drummer give him the money, and then he stood there in the hot sun and waited.

He waited pretty near two hours, but the farmer did not come back. And after while he set down on the curbstone, and he was feeling mighty low. So then the sheriff come along and he says, "What is the matter with you?" And the drummer says, "One of these apple-knockers has took me for ten dollars, that's what is the matter." And the sheriff says, "What have you got in that there jug?" The drummer says, "If you knowed how to read you could see it is pure cider vinegar with artificial color added, as that's what it says on the goddam label." The sheriff he pulled out the cork. "It don't smell like vinegar to me," says he, "and I will have to put you in the jailhouse."

And so the drummer pulled out his wallet again and showed the little cards, all about how he is a Odd Fellow and a Elk and a Mason, and he belongs to the Commercial Club and the A.H.T.A. and the First Baptist Church besides. And he told the sheriff the same thing as he told the farmer. So then the sheriff says, "Well, brother, I reckon you are all right. But you got to stay in your room at the hotel. It won't do to have people setting around in the street with jugs of whiskey, and not even wrapped up. We're all law-abiding citizens here in Polk county," he says.

The drummer didn't let his shirttail touch his butt till he got back to the hotel, and then he begun to holler for ice water, and pretty soon he was feeling better. And before sundown he says everybody in town is Nature's noblemen and Polk county is the garden spot of all creation, and so they lived happy ever after.

UNCLE JOHNNY'S BEAR

ONE TIME when this town was a-booming we had a fine big whorehouse up on the hill where Sam Leath's tourist camp is now, and they called it the White Elephant. There wasn't no waterworks in them days, and the girls had to carry water from Oil Spring. Two of them girls come running back up the hill one evening, and they kept hollering about a big bear down by the spring. Another woman went down to get the buckets, and she seen the bear too, so after that the girls that lived in the whorehouse would not go to the spring, because they was afraid of the big bear. The old lady that run the place says the girls must be crazy, because no bear is going to come right into town like that. But she knowed something had to be done, so she sent for Uncle Johnny Hickson.

So finally Uncle Johnny come over with his shotgun, but he says it is all damn foolishness. "There ain't no bears in this town," he says, "and if anybody is looking for bears they got to go way out in the hills with dogs, and even then they might not find any, because bears is getting scarce. Also," he says, "it don't look right for a man to be hanging around places like this at my time of life. And if anybody was to hear how Johnny Hickson is hunting bears at the White Elephant, people would laugh at me all over town," he says.

"I told them fool girls there wasn't no bear," says the old lady. "But they claim they seen it with their own eyes, and now we ain't got no drinking water." So Uncle Johnny says give me the goddam bucket, and he started down to the spring. He seen tracks in the path, and a big she bear jumped right out pretty near on top of him. Uncle Johnny was a man that always had both hammers cocked, but he got tangled up with the water-bucket some way, and it slowed him down considerable. Next thing he knowed, the bear had the muzzle of the shotgun in her mouth, so Uncle Johnny pulled the triggers and fell over backwards into a mess of green brambles.

The bear was dead, all right, and Uncle Johnny was not hurt, except he was scratched up considerable in them briars. But when he picked up the shotgun he seen that the barrels was both busted at the end, and he figured the White Elephant people ought to give him twelve dollars to buy a new gun. But the old lady said, "You are a bear hunter, and you have got the bear, so you ought to be satisfied. And if anybody has fooled around and broke their gun it sure ain't my fault," she says.

Uncle Johnny wasn't satisfied by no means, and he says that is what a man gets for trying to be neighborly, specially if the neighbors ain't got nothing better to do except run whore-houses. And he says there is a lot of undesirable citizens in this town, and the fact is damn near all of them are undesirable. So then he went and skinned the bear and cut off the best meat to sell down at the hotel. After he left there was some foreigners come and got the rest of the meat, and that was the end of Uncle Johnny's bear.

THE NEWFANGLED CAPSULES

ONE TIME there was a new doctor come to town, and he give most of his medicine in capsules. Folks did not like the look of these here capsules, because they had never seen any capsules before. In the early days we just took our quinine straight and washed it down with coffee. And when we had to take calomel, we put it in a spoonful of jelly. If there wasn't no jelly in the house, we took calomel just like quinine, with a little whiskey-and-water for a wash. Some of the old-time doctors used to make big pills out of bread, or slippery-elm bark. That's why doctors was called pill-rollers in them days. But nobody in the settlement had ever heard tell of capsules.

So when this young doctor come along with his capsules, folks was kind of dubious, but they swallered them the best they could, and the medicine worked all right. It seemed mighty funny, though, to be taking quinine without no bitter taste. And some thought maybe the stuff wasn't quinine at all. They figured the doctor was maybe giving them soda, or some other white powder that was cheaper than quinine, so he could make more money. But one fellow busted a capsule open and put some on his tongue, and he says it tasted like quinine, all right.

One day Doc stopped by to see a old man he had give

medicine to, and asked how he was getting along. The old man says his malaria fever is lots better, and he ain't a-chilling no more. But it seemed like he was mighty worried about something, and Doc says to him, "What are you a-fretting about?" The old man he looked mighty solemn, and he says he figured his bowels must be damaged permanent. "You know I took fourteen capsules, Doc," says he. "Well, I ain't passed a single one of them hulls yet!"

HIGH WATER AT TURKEY FORD

ONE TIME there was some Holiness people held a big meeting at a place called Turkey Ford, right close to the Oklahoma border. They had a campground down by a little creek. It was a terrible dry summer, and the corn was a-hurting all over the country, so the Holiness people was praying for rain. They run three eight-hour shifts, and some would sleep while the rest of them was a-praying. They kept it up for three days and nights, but nary a drop of water fell. Finally they just kind of give out, and old Preacher Garvin says, "If it's God's will to burn up the corn there ain't nothing anybody can do about it."

That same evening a bunch of draggle-tail Indians come along, and they climbed a bluff right across from the campground. One old Indian come over, and he says, "We are going to have a rain dance, and the white people better move up on high ground, because there will be a lot of water in the creek before sun-up." The preacher he thanked the old Indian polite enough, but he had to laugh when them draggle-tails begun to holler and thump on drums. And he says, "If three days and nights of honest Christian prayer don't fetch a shower, there ain't nothing more to be done. Them poor benighted savages can stomp and holler till hell freezes over, but they won't get no rain out of a dried-up sky," he says.

So the Holiness people just sung a few hymns, and then they all went to bed. The women and children slept in the wagons mostly, but the menfolks just bedded down on the ground. Whenever one of 'em would rouse up a little, he could hear them Indians a-trying to make rain-medicine on the bluff. The Indians would holler "Yip-yip-yoe" every little bit, and them drums just kept a-mumbling "Tum-tiddy-um-tum, tum-tiddy-um-tum" all night long, and never missed a beat. The preacher he says, "This is a free country and everybody has got a right to their own belief, even them poor ignorant heathens. But it's too bad they got to be so noisy that God-fearing Christians can't get no rest," he says.

Well sir, just about daybreak the sky clabbered up, with the awfullest clap of thunder a body ever heard. Then come the rain, a regular cloudburst, and the creek a-rising so fast them wagons was hub deep before they could get the teams geared

76

up. The wind was blowing a regular hurricane by this time, and big limbs a-falling all over the place. The women and kids was a-hollering, and the menfolks a-splashing round in the water, and some of the horses broke loose, and there was hell to pay generally. Right in the middle of the whole mess old Preacher Garvin was up on a high stump, a-praying at the top of his voice. "Hold on, Lord! No more water, Lord!" he hollered as loud as he could. "You want to drownd us like a bunch of goddam polecats?"

The Holiness folks got out all right, and saved most of their stuff, but it was God's own luck and no credit to Preacher Garvin. When they finally got back up into the road and started for town, they was a mighty sorry looking crowd. Pretty soon they come to a open space, and they could see the Indians across the creek. Them Indians was all setting under a big ledge, where it was dry as a bone. They had fires in there too, and was a-cooking their breakfast. Old Preacher Garvin stopped and looked at them for a long time, but he didn't say nothing. He knowed some of the young folks was tickled to see him make a fool of himself climbing up on a stump and hollering to the Lord about polecats. It all happened a long time ago, but the Holiness people ain't forgot the big flood at Turkey Ford. And some of them call the old man Polecat Garvin to this day.

THE ABOLITION OF SCOTT COUNTY

ONE TIME there was two fellows elected to the legislature, so they went down to Little Rock. The Representative from Scott county was a solemn-faced man, and he took everything mighty serious. But the fellow from Polk county was a joker, always playing tricks on somebody. One day he got up in the House and introduced a bill to abolish Scott county, and add the territory to Polk county. Scott county was very sparsely settled, he says, and they don't need no courthouse out there in the woods, just for a bunch of possum-hunters. All the best people lived in Polk county anyhow, and they could just drive out in a wagon some day and fetch the county records over to Mena.

The Polk county fellow had went around beforehand and told everybody that his bill was just a joke, and he passed the word to the Governor, too. The Representative from Scott county didn't think such a fool bill could possibly pass, but he soon found out that pretty near everybody in the Legislature was going to vote for it. He begun to talk against the bill all over Little Rock, but people just laughed at him. He went to the Governor's office, but even the Governor seemed to think it might be a good idea to abolish Scott county, and he wouldn't promise to veto the bill. The Committee on County Lines recommended that the measure be enacted into law. It looked like Scott county was going to be wiped out over night, and there wasn't nothing anybody could do about it.

The Representative from Scott county figured that him and his constituents was ruined forever, but he got up in the House and made one more speech. "I can see that this outrageous bill is going to pass," he says. "But in the interest of my people's peace and welfare, in the interest of law and order, I want to offer an amendment that my county may be added to the Indian Territory and not to Polk county!" The solemn fellow from Scott county was in dead earnest, and it was a terrible slam at Polk county, because the Indian Territory in them days was full of robbers and outlaws from all over the United States, and it was the toughest place in the whole country. So everybody laughed to see how the Polk county man's foolishness had done backfired on him, and the bill was dead as a wagon tire from then on out. The Representative from Polk county looked mighty sick, and spent considerable money to keep the story out of his home-town newspaper. And he never did play no more jokes on the solemn fellow from Scott county, neither.

HUNTING THE OLD IRON

ONCE UPON A TIME a man went out into a big, dark, dense forest. He had his dogs with him, and his rifle, because he was hunting the old iron. He went deeper and deeper into the woods. Finally, way up in the top of a big oak tree he seen the old iron. And he *called* the dogs: "Hyar, Shep! Hyar, Tray! Hyar, Bruce! Hyar, Rover! Hyar, Caesar! Hyar, Ring! Hyar, Nero! Hyar, Horace! Hyar, Pinder! Hyar, Belt! Hyar, Ponto! Hyar, Bugler! Hyar, Buck! Hyar, Zip!"

But the old iron jumped into another treetop, so the man follered along, and he *called* the dogs: "Hyar, Shep! Hyar, Tray! Hyar, Bruce! Hyar, Rover! Hyar, Caesar! Hyar, Ring! Hyar, Nero! Hyar, Horace! Hyar, Pinder! Hyar, Belt! Hyar, Ponto! Hyar, Bugler! Hyar, Buck! Hyar, Zip!"

But the old iron jumped into another treetop, so the man follered along, and he *called* the dogs: "Hyar, Shep! Hyar, Tray! Hyar, Bruce! Hyar, Rover! Hyar, Caesar! Hyar, Ring! Hyar, Nero! Hyar, Horace! Hyar, Pinder! Hyar, Belt! Hyar, Ponto! Hyar, Bugler! Hyar, Buck! Hyar, Zip!"

But the old iron jumped into another treetop, so the man follered along, and he *called* the dogs: "Hyar, Shep! Hyar, Tray! Hyar, Bruce! Hyar, Rover! Hyar, Caesar! Hyar, Ring!

Hyar, Nero! Hyar, Horace! Hyar, Pinder! Hyar, Belt! Hyar, Ponto! Hyar, Bugler! Hyar, Buck! Hyar, Zip!"

But the old iron jumped into another treetop, so the man follered along, and he *called* the dogs: "Hyar, Shep! Hyar, Tray! Hyar, Bruce! Hyar, Rover! Hyar, Caesar! Hyar, Ring! Hyar, Nero! Hyar, Horace! Hyar, Pinder! Hyar, Belt! Hyar, Ponto! Hyar, Bugler! Hyar, Buck! Hyar, Zip!"

But the old iron jumped into another treetop, so the man follered along, and he *called* the dogs . . .

THE DEAF MAN'S ANSWERS

ONE TIME the acorns failed in Arkansas, and the squirrels all come a-trooping up into Missouri. There was thousands of 'em, and they eat up pretty near everything in this country. Old man Hodges was a-standing out in the road, looking up at the squirrels in a big white-oak. The old man was deaf as a post, so he didn't hear them two fellows that come a-walking up the road behind him. They had come afoot from way down around Batesville somewheres, and they was looking for a place to stay all night.

The boys says "Howdy" polite enough, and then they wanted to know how far it is to the next town. But old man Hodges thought they must be talking about what was going on in the white-oak tree. "Yes, they act like minks," says he, "but I reckon they're both fox-squirrels." The two fellows from Batesville looked at each other kind of funny, and then one of them says, "How far is it to the settlement?" Old man Hodges was still a-looking up the white-oak. "A fox-squirrel is mighty good with dumplings," he says. Them Batesville boys wasn't in no mood for jokes. They was tired and hungry, and they had asked the old man a civil question. The biggest one begun to get pretty mad. "Mister," says he, "I believe you're a damned old fool!" Old man Hodges just nodded his head. "Yes, the woods is full of 'em," he says, "and more a-coming in from Arkansas every day."

The least boy he busted out laughing when he heard that, and he says, "Yes sir, you took the words right out of my mouth!" And the other fellow he seen the old man was deef by that time, so they just grinned at him and went on down the road.

A PALLET ON THE FLOOR

ONE TIME a fellow was traveling through the country, and it was a-raining, and he was looking for a place to sleep. Just before sundown he come to a little old log house. There was a man and a woman there, with three young-ones. They only had one bed, but the man he allowed there's always room for a traveler. "You can have the bed," says he. "Me and my woman will sleep on a pallet with the kids."

After supper they set around and swapped whoppers awhile, and when the children got sleepy, the woman put them in the bed. Pretty soon two of the kids was sound asleep, and the man he picked them up careful and moved them to the pallet on the floor. So then the folks talked some more, and the other boy he went to sleep, and they laid him on the pallet, too. "The bed's all your'n, stranger," says the man. "You just turn in whenever you get ready. There's plenty of room on the pallet for me and the old woman." So the fellow went to bed. He was tired from riding all day, and he slept fine.

When the traveler woke up next morning it was still pretty

dark, and seemed like the bed had got awful hard. But he just laid there till dawn. And then he seen that he wasn't in the bed at all. He was laying on the pallet with the kids. The man and the woman was in the bed, both of them a-snoring like they was sawing gourds. The fellow got up quiet and went outdoors awhile. He set out by the barn till he heard somebody splitting wood. When he come back to the house everybody was up and the woman was cooking breakfast. "You sure do get up early, stranger," says the man. "If you'd slept a little longer, me and the old woman would have put you back in bed. We always do strangers thataway, and mighty few of 'em ever know the difference."

THE RAIL SPLITTER

ONE TIME a fellow was splitting rails to build him a fence, as they did not have no wire fences in them days. He got his wedge into a white-oak log, and had just drove in the glut, when all of a sudden there was four big Indians a-standing right beside him. They had their war-paint on. One was carrying a big brass pistol, and the others had tomahawks in their hands. The rail splitter's rifle was standing against a tree ten foot off, on the other side of the log. He seen he didn't have no chance.

One of the big Indians says, "Come with us," and motioned towards the pineries. "Help me split this here rail-cut," says the fellow, "and I'll go wherever you say." Then he reached down and grabbed a hold of the log, like he figured on busting it open with his bare hands. The Indians grinned, as they thought all white men was crazy anyhow. So all four of them took a hold of the log and made out like they was pulling hard as they could. They thought it was a good joke, but the rail-splitter knowed what he was doing. Soon as all four Indians got their hands in the crack, he grabbed his maul and knocked out the glut. Them Indians yelled like a steamboat whistle, but they could not do nothing, because their hands was caught in the crack.

So then the rail-splitter took his maul and knocked them four Indians in the head. "That'll learn these here savages not to fool with me," he says. And when he got home he told his wife a big windy about how four Indians jumped on him, and they fit a long time, but finally he killed them all. The woman she just laughed at first, like she didn't believe it. But when he showed her the big brass pistol and the three tomahawks and some other things he took off the dead Indians, she didn't have no more to say.

DIVIDING UP THE DEAD

ONE TIME there was a preacher come through the country, and he was making too free with the womenfolks. Finally it got so bad that something had to be done, so two bear-hunters laid for him in the burying-ground, right next to the big road. One was a little dried-up fellow, and the other one was pretty fat. They had their rifles ready, and a little jug to keep off seedticks. Them bear-hunters figured the preacher would come along the road about four o'clock, but he never showed up. They waited a long time, and drunk the jug plumb dry. The fat man got kind of chicken-hearted, and he says maybe it's bad luck to kill a preacher anyhow. And the little dried-up fellow says he don't mind killing preachers, but this here setting on the ground is bad for the rheumatism.

Just about that time a couple of boys come along with a sack of pawpaws. They slipped into the graveyard by the back way, and set down by the stone wall. They did not see the bear-hunters on the other side of the wall, and the hunters could not see them, neither. The boys spread their pawpaws on the ground, and begun to divide them up. "You take this one, I'll take that one," says the oldest boy. "You take this one, I'll take that one," says he. He said it kind of sing-song, like boys naturally do when they are dividing up pawpaws. The two men heard all this, but they couldn't see nothing, and they didn't know who it was doing the talking. They thought maybe there was devils in the graveyard, dividing up the dead.

The boys had got the pawpaws in separate piles by now, and the oldest boy says, "Well, that's all, except them two over by the wall. You take the dried-up one, and I'll take the fat one." The bear-hunters heard this plain, and it sounded like they was being counted in with the corpses. The little dried-up fellow give a whoop and lit out for home. The big fat bear-hunter didn't do no hollering, but he sure tore down the brush a-getting away from there.

That same night, it seems like a woman told the preacher how the menfolks was fixing to kill him, and the next morning he showed up missing. Some say maybe the bear-hunters got him, and buried him out in the woods somewheres. But most folks figure he just skipped plumb out of the country. Nobody in them parts ever seen him again, anyhow.

THREE LITTLE PIGS

ONE TIME there was three little pigs. One pig built him a chip house, one built him a stick house, and one built him a rock house. When the old fox come to the chip house he says, "Let me in, Piggy-Wee. If you don't, I'll puff and I'll blow till I blow your house down." But the little pig was afraid, and he wouldn't open the door. So the old fox he puffed and he blowed till the house fell down, and then he et the little pig up.

Next day the old fox come to the stick house and he says, "Let me in, Piggy-Wee. If you don't, I'll puff and I'll blow till I blow your house down." But the little pig was afraid, and he wouldn't open the door. So the old fox he puffed and he blowed till the house fell down, and then he et the little pig up.

Finally the old fox come to the rock house, and he says, "Let me in, Piggy-Wee. If you don't, I'll puff and I'll blow till I blow your house down." But the little pig was afraid, and he wouldn't open the door. So the old fox he puffed and he blowed, but the rock house wouldn't fall down. Then the old fox says, "Let me get the end of my nose in," and the little pig opened the door a crack. Then the old fox says, "Let me get a little more of my nose in," and the little pig opened the door another crack. Then the old fox says, "Let me get my eyes in," and the little pig opened the door another crack. Then the old fox says, "Let me get a little more of my eyes in," and the little pig opened the door another crack. Then the old fox says, "Let me get my ears in," and the little pig opened the door another crack. And so it went, with the old fox getting a little more of his ears in. Then his neck, and a little more of his neck. Then his front feet, and a little more of his front feet. Then his ribs, and a little more of his ribs. Finally the old fox was all inside the house but his tail, and then he just busted on in without asking the little pig nothing.

Next the old fox set down by the fire, and he says, "Warm belly gut. Eat a pig pretty soon." Just then they heard the hounds a-coming round the mountain, and the old fox says, "Piggy-Wee, where can I hide?" And the little pig says, "Jump in that big trunk." So the old fox jumped in the big trunk, and Piggy-Wee slammed down the lid and locked it.

The little pig he set and thought awhile. Then he got some hot water out of the kettle and poured it through a little hole, and the old fox says, "Piggy-Wee, there's a flea biting me." Then the little pig poured in some more water, and the old fox says, "Piggy-Wee, there's a fire burning me." Then the little pig poured in the whole kettle of hot water, and the old fox hollered something terrible, but it didn't do him no good. Pretty soon the old fox was scalded plumb to death, and the little pig lived happy in his rock house till the butcher cut him down.

THE PIN IN THE GATEPOST

ONE TIME there was a good-looking girl with a fine figure, but her eyes got so weak she could not see nothing hardly, and she would not wear specs. Her mother was trying to get her married off, and she set her cap for a rich old man that had two big farms. The old man didn't know the girl was almost blind, and they did not aim to let him find out. Whenever he come to see her they set everything exactly in the right place, so she could reach out and pick up whatever she wanted. And when he asked her to go buggy riding, she says no. She says her mother did not think it was right for a girl to go buggy riding with a man until after they was married.

One day she stuck a pin in the gatepost, and when the old man come to see her they was setting out on the porch. Pretty soon she says, "What's that on the gatepost?" The old man looked, and he says he don't see nothing. "Well," says the girl, "it looks to me like a pin sticking in the gatepost." So they walked down the path, and sure enough there was the pin.

And the old man says, "My Gosh, you have got sharp eyes!" The girl she just grinned, and put the pin in the front of her dress for luck.

Everything would have been all right except they had a big white cat. Mostly it would just lay by the fire all day, but sometimes it would take a wild spell and jump right up on the table. Well, when they set down to supper that night, the rich old man he returned thanks. Soon as he says "Amen" somebody set a pitcher of buttermilk right in front of him. The girl hollered "Scat, you brute!" and knocked the pitcher off the table, because she thought it must be the cat.

The rich old man seen how things was, but he did not say nothing. He just wiped the buttermilk off of his pants, and then got in his buggy and went home. He never did come back there no more, neither. It served the old girl right, for trying to fool him with that pin on the gatepost.

THE LITTLE BOY AND
THE SNAKE

ONE TIME there was a woman, and she had a little boy. Every day she would give him a bowl of bread and milk. He always carried the bread and milk out in the brush to eat it. She thought it was kind of funny he wouldn't eat in the house, but she did not say nothing. Every day she heard the little boy talking and laughing out in the brush, but she figured he was talking to himself. He could talk pretty good for his age. A girl told her that the little boy was all the time playing with a snake, but the woman didn't believe it.

One day she slipped through the fence to find out what the

little boy was doing, and she seen him setting on the ground with a big yellow rattlesnake wrapped around his legs. He would eat a little of his bread and milk, and then give some to the snake. They was having a fine time together. That was why the little boy always took his bread and milk out in the brush that way and would not play with the other children.

The woman did not say nothing, but she went back to the house and got the shotgun. Pretty soon the rattlesnake seen her coming. It moved away from the little boy, and then reared up and begun to rattle. So then the woman shot the big snake and killed it.

The little boy did not make no fuss. He just looked at his mother once, and his eyes was like snake eyes. Then he went back to the house, and he never spoke another word to anybody. He never laughed no more, and he never eat another bite except some leaves off of a weed. Nobody knowed what kind of a weed it was. On sunny days he laid still in the sunshine, with his eyes wide open. He just kind of pined away and got thinner. They had the town doctor come out, but it didn't do no good. About three weeks after she killed the big snake, the woman found her little boy laying in the path, and he was dead. His mouth looked kind of funny, and his eyes was not like other little boys' eyes.

The town doctor said maybe the little boy was poisoned by eating weeds. But the home folks did not believe no such foolishness. Everybody knowed that the woman's first husband was part Cherokee, and he was kind of a snakey-looking fellow. It was against his religion to kill snakes. Some folks thought there might be a little cross of rattlesnake in the family.

BELLE STARR AND JIM REED

ONE TIME there was a pretty girl named Belle Shirley lived at Carthage, Mo., and she married a fellow that called himself Jim Reed. He learned her to steal horses, and they done a lot of hell-raising along the border between Arkansas and the Indian Territory. It was a pretty tough country in them days, and they say Jim killed three or four fellows that crowded him. So him and her run off and went to Texas. There was a big reward out for Jim, dead or alive. Plenty of people knowed about the reward, and Jim got so he wouldn't go no place without a Winchester carbine in his hand. Belle she always wore a six-shooter, just for protection. But there was a no-good fellow by the name of John Morris caught up with them in Collins county. Morris got behind Jim some way, while he was eating dinner in a farmhouse, and killed him.

Well, there wasn't no way for this fellow Morris to get the reward money unless he could prove that the dead man was Jim Reed. Lots of folks in the neighborhood knowed Jim well, but they didn't want no part in this here killing. So they all says they never heard of Jim Reed, and they didn't have no idea who the corpse was, neither.

Finally the sheriff went and got Belle to come in and take a look at the dead man. He figured if it really was her man, Belle would maybe bust out a-crying or something. There wasn't no undertaker, and the weather was kind of warm, so the corpse looked pretty bad. Belle stared at the dead man's face a minute, and she knowed him all right, but she didn't let on. "I never seen this fellow before," she says, "but it sure ain't Jim Reed." Then she walked out with her spurs a-jingling, and she got on her black horse and rode off. The sheriff had to bury the body, and John Morris never got a cent of the reward. Some say he come pretty near getting lynched besides.

Belle felt pretty bad for a long time after that, and she says if Jim's brother Solly was half a man he would run down John Morris and kill him. "Well," she says, "I kept that murderer from getting the blood-money, anyhow. It was all I could do."

She moved up to Joplin for awhile, and run around with Bruce Younger, that claimed to be a cousin of Cole Younger. Then she took up with a Cherokee named Sam Starr, and they lived out at Younger Bend, on the Canadian River west of Fort Smith. That's when everybody got to calling her Belle Starr. There was a lot of lies in the papers about Belle being "Queen of the Bandits," and how many men she killed, and all like that. Some people said Belle's place was headquarters for the worst gang of outlaws in the whole Territory. She was a mighty pretty woman, not near so chunky as the pictures in the magazines, and she come of a fine family. It's too bad she had to get mixed up with all them tough characters.

THE MAN FROM
HOCKEY MOUNTAIN

ONE TIME there was a big fellow lived up on Hockey Mountain who was always singing hymns and praying. Whenever he seen anybody doing something wrong, he would flop right down on his knees and pray so loud you could hear him two miles off. That fellow busted up dances and card games and drinking parties all over the country, just by praying and singing hymns. "Prayer is a great power in the world, specially if a man is blessed with a good voice like I got," he says.

Folks was getting pretty tired of this Hockey Mountain business, but nobody done anything about it. After all, a man has got a right to pray, if he feels like praying. Things just kind of rocked along till they caught Slim Pemberton making whiskey. Slim's wife was a terrible pretty woman, and so Nick Bradley come over to see her while Slim was serving out his time. Nick and Sally Pemberton was getting along fine, till one night the big fellow began to pray right outside the door, and you could hear him all over town. "God damn it, there's old Hockey Mountain a-bawlin' at the moon!" says Nick, and then he slipped out the back door and run home through the cornfield. Soon as Nick was gone the praying stopped, but the more he studied about it the madder Nick got. And he says he is going to whip this here troublemaker within a inch of his life.

The Hockey Mountain fellow was setting on the hotel porch when Nick Bradley caught up with him. "Take off your coat," says Nick, "I'm going to batter you down to my size." The big fellow just looked at him for a minute. "You mind if I pray?"

he rumbled way down in his gizzard. Nick laughed. "Go right ahead," he says, "you're a-standing in the need of prayer, right this minute."

The big man stepped off the porch and got down on his knees in the dusty road. "Oh Lord," he says, "you know the time I killed Lon Witherspoon it was in Your service, and that's why the jury turned me loose. You know I butchered up Newt Allsopp in self-defense, and it warn't no fault of mine. And You know I had to kill Andy Calvert, after he drug our preacher out of the pulpit and shot off his pistol right in the church house. And that gambler in Hot Springs was neglecting his family, Lord, and running after married women, so I was forced to de-horn him." There was quite a crowd gathered round by this time, and they all heard the Hockey Mountain fellow's prayer. "And now, Lord, I've got to cut down this poor misguided sinner right in the bloom of youth. You know what he's guilty of, Lord. But I hope and pray that You'll have mercy on his sin-blackened soul. In Christ's name I ask it, Amen!"

Then the Hockey Mountain fellow stood up, and there was a big homemade bowie knife in his hand. "Well, young man, let's get it over with," says he. With that he looked around in the crowd for Nick Bradley, but Nick wasn't nowheres in sight. "A guilty conscience makes a coward of us all," he says, and put the bowie knife back under his overalls. "I never seen a adulterer yet, but what he was afraid to meet his Maker face to face."

Nick Bradley never showed himself around town for a long time after that. A lot of other young fellows was scared pretty bad, too, and they say Sally Pemberton didn't have no company all summer, except maybe a few outlanders from the tourist camp.

ONE TIME a stranger come out to old man Kerr's place on Shanker Branch, to see about buying some hogs. There was two little boys a-setting on the gallery, and they didn't have a stitch on except their homemade shirts. Pretty near all little boys wore long shirts in them days, without no pants. When a youngster was about twelve years old, the folks give him his first pair of jeans.

Well, the stranger knowed all about that, and he never paid no attention to them little shirttail boys. But when him and old man Kerr went to look at the hogs, there was a full-growed man out there, and he didn't have nothing on but a shirt neither. The big fellow was setting on a stump, with his long hairy legs a-sticking out, and he looked like one of these here tarantulers. The stranger never had seen no shirttail boy that big before, and he thought it was mighty funny, but he knowed better than to laugh. So he just kept on a-talking about hogs with old man Kerr, and never let on like he seen anything out of the way.

After the hog-buying was done, though, he stopped one of the little boys out by the gate, and asked who was the big fellow without no pants on. "Looks like he's kind of old, for a shirttail boy," says the stranger.

"Oh, that's my brother Lem," the boy says, grinning like a young possum. "Lem's got kind of stuck up since he went to business-college in Springfield, and this morning he done something at the table that hurt Aunt Ethel's feelings. So paw just hauled off and knocked him back fifteen years!"

THE WOOL ON PAPPY'S FILLY

ONE TIME there was two boys, and they wanted a horsehide coat like they seen on cowpunchers from Oklahoma. They didn't have no money to buy coats like that, so they sneaked up behind their pappy's bay filly, and whooped and hollered loud as they could. It scared the filly so bad she jumped plumb out of her skin. They had a fine horsehide, all right. But the old man just went wild when he seen the filly running around bare that way. He whupped them boys something terrible, and booted them right out in their shirttail. He told 'em never to come in the house no more till they figured out some way to fix up his prize filly.

Well, the boys killed two sheep and skinned them, and then they put the sheep pelts on the filly the best they could. The skin growed on all right, but the filly always looked kind of funny after that. She didn't grow much wool the first year, but the second year she had wool four foot long and pointed three ways for Sunday. The whole family worked seven days a-shearing her. Just about time the job was done, the filly kicked pappy into the pile of wool, and it took all day and half the night to find him. He pretty nigh sultered under all that wool, and they do say he suffered terrible with the asthma all the rest of his life.

THE FELLOW THAT STOLE CORN

ONE TIME pappy figured somebody was stealing corn out of his crib, so he put a padlock on the door. Everybody left their houses and barns unlocked in them days, and folks thought the country must be in a bad way when it got so a man had to lock up his corn. But even after he put the lock on the crib, pappy kept a-missing corn just the same, and he found where the thief had reached through a hole betwixt the logs and pulled out one ear at a time. He never said nothing to nobody, but that night he set a wolf-trap inside the crib, right next to the hole in the wall.

Next morning when pappy went out to milk, there was a fellow standing by the corncrib, with his arm stuck through the hole betwixt the logs. Pappy just says, "Howdy, it looks like rain," and went right ahead with his chores. After while he got a couple of neighbors to come over, and they all seen the fellow a-standing there. There was a tow sack on the ground beside him with a few ears of corn in it, and his hand was caught in the wolf-trap. "It must be some kind of a varmint," says pappy. The biggest neighbor he says, "No, it seems to favor one of them Spelvin boys that lives down the road a piece." And the other neighbor says, "I reckon he was going to the spelling bee

95

last night, and got off the road, and mistook your corncrib for the schoolhouse." So they all nodded their heads, like they thought that must be how it happened. The thief he just stood there, and never opened his mouth.

Well, pretty soon they let the fellow out of the trap, and made him go in the house and eat breakfast with the family. He didn't seem to have no appetite, but they told him to eat, so he set down to the table and done the best he could. Pappy and the two neighbors just watched him. When he got done eating they took him out to the corncrib again, and pappy filled up the tow sack with corn. "You reckon we'd know the critter, if we was to see him again?" says pappy. The two neighbors just looked at the thief careful, and nodded their heads. "Yeah, but maybe it would be better if we don't see him no more," says the biggest one. The other neighbor kept a-fiddling with his gun. "I reckon it would be a lot better," he says, and scowled so as to show his teeth like a wolf.

The thief thought they was going to kill him, and he wanted to run right off through the timber. But pappy made him put the sack of corn on his shoulder and march out of the gate like a gentleman. He must have skipped the country right away, because nobody ever seen him in the neighborhood after that. If they had caught him sneaking around there again, it's likely somebody would have done him harm. Folks was awful set against stealing in them days. There was men right in that holler that would kill a thief just as soon as they'd shoot a chicken hawk, and never give it a second thought. Things is different nowadays, of course.

JASPER ACTED
KIND OF FOOLISH

ONE TIME there was a boy named Jasper that lived up on Crane Creek, and he acted kind of foolish sometimes. So whenever anybody wanted to tell a story about what some fool boy done, they generally laid it on Jasper.

His own uncle told it around that when Jasper was seventeen years old they had to throw him down and put shoes on him. Jasper broke loose and run through the woods till he was plumb wore out, and then he went to sleep. When he woke up it was dark, and his feet hurt so bad he thought he was caught in a bear-trap, so he just laid right there till daylight.

They used to tell another one about how somebody give Jasper a collar and necktie for Christmas. He never had no collar before, and when the folks put it on him Jasper just stood still all evening, because he figured he was tied up.

Jasper went to school all right, but he couldn't learn nothing, and he acted like he was scared of the other scholars. The folks tried to tell him there wasn't no sense in it, because he was bigger than anybody else in school and could lick the other boys easy. Finally they found out he was afraid they might gang up on him and fasten a tin can to his shirttail. If they done that, Jasper thought he'd have to run down the road and holler, like a dog does when the boys tie a can on his tail.

When his pappy told him to grease the wagon, Jasper done a fine job with the front wheels, but he didn't put no grease on the rear wheels at all. "The main thing in greasing wagons," says he, "is to keep the front wheels a-running good. It stands to reason that them hind wheels has *got* to foller."

Folks used to tell about the time the boys got to skylarking around and busted the glass in old man Hedgepeth's window. They sent Jasper to town after a pane of glass, ten inches by twelve inches. The clerk in Tipton's store was a smart aleck, so he says they ain't got any ten-by-twelve glass, but how would a twelve-by-ten piece do? Jasper studied about it for a long time. "Well, we can try it," he says, kind of doubtful. "Maybe if I slip the glass in sideways, old man Hedgepeth won't never know the difference."

When it come to plowing Jasper was a pretty good hand, provided he got started off right. One day he plowed his first furrow by sighting on a big brown rock. The trouble is that it wasn't a rock at all, it was a cow. When the cow moved it throwed Jasper out of line, so his furrow was crooked as a dog's hind leg. Jasper he looked at that furrow a long time, and then he unhitched the team and went home. When the folks got to looking for Jasper they found he had went to bed, at nine o'clock in the morning. Jasper says when a fellow can't plow no straighter than that he's a mighty sick man, and liable to die any minute.

One day there was a schoolmarm over at Hurley wrote Jasper a letter, but he couldn't read good enough to make out what it was about. Jasper studied a long time, and then he got one of the Dunlap youngsters to read the letter out loud. Whilst the Dunlap boy set on the ground a-reading, Jasper made him plug up both his ears with moss. "Nobody but me is going to hear a word of that there letter," he says. "Do you think I want them Dunlaps to know all about my private business?"

Jasper never was no hand to go with the girls, but his pappy thought maybe they could marry him off to a widow woman about seven miles down the creek. So they dressed Jasper all up, and made him go over to her place. Jasper didn't know how to spark no widow woman, and he set there three hours without saying a word, just a-looking at her. She wasn't much to look at, neither. Finally Jasper got to thinking how he had to walk all the way back home, and him tired out already, and it a-raining besides. "Well by God!" says he, "I wish I was home in bed! And I wish pappy was here, *in his sock feet!*" The widow woman was pretty mad, but she couldn't keep from laughing. Next day she told the neighbors about it, and that's how the story got out.

To hear all them tales they used to tell on Jasper, you'd think he wouldn't never amount to much, and lucky if he didn't end up in the poorhouse. But the fact is, he done pretty good. He married one of them Pinkley girls, and raised a big family, and owned the best bottom farm on the creek. It just goes to show that you can't never tell about a fellow like Jasper.

THE POPPET CAUGHT A THIEF

ONE TIME the people that was sleeping in a tavern all got robbed. It looked like somebody must have put powders in the liquor, and stole their stuff while they was asleep. There wasn't no banks in them days, so travelers had to carry their money in gold. They claimed there was three thousand dollars missing, besides four good watches and a snuffbox which the man says he wouldn't have took a hundred dollars for it. The fellow that run the tavern would not let nobody leave, neither. "Them valuables must be got back, or else I will wade knee-deep in blood," he says, "because the honor of my house has been throwed in jeopardy!"

The travelers was getting pretty mad, but just then an old

woman come along and she says, "What is the matter?" The tavernkeeper he told her, and the old woman says, "My poppet can catch any thief in the world, and it won't take ten minutes." She pulled a little wooden doll out of her saddlebag, and rubbed some walnut-juice on it, and set it on a stand-table. "Them travelers can come in here one at a time," she says, "and the rest of us will set just outside the door. Every one of 'em must grab that there poppet and squeeze it. If the man's honest you won't hear a sound, but if he's a thief the poppet will holler like a stuck pig." The travelers says it is all foolishness, but they will try anything to get away from this lousy tavern. So they went in one after another, but the poppet didn't holler at all.

The old woman looked considerable set back. "Did you all pinch the poppet?" she asked. The travelers all says they squeezed it hard as they could. "Hold out your hands," says the old woman, and she studied each man's fingers mighty careful. Pretty soon she pointed at the traveler that done all the hollering about his snuffbox. "That's the thief," she says. The fellow tried to lie out of it, but when they got the rope round his neck he begun to holler. "If you turn me loose I will give everything back," says he. "But if you hang me you will never get a penny, because that gold is hid where you couldn't find it in a thousand years." Well, the tavernkeeper was unanimous for hanging him anyhow, but them travelers naturally wanted to get their money back. They promised to put the robber on a good horse and give him three hours' start. He made everybody swear with their right hand on the Book, and then he showed them where the stuff was hid under a woodpile. So pretty soon they turned the son-of-a-bitch loose, and off he went down the road at a dead run. Nobody ever did catch up with him, neither.

Soon as the people got their money and watches, they begun to feel pretty good again. The tavernkeeper set up a big dinner, and everybody eat and drunk till they was full as a tick. Pretty soon they raffled off the robber's watch to pay for the dinner, and the man that won the watch give it to the old woman. Finally a fellow passed the old woman's bonnet around for a silver collection, and then he says, "You can have all this money, if you will tell us how you knowed which one was the thief."

The old woman just grinned at him. "Didn't you hear my poppet holler, when that scoundrel grabbed it?" she says. The fellow says of course not, and everybody knows a wooden doll can't holler. "A thief don't know nothing for sure," says the old woman. "Every one of you honest men squeezed that poppet. But the robber figured there might be a trick to it, so he never touched the poppet. All I done was to look for the fellow that didn't have no walnut juice on his hands."

THE QUEEN'S WHITE GLOVE

ONE TIME there was an old king, and the queen was a lot younger than he was, and she was the prettiest woman in the whole country. They didn't have no children, but the king had a little dog that was trained, and could do all kind of tricks. Sometimes the king would hide his handkerchief or something like that, and then tell the little dog to go fetch it. The little dog would smell the king's hand just once, and away he went over hills and down hollers till he found the handkerchief, and then he would bring it back mighty proud and give it to the king. And all the people would brag about what a smart dog he was, and what a good nose he had, and how he could smell out everything and never made no mistakes.

Well, one night the king and queen went to a big dance, and the queen says she has lost one of her white gloves. She wanted to go back home and look for it, but the old king says no, we will send the little dog instead. So the little dog smelled the queen's hand just once, and away he went over hills and down hollers. They waited awhile, and the queen says, "Maybe I better go back and look for the glove myself, because I know right where I lost it." But the king says, "Don't you worry, my little dog will fetch it pretty soon, because he has got the best nose of any dog in the world, and he never makes no mistakes."

After while they could hear the people hollering outside, and they knowed the little dog had got back. So here he come into the room with something in his mouth, but not the queen's white glove. No sir, it belonged to the young servant man that lived in the king's house, and it was not the kind of thing the queen ought to be putting her hand on, neither. The king stuck it in his pocket right quick, so the people did not get much chance to see what it was. The queen laughed and she says well, your little dog sure made a mistake this time! The old king just looked at her, but he did not laugh. "Somebody has made a mistake, all right," says he, "but I ain't sure if it was the little dog or not."

So then him and the queen went out on the floor and led the dancing same as they always done, and all the people had a good time. But next day the young servant man that lived in the king's house was gone, and the king got another fellow to take his place. The new servant was pretty near seventy years old, and he was fat and bald-headed besides. The king was a very smart man, and he never said one word to anybody about the time his little dog made a mistake. But from that day on if the queen lost anything the king just let her go and find it herself, which was what she wanted to do in the first place. And so they all lived happy ever after.

STRAWBERRIES ARE
EASY WITCHED

ONE TIME old Judge Culpepper set out a big patch of strawberries, and they done fine at first. But the Judge's wife was mean and hard to get along with, always having trouble with the neighbors. Old Gram French come along the road selling sassafras roots, but Mis' Culpepper didn't want no sassafras roots, and she says Gram French don't know enough to dig sassafras anyhow. One word led to another, and pretty soon both of them women was cussing and blackguarding loud as they could. So Gram went out in the road and drawed a little circle in the dust. Then she marked a cross in the circle, and spit on the cross. Everybody knowed Gram French could talk the Devil's language, and they figured she was throwing a spell on Judge Culpepper's berry patch.

Next morning the Judge got up early to look at his strawberries, and it looked like they was doing all right. The next day he was out early again, but he couldn't see nothing wrong in the strawberry patch. Old Mis' Culpepper says this gabble about witching berries is all foolishness, and Gram French could draw circles in the dust every day if she wants to, and it won't make no difference. The Judge didn't say much, but when he went out the third morning he seen that the leaves didn't look right, and by four o'clock that evening every one of them fine strawberry plants was dead.

Old Mis' Culpepper had changed her tune by this time, and she says Gram French is a witch sure enough, and the folks ought to run her plumb out of the country, or maybe shoot her

103

with a silver bullet. But the Judge he says you come with me, and they went out to the patch, and he showed her some little white grains in the dirt. "Taste that stuff," says he. So Mis' Culpepper put some on her tongue, and she says it tastes like salt. "It *is* salt," says the Judge, "and salt is death on strawberries, and the ground won't grow nothing but sparrowgrass from now on. That's what comes of cussing Gram French," he says.

So then Mis' Culpepper begun to holler how she is going to fix Gram, but the Judge says you have done enough fixing already, and from now on you better keep your big mouth shut. And next time Gram French comes along selling sassafras, you just give her the nickel or the dime or whatever it is she wants. Fooling with them people is bad luck, he says. Do you want my new barn to catch fire mysterious and burn plumb to the ground? How would you like to see all our chickens poisoned, and the ducks too? Maybe you would rather have a dead snake in the well every few days, or some buckeye juice throwed in to drive us both crazy, he says.

It was on a Wednesday the Judge told Mis' Culpepper all this, and Saturday morning here come Gram with a little bundle of sassafras roots. They was not red ones neither, but thick white roots that ain't fit for nothing. But old Mis' Culpepper she took them just the same, and give Gram ten cents, and says she is mighty glad to get some good sassafras roots. So then Gram just grinned at her and went on down the road. The Judge he grinned too when he heard about it. "I ain't educated like my wife is, but I know better than to cuss Gram French," he says. "It's a lot cheaper to buy the goddam sassafras." Mis' Culpepper figured she better do what the Judge told her about things like that, and they all been getting along pretty good ever since.

NAKED ABOVE THE WAIST

ONE TIME there was a fellow that run a little store. He sold novelties and ice-cream cones and soda pop to the tourists in the summer time. He was making pretty good money, and it looks like he would be satisfied, but he was one of them fellows that is always uneasy about something.

There was one year he took up worrying because the tourists don't wear enough clothes. He says them women running around half naked is a bad example for our young folks, and makes my store look like a three-ring sporting-house. And when grown men got to coming in without a stitch on but them little bathing trunks, he thought it was worse yet. "One more summer, and they'll all be stark nude," he says. Finally he went and asked the mayor to pass a ordinance against bathing suits in the street, but the mayor says nobody gives a damn what kind of clothes the tourists wear, so long as they got pockets. The main thing is to keep them coming here and spending their money, says the mayor.

But the fellow that run the store went right on worrying about them bathing suits. He knowed it wasn't no use telling women what to wear, but he figured something might be done with the menfolks. He thought about it a long time, and finally he put up a big sign: MEN NAKED ABOVE THE WAIST NOT WANTED HERE. The tourists just took one look at that sign, and they all busted out laughing. One big fat fellow he says, "Mamma, bring me my shirt out of the car." And then he put on the shirt, and stood up beside the sign to have his picture took. He pulled the shirttail down over his swimming pants, so it looked like he didn't have nothing on except his shirt. Pretty soon the whole place was full of men strutting around in their shirttails, and the women was taking pictures, and everybody laughing and cutting up. They was all buying novelties too, and drinking soda pop, and eating ice-cream cones. The other businessmen that sold novelties and soda pop and ice-cream cones was getting pretty mad. And the fellow that run the store was not happy about it neither, because things was not working out the way he expected.

After while two couples come busting in through the crowd and set down at a table, but the men did not have no shirts on. So the fellow that run the store he showed them the big sign. One of the men went and got a shirt out of his car, but the other fellow did not have no shirt in the car, and he says, "You mean I got to go clear back to the hotel after my shirt, before I can buy a bottle coca-cola?" The fellow that run the store says, "You can go wherever you want, but if a man is naked above the waist we don't serve him nothing here." The tourist he says to his girl friend, "Mabel, give me that blouse!" Mabel was not going to do it, as she ain't got anything on underneath, but the man says that don't make no difference, because the sign don't say nothing about women, it is only men that has got to wear shirts. All of a sudden Mabel busted out laughing, and she says "Okay, if that's the way you want it," and she pulled off the blouse. The man he put it on, but it was pretty tight. "I feel like a fool," he says, "but we got to respect these here local customs." And Mabel says, *"You* feel like a fool! How do you think *I* feel, with everybody gawking at me, and half of them taking pictures?" And she says people sure have got funny notions in Missouri, and I see why they call it the Show-Me state. All this for a bottle of coca-cola, and it sure is lucky you didn't order champagne, she says. And then they all laughed like fools, and there was flash-bulbs a-popping everywhere, and the crowd hollering till you could hear 'em clear to the court-house. The fellow that run the store was hollering too, but he was plumb drownded out, and nobody paid him any mind.

Just then the mayor come pushing in, and he says, "Excuse me, lady, but will you please put your clothes on? The highway is blocked for pretty near a mile, and somebody has called the sheriff, and it looks like we are getting too much publicity here." So Mabel she put on her blouse, and the two couples went outdoors, and you could hear them laughing away down the street. Then the mayor says "What the hell is the matter with all these men, coming into stores barefooted and without no pants on?" The tourists says of course we have got pants on, and they all pulled up the shirts to show their swimming trunks. "It seems they've passed a law in this town," says one fellow, "that everybody has got to go around in his shirttail or else he can't buy no novelties, or even soda-pop."

The mayor started to holler how there ain't no such a law, but just then he seen the big sign: MEN NAKED ABOVE THE WAIST NOT WANTED HERE. "So that's it!" says he, and he drug the fellow that run the store out from behind the counter. "I hope you're satisfied, and if you don't tear that silly sign down in two minutes, I'll take your license away!" says he. "Yes, and throw you in jail for running a nudist camp! Didn't you see them fools taking pictures? Don't you know this will be in the Joplin papers tomorrow, and people laughing at us all over the goddam country?"

The folks watched the newspapers for two or three days, but they never did see no story about it, nor no pictures neither. So the mayor he says well, we got off mighty lucky. And the fellow that run the store says he has give up the whole business, and from now on everybody can run around naked as jaybirds for all he cares. That's just about the way the tourists do run around, too. But folks has got kind of used to it, and they don't pay no attention to them things nowadays.

THE STUPID SCHOOLMASTER

ONE TIME there was two boys raised down in the Sassafras Bottoms, and they was brothers too, but you never would have knowed it to look at them. The oldest one was Jeff, and he was smart as a whip. The other boy was named Gabe, and it seemed like he wasn't much good. Jeff had sense and book-learning with it, but Gabe didn't know nothing at all hardly, and the whole family was kind of worried about him. They seen he wasn't smart enough for a horse trader, and he didn't have sense enough to farm, and he couldn't get no regular job because he looked so foolish. So finally the folks made up their mind that Gabe would have to be a preacher, or else teach school for a living.

Gabe says right off he won't be a preacher, because preachers all smell funky in damp weather. And anyhow, he always figured on robbing banks, or else he would run one of them big engines on the railroad. But the old man says bankrobbing ain't safe nowadays, and neither is railroading, and you got to know arithmetic besides. Gabe got to thinking how there is always pretty girls around a schoolhouse, and maybe he could get next to some of them. So he says, "Well, I'd just as soon foller school-teaching as anything else."

The first thing Gabe had to do was get some book-learning, so the folks made him go to the high school in town. They thought he better kind of brush up on what he learned in the district school, because it seemed like he had forgot pretty near everything. He could read and cipher a little, but he was a mighty poor hand when it come to writing. Gabe didn't like to go to school because the shoes hurt his feet, but he never uttered no complaint. The old man made him study every night till way after bedtime, and brother Jeff done all he could to help out. But Jeff says he don't think Gabe can pass any kind of examination. And if a fellow can't pass the examination, the County Superintendent won't give him no certificate. Nobody can't get a job teaching school unless he has got a certificate, because there is a law against it.

Jeff got hold of some papers they had used last year, and he knowed Gabe couldn't answer no such questions as that. Him and Gabe went down to the courthouse and looked through the window, so they could watch how them examinations is run. They seen how everybody had to set four seats apart, and write down the answers, and then fold the papers up and hand them to the Superintendent. The Superintendent set on a high stool like a goddam chicken-hawk, and he watched everything mighty close. Jeff says there ain't no way to beat that examination, and if Gabe don't learn to answer them questions in the next three months he can't get no certificate. Jeff says Gabe ain't smart enough to learn that stuff, and he might as well give up the whole business. Maybe preaching the Gospel ain't so bad anyhow, he says.

Gabe studied awhile, and then he says, "Jeff, could *you* pass that examination?" Jeff says, "Sure I could, but that won't do no good, because you're the one that has got to have the certificate." Gabe he just grinned like a possum, and never said no more about it.

When the time come, Jeff told it around that he was fixing to be a schoolmaster too, and so him and Gabe both went in to take the examination. They wrote out them answers the best they could, and then they folded the papers, and the Superintendent put the papers in a big pile with the others. Next week the news come out that Jeff didn't do no good at the examination, but Gabe answered them questions fine, and so they give him the certificate.

Folks was kind of surprised at Gabe getting the certificate, but the Board hired him to teach the Big Piney school. He done a good job with it, too. They say he was just one jump ahead of the scholars at first, but he figured out every lesson at night, and by the last day of school he could start in anywhere and rattle off the whole book. Gabe was a fellow that learned everything by heart, just like it was Bible texts or some kind of Lodge work. Next year he got a better school over on Chicken Ridge, and he kept on till he was Principal of the big Consolidated School in town. And when he run for County Superintendent, the folks turned out and elected him easy. Gabe was one of the best-liked schoolmen we ever had in these parts.

After Gabe got to be County Superintendent, everybody took note how he talked mighty careful to everybody that come to take the examinations. Some say he graded on what they said, more than what they wrote down. Jeff always laughed at the way Gabe handled the school examinations. Finally he told some of the kinfolks what he was laughing about, and how Gabe got his first certificate. "We both took the examination," he says, "but it was *me* that passed." The folks just looked at him goggle-eyed. "Gabe knowed he couldn't answer them god-dam questions," says Jeff, "so he wrote my name on his paper, and I wrote his name on mine, and that's how come him to get the certificate."

Somebody made bold to ask Gabe about it one time, at a Fourth-of-July picnic. Gabe just grinned, and says that his brother Jeff always did like to tell a good story. "That examination was so many years ago," he says, "that I can't seem to remember much about it."

JOHNNY APPLESEED

ONE TIME there was a fellow named Johnny Appleseed, and some thought he looked like a Dutchman, but most folks figured he must be part Indian. Any fool could see he was raised with the Indians, because he always got onto a horse from the wrong side. Some fellow wrote in the paper how Johnny Appleseed come out from Pennsylvania barefooted, with a gunny sack round his middle and a tin pan on his head.

But them old hunters that knowed Johnny all say he wore Choctaw moccasins, and dressed just like anybody else. He sure didn't go around with no tin pan on his head, nor nothing like that. There ain't no use denying, though, that Johnny Appleseed was a mighty curious fellow. He could read print better than most schoolmarms, and carried books in his warbag, and somebody had learnt him to play the fiddle.

Johnny's wife was a fullblood Choctaw, and every time he started to play his fiddle she would go out in the woods somewhere, and not come back till he was done. A fiddle-tune sets an Indian's teeth on edge, just like these here steam whistles will run a dog crazy. Them Choctaws set around all night sometimes a-thumping on drums, and they like flute music when the moon is right for it, but they can't stand no goddam squeaky fiddling.

When his woman got in a family way, Johnny was so tickled he run through the woods a-howling like a wolf. The baby was the spitting image of Johnny, according to the old-timers. But the Choctaw woman got to chilling, and pretty soon she was dead, and the baby it died too. Johnny Appleseed went kind of crazy after that, and he just tramped around the country, reading them fool books out loud to anybody that would listen. He never played the fiddle no more, and he says the rattlesnakes are his brothers, and he is going to marry three angels in Heaven, and all kind of foolishness. Finally he went back east somewhere and got a lot of feverweed, which is the same stuff they called dogfennel nowadays. There wasn't no dogfennel in this country then, and Johnny claimed dogfennel tea would cure the malaria fever. He says the reason his wife died was because he couldn't get her the right kind of tea. And now he was bound to plant dogfennel at every settlement in the whole goddam country, so other fellows won't lose their wife and baby like he done. He planted some apple cores around too, because apples is healthy for people to eat, specially little children. But

112

the main thing in a new country like this, he says, is to make sure that everybody has got plenty of feverweed handy.

That fool story in the paper made out like folks called him Johnny Appleseed because he planted them apple trees. But Appleseed is an Indian name, and there's lots of fellows with names like that among the Choctaws. If it was planting seeds that give poor Johnny his name, he would have been knowed as Johnny Dogfennel or Johnny Feverweed to this day. It just goes to show, that you can't believe nothing you read in the goddam papers.

THE SINGING TEACHER
AND THE BEAR

ONE TIME there was a young fellow from the academy at Pea Ridge come up into Missouri afoot, because they was looking for somebody to teach a singing school on Sugar Creek. He had a celluloid collar with one of them little neckties on it, and he was walking along the public road in broad daylight, a-minding his own business and not bothering nobody. All of a sudden a big she-bear come busting out of the brush, a-growling and showing her teeth. You could tell she had cubs hid out somewheres, and she was just natural-born mean, anyhow.

The big bear looked plumb dangerous, but the young fellow spoke up like a man. "Listen," says he, "I ain't no bear hunter. I'm just a singing teacher from Pea Ridge, not looking for no trouble." The bear just come right on, a-slavering and a-faunching like she was going to eat him up. "I never seen your cubs, and I ain't got so much as a pocket pistol on me," says he. "You go your way, and I'll go mine, without no hard feelings." But the old bear she just kept on a-coming, with her mouth open big as a soap kettle.

Anybody who has been around much knows that them Pea Ridge boys ain't going to be pushed off the road, no matter what happens. When this fellow seen the bear wouldn't listen to reason, he just snatched up a flint rock and throwed it hard as he could. That rock hit the varmint square in the mouth, and knocked several teeth out, and drove right on down her gullet. The bear was hurt bad, and she swung round and run off, a-coughing and spitting blood. But the singing teacher's dander was up now, so he grabbed another flint rock and took after her. When he throwed the second rock it landed right under the bear's tail, and tore into her innards from behind. She let out a terrible roar and made a grab for the singing teacher, but it wasn't no use. When them two flints come together inside the bear, they struck sparks, and the critter was so fat she caught fire like a barrel of axle grease. The Pea Ridge fellow just stood back and let her burn, and pretty soon there wasn't nothing left but a big scorched circle on the ground and a pile of black-looking bones.

The singing teacher just wiped his hands with a red handkerchief, and then he rubbed a little speck of soot off'n his fine celluloid collar. "That will learn bears not to monkey with me," says he, and marched off down the road to the old barn where they was having the singing school.

GEOMETRY IS WHAT DONE IT

ONE TIME there was a fellow come from up around Joplin somewheres, and he says his name is Tandy Simpson. There was an old brass cannon in the courthouse yard, and the first thing Tandy done was hire some men to load it on a wagon. The sheriff figured Tandy was trying to steal it for the brass, but Tandy says he is just going down to the freight depot and he will fetch the cannon right back. The sheriff he went along to make sure, and Tandy had them fellows put the old gun on the scales. It weighed seven hundred and fifty pounds. So then Tandy hauled it back to the courthouse yard, and paid the fellows their wages, and bought everybody a drink besides. "I'm kind of crazy about brass cannons," he says, and then he got on the train and left. The sheriff says Tandy is crazy all right, but he figured there ain't no harm in him.

The next we seen of Tandy was way along in August, when he come down with a bunch of rich people from Kansas City. They all drunk whiskey like water and spent their money the same way, and some of them fancy women was worse'n the menfolks. The whole outfit danced and swum and fished and celebrated all over the place. And gamble? You never seen anything like it. Some of them fellows would bet on anything. If two birds was setting on a fence, they would bet maybe a hundred dollars which one would fly first. They must have bet thousands of dollars on shooting matches, and most of them was good shots, too. They had a little tin box that was knowed as the fishpool, and each man would put money in it every day, and the fellow that caught the biggest fish took the pot. And every night the whole bunch would make up another pool to bet on something, even if it was only what the weather was going to be like next morning.

One day a lot of them people was setting in chairs out front of the hotel, across the street from the courthouse yard. They got to guessing how much each other weighed, and somebody brought the bathroom scales out there, and they was betting how heavy people was, and then weighing them on the scales. Everybody took it good-natured except old lady Carleton, and she is too fat anyhow. Tandy says he was losing money at this foolishness. He says it ain't possible to guess a person's weight very accurate, because the human body is made of so many different kinds of stuff. If a man was solid meat clear through, says Tandy, a fellow could figure his height and girth and make a mighty close guess by geometry.

"Geometry, my eye!" says a skinny little man. "You see that statue over by the courthouse? Same kind of stone all the way through, ain't it? But I bet you couldn't guess within four hundred pounds how much it'll weigh." The two of them walked over to the courthouse, with the whole crowd trailing along behind. Tandy he studied the statue mighty careful. "There ain't no regular shape to it," says he. "Geometry can't get a hold of a thing like that. You show me something that's round, or square, or oblong—" The skinny little fellow stopped him right there. "All right," he says, "let's see what geometry can do with that brass cannon." Tandy studied the old gun mighty careful. "That's better," says he. "There's something that geometry can

116

sink her teeth into. I'll bet a thousand dollars I can guess its weight closer'n you can."

With that the whole bunch begun to argue, and finally they decided each man would put five hundred dollars into the box, and whoever guessed closest would take the pot. The sheriff heard about it, so he called one of them fellows outside. "I know exactly how much that gun weighs," says he. So the fellow give the sheriff some money, and the sheriff told him the cannon weighed seven hundred and fifty pounds.

They all watched while the boys loaded the cannon on a wagon and took it down to the freight depot. When they got it on the scales, the goddam thing weighed eight hundred and two pounds! And the cards showed that Tandy Simpson's guess was eight hundred, and the next best guess was seven hundred and fifty; the rest of them run all the way from six hundred to fifteen hundred. So they give the money to Tandy Simpson, and he says guesswork may be all right in its place, but geometry is more dependable. The fellow that guessed seven hundred and fifty was pretty mad, but he seen the weighing himself, and them scales was inspected by the Government, so he couldn't make no holler. The sheriff went fishing up on White River somewhere, and he never showed his face in town till them people had all went back to Kansas City.

The sheriff done a lot of thinking while he was on that fishing trip. Soon as he got back, somebody seen him a-poking a stick into the old brass cannon. Then he got the blacksmith to come over with a grabhook, and pretty soon they drug out a big piece of sheet lead, rolled up like a newspaper. "I see how this here geometry works," says the sheriff. "Tandy must have sneaked over here in the night, and rammed that stuff down the muzzle." The blacksmith sold the lead for junk, and it weighed just fifty pounds. The other two pounds was some kind of gummy plaster,

117

that Tandy had put in so the lead wouldn't come out while they was weighing the cannon.

THE BROWN MARE

ONE TIME there was a man named John Cecil, and he had a little mare that could run like the wind. She was kind of dun-colored, so they called her Brown Lady. The Cecil outfit matched her against a gray horse that had been winning races all over the country, and the gray horse belonged to a fellow they called Houston. Mister John thought maybe there was something underhanded going on, so he got another mare that looked just like Brown Lady, but she couldn't run. They put the other mare in Brown Lady's stall, and Mister John he stayed in the loft every night and waited for something to happen.

A couple of nights before the race he heard a noise outside, and here come three men into the stable. The leader was Houston, the fellow that owned the gray horse. The three men beat the mare with clubs until they knew she would be too stiff and sore to win any race, and then they went away. Mister John saw all this, but he just kept quiet.

When Saturday morning come around the Houston crowd was there, bold as brass. They brought all the money, cattle, and stuff they could get a hold of, and bet everything on the gray horse. The gray horse was pretty good, but Brown Lady was in fine shape, and she beat the gray horse by four lengths. So the Houston crowd lost all their money and other property, and it served them right.

The boys made up a song about the race, and it went something like this:

The race it was made, it was made on the square,
Between Houston's gray horse and Cecil's brown mare.

They clubbed her behind, they clubbed her before,
Saying now, Brown Lady, your racing is o'er.

On Saturday morning, the day of the race,
The horse-beating company looked bold in the face.

They bet all their money and property too
That the gray horse would beat the brown mare through.

The sun it was shining, the month it was June,
The jockeys were there, all gay and in tune.

The word it was given, the hickory too,
And the brown mare beat the gray horse through.

John Cecil's friends used to sing that ballad all around the neighborhood. The Houston crowd got pretty mad, but they couldn't do anything. Some of the boys kept on singing "The Brown Mare" right up to the time of the War between the States. After that, everybody was too busy to think of horse racing, or to sing any songs about such things.

SHE WOULDN'T BE A WITCH

ONCE UPON A TIME a crowd of country women were having a quilting bee, and they all got to talking about witches. One lady says she had heard a lot of peculiar stories about things like that. "I'd like to see one of those initiations," she said, "and maybe I'd even ride the broomstick myself." She was just a-talking for fun. But the joke seemed to fall kind of flat, so she didn't say any more about it.

When the party broke up the lady started for home, and one of the neighbor women walked along beside her. "Did you mean what you said, about becoming a witch?" she asked. The lady was a little sore because her joke wasn't appreciated, but she decided to carry it through. "Yes, I did," she answered, "I usually mean what I say." Just then they come to the place where the roads branched off, and the other woman said there would be a meeting at the schoolhouse early Friday night.

The lady thought for awhile she wouldn't go, but when the time came she was right there with the rest of the crowd. She knew most of them, and they were nice refined folks. They all walked over to a vacant house in a grove of trees, just at the foot of a hill. A lot of people were in the house already, and some had long gowns on, and masks over their faces. A fiddler was playing a strange tune, and eight couples were a-dancing. There was a big fellow setting at a table over in the corner. His mask showed a bulge at the front, and one of his feet looked like a cloven hoof. The lady had a pretty good idea who he was, and she begun to get kind of uneasy.

Pretty soon the music stopped, and the dancers all stood still. It was time to begin the initiation, and they led the lady over to the table. She had to kneel down and put one hand under her feet, and the other on top of her head. Then they told her to say, "All that's between my hands belongs to Satan." But right there is where the lady balked, because she would never say anything like that. She just drew a big breath and said, "All that's between my hands belongs to the Lord who rules on high!" That very minute the lights went out, and a big cold wind blew through the house. The Devil and all his witches was gone helter-skelter. The old house was quiet as an empty grave.

The lady picked up a long pine splinter and lighted it from the coals on the hearth. Then she held the torch over her head, and down the road she went. She never stopped a-running till she was safe at home. And that is the end of the story, so far as anybody ever knew.

THE HEIRLOOM

ONE TIME there was a town fellow went a-hunting, and he camped under a ledge on Owl Creek pretty near a month. He come up to a farmer's house one morning and says to the farmer, "I will trade you a mess of venison for a dose of Epsom salts, because I am not feeling very good the last four days." The farmer says he don't keep no salts in the house, and it ain't healthy for people to take drugs or loosening-weeds. The town fellow says, "Well, it ain't healthy for a man to be all constipated up like this neither, and what do you use for a physic?" The farmer reached up and got a big old round bullet off'n the fireboard. "Just swaller that lead ball," says he, "and you won't have no more trouble."

The town fellow didn't like the looks of it much. "You think this will do the work?" he says kind of doubtful. The farmer

121

just nodded his head, so the town fellow swallowed the ball, and washed it down with a gourdful of water.

Two or three days after that he come back to the farmhouse. "That remedy worked fine," says he. "I feel like a new man now." So he give the farmer a fine mess of venison and four squirrels to boot.

"Where's the lead ball?" says the farmer. The town fellow looked kind of funny. "Why, I don't know," he says, "I never paid no attention. Probably it's out in the brush somewhere, back of my camp." The farmer put on his hat. "We'll have to go look," says he. "I wouldn't lose it for a hundred acres of land. That ball has been in our family for three generations."

HOW THE STILL GOT BUSTED

ONE TIME there was a fellow that lived back on the ridge come into town to renew his mortgage, and he found out about the prohibition law. The saloons was all shut up, and you couldn't buy no Government whiskey, so the price of farm liquor had went sky high. Everybody knows that common moonshine ain't worth more than three dollars a gallon, but the people in town was paying ten dollars a quart, and glad to get it at that.

This fellow was not a drinking man, and he didn't know nothing about making liquor, but he figured here is a chance to get rich easy. What a fool I would be, he says to himself, to work my guts out hoeing corn for seventy-five cents a bushel, and chop wood for a dollar a rick! All I got to do is run one of these here stills, and make enough in one summer for us to live comfortable the rest of our life. And no interest to pay neither, and the bank can take the goddam farm for all I care, he says to himself.

When he got back home that night the fellow says, "Lizzie, I have done give up farming." And early next morning he drug the rain barrel down to the spring, and throwed in some cornchops with a handful of yeast, and then filled her up with water. He got a little old still somewhere, and soldered it up good. Soon as the stuff in the barrel got sour, he dumped the whole mess into the boiler and built a rousing big fire underneath. Pretty soon them cornchops plugged up the still some way. "I was just setting there a-smoking my pipe," he says, "when all of a sudden I seen that boiler was swole plump to a strut! Gentlemen, it was pooched out like a cat full of kittens! Next thing I knowed, the whole contraption blowed up louder'n the crack of doom, and throwed boiling corn mush all over the place. It's God's own mercy I warn't scalded plumb to death, and I sure taken it as a warning."

The boys tried to tell him how the still wasn't set up right, and he done wrong to solder the joints thataway, and he ought to have strained the mash, and built a slow fire besides, but he never paid them no mind. "Some folks is born to chop wood and live poor," says he. "The good Lord never intended for me to be a moonshiner."

THE LITTLE MAN AND THE GRANNY WOMAN

ONE TIME there was a thrifty farm woman that lived among hills and streams. She was a midwife, which is the same as a granny woman. While she was sewing there was a noise like little feet coming in the door, but she couldn't see anybody. All of a sudden she felt a stream of cold water shoot into her eyes. And then she saw a little man wearing a red cap with a white feather in it. She knew what he was, the minute she laid eyes on him, but he says for her not to be afraid. He just wants her to come and take care of his sick wife.

They walked along till they come to a cliff, and there was a cave that didn't look any bigger than a groundhog's den. The little man's wife was laying on a bed outside. Pretty soon she had a baby, and it was a boy. The little clothes they put on the baby was all handmade, wove out of thread as fine as spider webs. The granny woman drunk some of their coffee out of a cup that looked like china, but it was an eggshell with a gold frame on it. And then the little man took the granny woman back to her house.

It was about a week after that she was fixing supper, and she heard the little footsteps again. There was the little man up on the flour barrel, and he was shoveling out flour into a little bucket. "Well," she says, "how is your wife and baby?" The little man jumped and looked right at her. "They're doing fine, but how did you know I was here?" says he. And the granny woman says she could see him plain as day. "My goodness," says the little man, "I was so excited about my wife the other day that I forgot to fix things!" All of a sudden she felt a stream of hot water shoot into her eyes, and when she looked again the little man was gone. She never did see him any more, neither.

THE HORSELESS CARRIAGE

ONE TIME there was a fellow lived away back off the big road, and his name was Thompson. He was one of them fellows that never go to town, only once a year to pay his taxes.

124

Automobiles was a new thing then, and they was called horse-less carriages. We didn't have none in Christian county, because the roads was not suitable. There was always stumps in the middle of the road, just high enough so a wagon could clear them. Even people at the county seat that had seen horseless carriages figured they might work in cities where the streets was all paved with brick, but they would never be no good down here because of them stumps in the road. Nobody ever dreamed that we'd have concrete highways all over the country like we got now.

Living back in the woods that way, old man Thompson hadn't never seen a automobile, and maybe he never even heard of such a thing. One evening just before dusk there was a terrible commotion over by the big road, and here come a horse-less carriage down the trail right toward Thompson's house. It was one of them old high-wheelers that a fellow had traded for, and he was a-driving around the side roads to show folks how it could clear them stumps good as a buggy. There was two big gas lamps out in front, and a cloud of blue smoke behind, and the fellow that was running it had goggles on. The engine was a-popping and a-puffing and a-roaring, and you could hear chains a-clanking too. All automobiles in them days worked with a chain drive like a bicycle, only bigger.

The old woman just took one look, and then she run for the brush with the young ones. One of the big boys crawled under the house. But old man Thompson never run from anything in his life. He stood right there on the porch with the shotgun in his hands, and soon as the thing come even with the gate he give it both barrels. The horseless carriage wabbled on down the hill, because the wheels was in the ruts, but the fellow that was driving give a yell and jumped out. He took right through the pasture, a-running like a turpentined cat. If that fellow had one feather in his hand, you could have called it flying. He kept a-hollering, maybe because he had got a few birdshot in him.

Soon as everything quietened down, the big boy come a-crawling out from under the house. "Did you kill the varmint, pappy?" says he. The old man was a-loading his gun, and looking down the road to see if any more of them things was a-coming. "No, I reckon not," he says, "but I sure made him turn loose of that feller!"

OOLAH! OOLAH!

ONE TIME there was a fellow lived just over the line in Oklahoma, and he was running for Congress. There was a lot of Indian farmers out that way, and he got an old chief to round up a lot of them to hear him speak.

"The Government ain't treated you boys right in the past," says he, "but I aim to change all that soon as I get to Washington. After I'm elected, my Indian brothers won't be living in shanties and brush wigwams like they do now. No, siree! Not in my district! I'm going to see that every one of you fellows has got a good house, and fine furniture, and a new cookstove, and a electric ice-box if he wants it."

The Indians acted like they was mighty happy to hear this, and they all clapped their hands and hollered "Oolah! Oolah!" The old chief looked kind of surprised, but he did not say nothing.

"And furthermore," says the candidate, "my first act as your Congressman will be to get every Indian voter a good farm, if he ain't got one already. And I'm going to fix it so every one of you boys can have a nice late-model car, instead of some old jalopy. Yes, and we'll build roads fit to drive on, without no mud holes in 'em!"

The Indians was in a fine good humor by this time, laughing

and chuckling amongst themselves, and they clapped their hands louder than ever. They was all hollering "Oolah! Oolah!" till you could hear them half a mile off.

"I'm going to bring better livestock into the district, too," says the candidate. "I'll see that good bulls and stallions are available to every Indian stockman, so that our cattle and horses will be second to none in the United States." And with that he set down, and all them Indians was so happy they just laughed and slapped each other on the back. They kept a-hollering "Oolah! Oolah!" for five minutes anyhow, while the candidate was a-smiling and shaking hands with everybody that come within reach. He says it is the most enthusiastic audience he ever spoke to, and one of the best meetings of his whole campaign. The old chief he just set there poker-faced and never said a word, but anybody that knows Indians could tell he was just as tickled as the rest of them.

On the way back to town the candidate stopped at a big farm where the ranchman wanted to show him some fine cattle. There was one prize bull that they said was worth ten thousand dollars. "A magnificent animal!" says the candidate, and he started to walk right into the pen, but an Indian ranchhand touched his arm. "You better come around this other gate, Mister," he says. "The boys ain't cleaned up that side yet, and if you walk over there you'll get *oolah* on your shoes."

THE FOOTLOOSE FAMILY

ONE TIME there was a man and a woman that didn't have nothing but a team of horses and seven children. They never owned no land, and they never paid no rent, and they wouldn't raise a crop on shares neither. They just kind of piddled around, here today and gone tomorrow. Whenever them folks come to a deserted house they would move right in, and live there till somebody come along and put them out. If the talk was that some family was going to leave the country, these here wayfarers would be there a-waiting to move in. Lots of times they would get their stuff into the house before the chimney had cooled off.

The fellow would let the chickens loose and turn the horses out on the grass, and in five minutes he'd be a-chopping firewood, whilst the woman was fetching water and redding up the house. Two of the kids would run for the brush to set rabbit traps, and another one went to see if there was any potaters left in the garden patch. If it was close to the creek they would put out bank lines, and maybe have fish for supper. Every one of them kids knew exactly what to do, and they was all trained like a fire department or something. Even the dogs made for the timber soon as the wagon stopped, and the minute they barked treed the biggest boy took the rifle and went after a mess of squirrels. It sure was surprising how quick them folks would be all settled down, with a fire a-burning and victuals in the pot. If a stranger come along and seen them, he'd figure they was old settlers that had been a-living there for years.

Them folks was sure hard to get out of a house, no matter who owned it. Mostly they claimed they thought the place belonged to their Uncle Jethro, and then they would show how they had done planted a big crop, and if somebody won't pay cash for the crop then they got to stay and harvest the fruit of their labor. Or else the woman would lay in bed and holler that she is going to have a baby, and surely nobody would turn a poor woman right out in the road, and it a-raining. Sometimes they would put pokeberry juice on all the kids' face and hands, and how could anybody talk about rent when they all had the smallpox? One time the sheriff come to put them out,

128

and the whole family was down by the river a-crying because one of the girls got drownded, so the deputy dived in and dragged the river, and him and the sheriff worked four hours and got all wet and tired, but come to find out the girl had just went over to Puckett's Run and got a job with the berrypickers. And the man that owned the place was afraid to holler very loud, or else them people might set the house afire accidental, and folks didn't have no insurance in them days.

Everybody knowed this here footloose family, and the boys down at the store was always telling tales about how they done everything. One fellow said they planted their potaters on a hill, and when the time come to leave they would just cut off the end of the rows, so the whole crop would roll right down into the rain barrel. Another fellow told how they kept all their house plunder tied together with a rope, so that they just pulled the rope and drug everything into the wagon at once. Some claimed they always had the harness hung up right over the horses' backs, and when they knocked the trigger the team was hitched up automatic. Another story was that when they was ready to move, the old man blowed a horn, and here come the cow a-running, with the dogs right at her heels. Yes, and the postmaster himself swore he seen all their chickens lay down in a row with their feet sticking up to be tied, just like they knowed it was moving day.

Them fool boys kept on like that till it got so you couldn't hardly tell which was the truth and which was just a goddam lie. That's the way most of them big windy stories about the Ozark country get started.

SHOES FOR THE KING

ONE TIME there was a king, and he got sick. He couldn't eat very good, and something had went wrong with his head. The people didn't know what to make of it. You know if a common man goes crazy it don't make much difference, but a king has got to keep his wits about him, or he is liable to ruin the whole country. The king had lots of men to advise him, but one smart fellow would say something and then some other smart fellow told him just the opposite, so the king couldn't make up his mind what to do about anything. Sometimes it would take him all day to decide if he needed a hair-cut or not, and the Government was going to hell in a handbasket.

Finally they got the best doctor in town, and he says "Where do you hurt?" The king says, "Doc, my feet is killing me." So the doctor examined the king mighty careful, and after while he says, "Well, if a man's feet hurt he don't feel good, so his head don't work right neither, and that's what is the matter with you." Then the people wanted to put medicine on the king's feet, but the doctor told them it wasn't no use. "Medicine won't help none in this case," says he. "You got to find some fellow that feels good all over, and take his shoes off, and put them on the king. That will cure him in no time." And so the king give the doctor a sack of gold.

Soon as the doctor was gone, the folks started out to get the king some shoes. There was several fellows in the king's house that wore the right size, but there didn't none of them feel good all over. One fellow has got a boil on his neck, and another one says he is ruined by the pox, and the rest of them suffers terrible with kidney trouble, or bellyache, or rheumatism, or something. Next morning the king's servants went into town and says to everybody, "What size shoe do you wear?" And if the fellow says number ten, they ask him did he feel good all over? But every man of them says no. So the servants come back and told the king the people in town was sick, and they couldn't find nobody that felt good all over.

The third day the king sent his soldiers out, and they went to every settlement for miles around. But after while the soldiers come back and says the people are sick everywhere and they couldn't find nobody that felt good all over. "Well by God," says the king, "things is in a worse fix than I thought." So he had them saddle his horse, and he says he will go out and see about it himself. Two soldiers come along with him, and the king dressed up like a soldier too, so the people couldn't tell who he was.

They rode and they rode till the horses was plumb give out, but they couldn't get nobody to say he felt good all over. The king had to camp out every night, because he looked just like a common soldier, and the people would not let him stay in the hotels or the tourist camps even. "Just wait till I get home," says he, "and I will make a new law so soldiers can get the best beds everywhere, and it will do them fat drummers good to sleep on the ground." It seemed like camping out done the king good, anyhow, and he eat as much as anybody. His head was working better too, and he says it is the most fun he has had for a long time.

One day they rode up to a little shack out in the woods, and there was a fellow laying on the porch. The king says "Howdy," and the fellow just grinned and says "Light down, and rest your saddle." So the king ask him if he is sick, and the fellow says hell no, he never felt better in his life. "Do you feel good all over?" says the king. "You're goddam right I feel good all over, and what's it to you?" the fellow answers right back.

131

"Well," says the king, "us soldiers has been sent out to find a good healthy fellow like you, because the king is sick and maybe you can help him." The fellow says he is sorry to hear about it, but why don't the king take a big dose of mayapple root, and if that don't do no good they better send for the doctor.

"The doctor says he has got to get the shoes off of a man that feels good all over," says the king. "You just fetch me your best shoes, and I will give you a sack of gold." The fellow looked down at his bare feet for a minute, and he wiggled his toes, and then he busted out a-laughing. "Soldier," says he, "I ain't had leather on them feet in twenty years. Why, I can kick sparks out of a flint rock! A man like me don't need no shoes."

The king he thought about this awhile, and then he pulled off his shoes and wiggled his toes. "Well, maybe you're right," says he. And so him and the two soldiers rode back home. They didn't have much to say, but pretty soon the word got around that the king was cured. "The main thing is to ride every day, and eat plenty of victuals, and sleep on the ground of a night," he says. "And it's healthy for a man to go barefooted around the house, too." And so the king got along pretty good after that, and they all lived happy ever after.

JACK AND THE LITTLE BULL

ONE TIME there was three brothers named Tom, Will, and Jack. Jack was the youngest, so they made him the goat around the place. Tom and Will owned the farm, and they says it is time for Jack to make a place for himself in the world, so they turned him out with nothing but a little black bull that he had raised from a calf. Jack went on down the road, a-riding the bull. The bull looked round and says, "Take every road I tell you, and do just as I say." Jack was surprised, because the little bull had never done any talking before, but he says all right.

Just before sundown they stopped under a tree, and the bull says, "Get down, and unscrew my horns." So Jack unscrewed the horns, and they were hollow. One was full of rich milk, the other was full of good bread and meat. After supper Jack went to sleep, and he waked up at sunrise. The little black bull says, "Jack, I dreamed and I dreamed good. Pretty soon a great big bull will come along. When you hear him scream, you climb a tree, and wait there till I kill him." Jack done just as he was told, and the little bull killed the big bull, and then they went on down the road.

The second day the same thing happened, and the little bull killed another big bull. Then Jack got on the little bull's back again, and they went on down the road.

On the third morning the little black bull says, "Jack, this is the end. Pretty soon you will see a big bull with three heads, and he will kill me. But don't you grieve, because I am not really a bull, and I will not really die. But when it looks like I am dead, you cut two long straps of leather out of my hide, and tie them to my horns. Keep the straps and horns always with you, wherever you go. When any trouble comes, tell the straps to tie and the horns to beat, and you will get what is rightfully yours."

It all worked out just like he said, and Jack saw the big bull with three heads and six long horns. When the little black bull was dead, Jack cried for a long time. Then he took the straps and horns and went on down the road.

Jack met lots of trouble after that, but the straps and horns never failed him. Finally he came to a king's palace. There was a lot of young men on horses, and the king's daughter was sailing around over their heads in some kind of an airship. Whoever could get the gilded ball out of her lap was to marry the king's daughter; so the young men all tried, but none of them could get the gilded ball. Jack chose a tall horse, and then he reached up his faithful horn and hooked the ball out of her lap easy. Some people around there did not want a stranger to marry the king's daughter, but Jack called for the straps to tie and the horns to beat on several young men. And then he threatened the king himself, so the king let Jack marry his daughter, and they all lived together in the palace.

A long time after that Jack saw two tramps come to the back door, asking for something to eat. It was his two brothers that had run through their property, so now they was beggars. Jack give them some old clothes and some money, but he wouldn't let them in the palace. He told them to go somewhere, and not come back for a year and a day. Then maybe he would fill their purse again.

Everything went along pretty good after that, and Jack didn't

134

have any more trouble. Finally the old king died, and Jack was head of the whole country. And so him and the king's daughter stayed right there and lived happy ever after.

A COONBONE FOR LUCK

ONE TIME there was a fellow name of Waggoner, and he married the prettiest girl in the whole country, and so he was very jealous. Him and her was getting along fine, but somebody told him it was a good idea to carry a coonbone in his pocket anyhow, just to be on the safe side. So he cut part of the coon off and boiled it, but when he got the bone out it didn't look like no regular coonbone. Waggoner throwed it away and cut another part of the coon off and boiled it, but that was not the kind of a bone he wanted neither. "God damn it," he says, "what is the matter with coons nowadays?" And after that he give up his whole time to cutting pieces off of coons and boiling them, but he could not find no bone to suit him. People come along the road, and they all told him there is nothing to this coonbone business, but Waggoner did not pay them no mind.

The boys got to selling him skinned possums and groundhogs and skunks and even cats, because they found out Waggoner didn't know the difference, and that's the reason he could not find no coonbone. His wife tried to tell him about this, but he says, "Florence, you shut your goddam mouth," and so she went back in the house. It was pretty hot weather, and buzzards come from all over the country, and the whole neighborhood begun to stink something terrible, so the people going past in wagons had to hold their nose or else they would get sick. But Waggoner says he don't smell nothing out of the way, and things

135

has come to a pretty pass if a respectable tax-payer ain't got a right to boil coons on his own property. And he says there is a lot of other citizens in this town had better drop whatever they are doing and cut up coons too, if they knowed what was good for them.

One day Waggoner and his wife and some other people went to a Fourth of July picnic in a big cave over on the highway. The fellow that owns the place claims that cave men used to live in it a thousand years ago, and so he charged the tourists two bits to go in. Right at the entrance they had a glass case full of Indian relics. There was flint arrowheads and tomahawks and big spears and mortars and some busted pottery, and a few bone fishhooks and things like that. The crowd just looked at this stuff a minute, and then they paid their money and went on into the cave where it was cool.

All of a sudden everybody heard a lot of hollering, and they run back to see what was the matter. There was Waggoner a-jumping up and down in front of the showcase. "What's that?" says he, pointing to a smooth bone with a crook at the end of it. The fellow says that's a bone awl, and the cave men used it to mend their socks. Waggoner knowed this was a lie, because the cave men didn't wear no socks, but he wasn't in no mood to argue. "How much?" says he, and the man says it is a very rare piece, but he will sell it for ten dollars. So Waggoner give him the money, and put the bone in his pants pocket.

On the way home Florence didn't name no names, but she says anybody sure is a fool to pay ten dollars for a old bone darning needle, because you can go to the store and get a new steel one for a nickel. "That ain't no darning needle," says Waggoner, "it's the finest coonbone I ever seen, and there ain't a coonbone in this country can hold a candle to it." Florence says, "You ain't going to butcher no more coons, then?" Waggoner he just grinned, and shook his head. "Well," she says,

136

"I reckon it's money well spent, at that." Waggoner grinned at her again. "It's the best buy I ever made in my life, except the time I give two dollars for our license," he says.

From then on Waggoner did not cut up no more varmints, but every little while he would pull out the big coonbone, and he acted like he was mighty pleased about something. Florence was glad too, and so was all the neighbors, and even the people that come along the road in wagons, because Waggoner's place did not smell bad no more. It looks like the coonbone was lucky sure enough, and they all lived happy ever after.

THE END OF THE BENDERS

ONE TIME there was a family that called theirself Bender, and they used to keep tavern up in Kansas. They was doing pretty good at it, too. But one day an old gentleman shot a Yankee right in front of the Bender place, and when some folks went to bury the Yankee in the back yard, they found pretty near forty men was buried there already. It was men that come to the tavern to stay all night, and the Benders had cut their throats and stole their money. So the Governor of Kansas offered a big reward for the Benders dead or alive, but all four of them got away and come down into the Territory.

They stole some ponies in the Cherokee Nation, just about where Nowata is now, and started south. Old man Bender and his wife rode ahead, and then some Johnny and Katy. Them two was brother and sister, but they slept together just like they wasn't no kin. They didn't care who knowed it, either, and whenever she had a baby they would just knock it in the head. The Benders was not respectable people, and kind of tough. The folks that lived in the Territory didn't like them

137

much, and they never asked the Benders to eat dinner with them, or come to the dances.

There was gangs of men from Kansas riding round a-hunting the Benders, but everybody says they never heard tell of them. The folks knowed them Yankees was just after the blood-money, and they didn't want no part in such doings. But one day a bunch of these Kansas fellows run onto the Benders un-expected, and they tied all four of them up with rope. The Benders had more than forty thousand dollars in money belts and a hatful of watches and jewelry. The Yankees was so tickled to get all this stuff that some of them wanted to turn the Benders loose. But while they was dividing up the money they got to fighting among themselves, and two of them was killed.

The rest of the Yankees was pretty drunk, and did not trust nobody. If they took the Benders back to get the reward, the law might try to take the forty thousand dollars away from them. And maybe they would have to answer questions about how them two fellows got killed. They figured it might be better to let the reward money go, and just divide up the Benders' stuff and not go back to Kansas at all. So finally they killed all four of the Benders, and buried the six corpses in a big hole under a bluff. Then each one of them fellows took his share of the money and jewelry and rode off by himself.

The people up in Kansas never did find out what happened to the Benders, or what become of the posse. There was plenty of folks in the Territory that knowed all about it, but they never told nobody. They didn't give a damn about the Bend-ers, nor them Yankees neither. The folks that lived in the Territory was glad to see the end of the whole caboodle, and they didn't want to hear nothing more about it.

THE THREE WISHES

ONE TIME there was a man and his wife lived on a high windy ridge. They was both pretty old, and their children had all growed up and left. The meat had give out, and the meal barrel was plumb empty. There wasn't a bite of victuals in the house except a few potaters, and no grease to fry 'em in. The old man's money was all gone, and he couldn't get no credit at the store. It looked like the old folks was in a bad fix.

Pretty soon somebody hollered outside, and in come a hungry little man with a funny hat on. He looked like he ought to have been in bed hours ago, so the folks give him a 'tater out of the ashes. "Eat hearty, stranger," says the old man, "we got plenty more down cellar in a teacup." The little man seen how things was, but he told 'em their troubles was all over. "I ain't no tramp," says he, "I'm a king in a far-off land. You can make three wishes, and you'll get whatever you wish for." And with that he went out and slammed the door.

The old folks laughed after the little man was gone, because they figured he must be out of his head. "It sure would be fine, though, if a body's wishes really did come true," says the old woman. "I wish we had a good old home-cured ham." WHOOMP, and there was a fine big ham on the table. The folks just set there and gawped at it. The old man was the first one that come to his senses, and seen how things was. "You damned old fool," he hollered, "look what you've done now! Why didn't you wish for something sensible?" The old woman sassed him right back, and pretty soon they was cussing each other loud as they could. "A goddam ham, when you could have got a million dollars just as easy! By God, I wish you

139

had it down your throat!" says the old man. WHOOMP, and the ham was stuck in the old woman's goozle. She rolled on the floor, and kicked like a steer, and turned plumb black in the face. It looked like she was a-dying, and the old man was scared out of his wits. The only thing he could do was to wish the ham out again, and so he done it. WHOOMP, and there it was back on the table. The old woman was cured quick as a flash, and her and the old man just set there a-looking at each other.

"Well, we got our three wishes all right," says the old man, "but they didn't do us much good." The old woman just wagged her head. "It was all over so quick," she says, "we didn't have no time to think." After while she cut a couple slices of ham and cooked it, and then fried some 'taters in the grease. They both got to feeling better after they eat the ham and 'taters.

So pretty soon the old man went down to the road, and there was a letter in the box. It was from their married daughter, and she had sent them some money. She says there is plenty more where that come from, as her man has got a good job now. So it looks like everything turned out all right after all, even if the old folks did make a mess of them three wishes.

TWO SEEDS IN THE SPIRIT

ONE TIME there was a fellow come from down South somewheres, and he says he is a Baptist preacher. But he wasn't a Hardshell Baptist, nor a Separate Baptist, nor a Free Will Baptist, nor a Foot-Washing Baptist, nor a Missionary Baptist, nor a Seventh Day Baptist, nor no other kind of Baptist that the folks here knowed about. The regular preachers called him a Snake Baptist, and they wouldn't have nothing

140

to do with him. But the fellow himself says he's a **Two-Seeds-in-the-Spirit** Baptist, and he got mighty thick with some of them peckerwoods on Hardtail Mountain. Pretty soon they built a big brush arbor up there, and it was knowed far and wide as the Two-Seed Tabernacle.

The way this fellow told it, everybody in the world is children of Mother Eve, but lots of people ain't no kin to Adam at all. The Serpent that Eve seen in the Garden of Eden wasn't no regular snake. It was the Devil, dressed up slick and fancy. The Devil got next to Eve just like Adam did, so that Cain was the Devil's son, and Abel was the son of Adam. Abel growed from the good seed that God put into Adam, but Cain sprouted from the bad seed that the Serpent slipped into Eve. And to this day every growed-up woman has got two kind of seeds in her. Some children come from God's seed, and some are born from the Devil's seed. If a person grows from God's seed, he'll get into Heaven sure, no matter what happens. But everybody that comes from the Serpent's seed is bound to go to Hell, and there ain't a goddam thing anybody can do about it.

It looks like there wouldn't be no great harm in this here Two-Seeds doctrine, but them folks up on Hardtail Mountain kind of run it in the ground. At first they just hollered and jumped around at meetings, but that wasn't nothing out of the ordinary, because the regular Baptists done the same thing in them days, and so did lots of Methodists. But pretty soon they got to wallering on the ground and jabbering in the unknown tongue, like the Pentecostal folks do now. And then they begun to fetch big rattlesnakes into the arbor, and two or three women pretty near died from snake-bite. And there was one fellow that would stick his hand right in the fire, to show how the Lord kept him from getting burnt. The elders got to swapping wives mighty promiscuous, because they said

141

the end of the world was coming any day now, and such things didn't make no difference. Some of the young folks went plumb hog wild, and took up cavorting around stark naked, and next day the damn fools says they was possessed by the Holy Spirit and didn't know what was going on, and probably they never done it anyhow.

It wasn't no time till the girls was all knocked up, and married women would leave their family and take up with some other fellow. Most of the boys had got a dose of some bad disease, and wouldn't go to the doctor neither, because they didn't believe in doctors. They says Jesus Christ could cure anything, and so they just got the elders to pray and put holy oil on them.

One night the preacher didn't show up at meeting, and neither did Jeb Peevy's wife. The talk was that they just run off together, but some folks figured Jeb must have killed both of 'em, and buried them out in the woods somewheres. That same night some fool boys throwed a live hornets' nest into the meeting and stung the hell out of everybody, and one of the saints knocked the big lamp over and burnt the brush-arbor plumb to ashes.

The whole settlement kind of quietened down after that. It was getting too cold for revivals anyhow. Lots of the folks seen where they had made a damn fool out of theirself, so they just dropped the whole business. If you was to go up on Hardtail Mountain today and ask them people about the Two-Seeds-in-the-Spirit gospel, they'd just look at you. And every last one of them would say they never heard tell of such a thing.

UNDER GRAVEL I DO TRAVEL

ONE TIME there was a fellow got into trouble about something, and it looked like a gang of men was going to hang him. But the people was all great riddlers in them days, and they got to talking about riddles on the way to the hanging ground. So finally they told this fellow that if he could spin a riddle that nobody in the crowd couldn't answer, they would turn him loose. He says he wanted to think it over. So the boss of the gang says, "Well, we will ride slow, and you can think all you want. But when we get to the hanging ground your time is up."

After while the whole bunch come to the place where they was fixing to hang him, and the fellow set on his horse right under the gallows. He told them he could think better on horseback. When they started to put the rope around his neck he says, "Hold on, boys. I have thought up a riddle." So then he sung it out like this:

> Under gravel I do travel,
> On oak leaves I do stand,
> I ride my pony and never fear,
> I hold my bridle in my hand.

They made him sing the riddle over three times, and everybody thought about it awhile. But there wasn't nobody that knowed the right answer, so finally they all give up. Then the fellow pulled off his hat and showed them where he had stuck some gravel in it, and he pulled his boot out of the stirrup and showed some oak leaves he had put in. And he says I'm a-riding my pony, and I ain't scared of nothing, and I have got my bridle in my hand this minute.

143

The folks kind of grumbled about it, but they seen the fellow had got the best of them, and so they turned him loose. And that's all there is to the story.

THE MARE'S NEST

ONE TIME there was a boy come out from town, and he was visiting some people that lived on a farm. Soon as the country boys found out he didn't know much, they got to playing jokes on him. They would tell him the awfulest big lies you ever heard tell of. The town boy believed them stories, because he was raised in town and never had no chance to find out about things. It seemed like he didn't know nothing at all, except book-learning. There ought to be a law against people who would let a boy grow up ignorant like that.

When the neighbor boys told him that horses hatched out of eggs just like turkeys, he didn't see nothing unreasonable about it. So then he come across a pumpkin out in the field, and they says, "There is a mare's nest right now." The town boy could see there was a crack in the pumpkin, so he figured it was just about ready to hatch. After while he come back and looked at it some more, and he put the pumpkin on a big stump in the sunshine. Then he got up on top of the pumpkin like a hen setting on eggs, as he thought maybe that would make it hatch quicker.

Some of the country boys seen all this, but they just kept out of sight and didn't say nothing. Pretty soon the town boy begun to get drowsy, and finally he slumped over and went to sleep. All of a sudden he fell right off the stump into a pile of brush. When he opened his eyes, there was the pumpkin busted all to hell, and just then a big swamp rabbit jumped out of the brush pile. The rabbit took out across the pasture, and the town boy run after it, hollering, "Coltie! Coltie! Nice coltie!" loud as he could. That fellow figured he'd hatched a colt out of that there pumpkin, and there wasn't no use trying to tell him any different.

Them neighbor boys just rolled on the ground and laughed theirself plumb sick. Some of them tried to tell the crowd down at the store what happened, but everybody thought it was just another of them big lies. The folks down at the store was smart, and they didn't believe anybody in the world was such a fool as to think he could hatch a colt out of a pumpkin.

A NOTCH MARKS THE SPOT

ONE TIME there was two fellows come down from St. Louis to go fishing. They rented a boat from the man that run the hotel, and they fished all day, but didn't do no good. Next morning they started out again, and they fished all day, but didn't get nothing but a mud turtle. On the third day they took a jug along, and pretty soon they didn't care if they caught any fish or not. They just drifted around in the boat, and swapped stories, and sung foolish songs, and every little bit they would take a good snort out of the jug.

About the middle of the morning they come to the mouth of Bull Creek, and all of a sudden the fish begun to bite. It wasn't no time at all till they had a fine string of big bass. The two fellows was feeling mighty good about this, and they wanted to mark the place so they could come back next day. They talked about it awhile, and finally the biggest one pulled out his knife and cut a notch in the side of the boat. Then they started back to the hotel. Pretty soon the little fellow jumped up. "My God,

it won't work!" he says. "We'll never find that place again!"
The other fellow just looked at him. "What do you mean, it
won't work?" says he. "All we got to do is drop our lines right
under the notch." But the little fellow just kept on a-hollering,
and pretty soon he begun to cry like a baby. "You and your
goddam notch!" he says. "Don't you know the man has got a
whole string of these boats, and the hotel is a-swarming with
tourists? Don't you realize there ain't one chance in fifty that
we can rent the same boat tomorrow?"

The tourists was all laughing about this next day, but the
man that run the hotel says he don't see nothing funny about it.
He says bass won't bite in the same hole two days a-running,
so what's the difference if them damn fools can find the place
or not? It ain't much use to tell stories to anybody like that.

HE THROWED DOWN HIS GUN

ONE TIME there was a cowpuncher come to town,
and he was from the Indian Territory, and pretty soon he got
to drinking. He went into a saloon and give a few loud yells,

and then he begun to shoot around so the people all run out. After they was gone he loaded up his six-shooter and went to another saloon, and he done the same thing in there. The cowpuncher did not hurt anybody, but he busted two big mirrors, and scared some of our best citizens out of a year's growth. He kept on yelling and shooting till the saloon-keepers begun to complain about it, and so the marshal come down the street to arrest him.

The marshal was a pretty tough character, and he had a ten-bore shotgun with the barrels cut off short. When the cowpuncher come tearing out of a saloon, the marshal says, "Drop that gun!" The fellow says, "All right," and he throwed his six-shooter down in the street. When the pistol hit the ground it went off, and the bullet drilled the marshal right through the heart. Some of the boys wanted to hang the cowpuncher right there, but the sheriff come along, and he says, "This man is my prisoner, and I will kill anybody that lays a hand on him." And so everybody stood back, and the sheriff locked him up in the county jail.

When they got the cowpuncher in court, he was sober as a judge, and all cleaned up. "I got drunk and made a fool out of myself, and maybe I busted some looking-glasses, but I sure didn't murder nobody," he says. "There was a big crowd seen the whole thing. That marshal told me to drop my gun, and I done just what he said." And his lawyer proved that the cowpoke had dropped his gun before the marshal got shot, so how could he be guilty? The jury scratched their head awhile, and then they said the marshal was killed accidental, and turned the defendant loose.

After the cowpuncher went back to the Territory the folks heard a story about how he had killed two other fellows, and both times he throwed the six-shooter down on the ground so it went off accidental. Some fellows said he had his gun filed down to a hair-trigger, and he used to practice throwing it every day. They said he had a cooling-board set up for a target, and he could throw his gun down that way and hit the board three times out of five.

Well, we have got men here in town that carry guns without no triggers, and it is surprising how quick they can pop the hammer with their thumb. Maybe some of them know how to fan a pistol with both hands, and flip derringers out of their sleeves, and do tricks like that. But them old gun-fighters all say there ain't nobody in the world could hit a man by throwing his gun down on the ground like that cowpuncher done. So maybe the jury was right, and it must have been a accident after all.

JACK AND OLD TUSH

ONE TIME there was three boys lived on a farm by themselves. Each boy would take his turn to cook dinner, while the other two worked in the field. One day it was Joe's turn, and just as he was ready to put the dinner on the table a funny-looking man come running in, and he had a big tush in the front of his mouth. The man with the tush says, "Dinner done? Dinner done?" Before Joe could say anything the man dumped the whole dinner in a big bucket and run off with it.

The next day it was Will's turn to cook dinner, and the same thing happened again. Jack says, "You just wait till tomorrow, and see how I fix old Tush." So he got a little short crowbar, and put it where he could get hold of it handy. Next day Jack had the dinner ready, and when the man with the tush come running in, Jack hit him with the bar, and he knocked the tush out. The man dropped the bucket and run, with Jack right after him. Pretty soon old Tush run down a hole in the ground, and Jack come on back to the house.

Jack told his brothers what happened, and next morning he laid off work and went to the hole in the ground. He slid down a long ways before he come to a ledge, and there stood a little man. Jack knew he was one of the good people. The little man says, "Jack, you have proved yourself brave. Now you must rescue three lovely ladies that the giants have got down here. Always choose a rusty sword to fight with."

The first house Jack come to there was a pretty lady, and she says, "Oh Jack, I'm sorry for you." Jack looked at her and he says, "Why are you sorry for me?" She says, "There is a giant here with a great big head, and he kills everybody that comes along." Just then the big giant come walking out. There was some swords laying there, and one of them was rusty. So Jack picked up the rusty sword and cut the giant's big head off.

Jack was looking at the lady, and she sure was pretty, but she says her sister is lots prettier, and she lives down the road at a house where there is a golden gate. So Jack went on down the road to have a look at the sister, but while he was talking to her, out come another giant, and this one had two big heads.

Jack picked up the rusty sword, and they had quite a battle, but finally he got both of the giant's heads cut off.

Jack was looking at the lady, and she was prettier than the first one, but she says her youngest sister is the prettiest of all, and she lives down the road at a house where there is a set of golden bars. So Jack went on down the road to have a look at the sister, and while he was talking to her, out come another giant, and this one had three heads. Jack took the rusty sword and tackled the giant, and they fought a long time. But finally he got all three of the giant's heads cut off.

Soon as he got his breath back, Jack gathered up all the gold he could carry, and he made the three pretty girls bring all they could pack too, and then he took them back home with him. Jack married the one he got off the three-headed giant, because she was the youngest and the prettiest. Joe and Will married the others, and they all lived happy ever after.

THE FIDDLER'S WIFE

ONE TIME there was a fiddler that didn't amount to much, but his wife was a mighty fine woman. She was good looking too, and the boys was all after her like buzzards after a gut-wagon, but she wouldn't have nothing to do with nobody only her own husband. That's why all the men for miles around used to wish their wife was more like the pretty girl that married the fiddler.

A big steamboat used to come up the river every so often in them days, and the captain was a rich man. He owned the whole outfit himself, and always got the best girls every place the packet stopped. He figured he could have any woman he wanted. The captain heard about the fiddler's wife, but he just laughed. "She will fall like a apple, when the right man comes along," says he.

Him and the fiddler was drinking in the tavern one day, and pretty soon they got to talking about women. The captain says he can ride any mare on the river, and finally he bet his steamboat against an old fiddle that he could get the fiddler's wife in two hours easy. So he went up to the house one day, when her husband was away. But the fiddler sneaked back home and hid in the kitchen, where he could hear what was going on.

So long as they kept a-talking and laughing, the fiddler figured his wife was doing all right. But he heard the captain pour out some drinks, and after that everything was quiet. Pretty soon the fiddler heard a little bit of a noise that made him mighty uneasy. So then he begun to sing:

> Be true to me, be true to me,
> Be true, my love, be true,
> Be true to me till the clock strikes four
> And the boat belongs to you.

Nobody said anything for a minute, and then the fiddler's wife sung out kind of breathless:

> Too late, too late, my own true love,
> He's got me round the middle,
> He's got me once, he's got me twice,
> And you've lost your damned old fiddle!

So the captain he just put the fiddle under his arm and went a-whistling down to the boat landing. The fiddler didn't say much, but him and his wife never done no good after that. It wasn't long till the fiddler went over to Batesville, and some people say that him and the captain met up and got to fighting about something. The talk was that the captain killed the fiddler, or else maybe it was the other way round. Them things happened a long time ago, and the folks never did find out for sure.

RICK TYLER AND THE LAWYER

ONE TIME there was a lawyer down at the county seat, and he didn't know much about law, but he was the smartest man in town, and he could get anybody out of jail no matter what they done. A fellow by the name of Rick Tyler got caught stealing chickens in the middle of the night. That's what made it bad, because the Missouri law says that if a man steals chickens in the daytime it don't amount to nothing, but if he steals chickens at night they will put him in the penitentiary. But it ain't practical to steal chickens in the daytime, because you got to wait till they go to roost. And everybody knows chickens won't go to roost till it begins to get dark.

Well, when Rick Tyler seen the lawyer, he says what had I better do? And the lawyer says you better pay me fifty dollars, or else they will put you in the pen for a couple of years. Tyler didn't have no fifty dollars, but he says I will give you twenty-five dollars right now, and after the trial I will go out and raise the rest of the money. So the lawyer took the twenty-five dollars, and then he says, "Did anybody in your family ever lose their mind?" And Rick says, "Well, my Uncle Jaybird is kind of peculiar and they have got him in the asylum, but he ain't what you might call crazy."

"That's fine," says the lawyer. "All you got to do is play off insane, and the jury will turn you loose." Tyler didn't like it much, but the lawyer told him what to do. "Just put a piece of soap in your mouth so you can slobber good, and throw a fit right in the courtroom," says he. "And if anybody asks you a question, you better just holler *ba-a-ah* like a sheep." So Rick done it, and the lawyer says to the jury, "This poor boy is crazy as a bedbug, just like his uncle Jaybird that is in the asylum this minute, and any fool can see he ain't responsible." The town doctor he testified it is all damn foolishness, but the jury seen Rick Tyler a-rolling on the floor and frothing at the mouth and blatting like a sheep, so they all says, "Not guilty." Tyler spit out the soap and took a chaw of tobacker, and then he went on home.

About a month after that he come in to do his trading, and the lawyer seen him standing in front of the pool hall. "Well, Tyler," says he, "don't you think it's about time to pay something on my bill?" Rick just looked at the lawyer like he never seen him before, but he didn't return no answer. Pretty soon he grinned and spit out his tobacker. *"Ba-a-ah!"* says he.

The boys around town was all a-laughing about it, and even the lawyer had to chuckle a little. But he never did get no more money out of Rick Tyler.

HOW BETSEY GOT DROWNDED

ONE TIME there was a woman named Betsey, and she married an old man, but she wanted to get rid of him so she could go with a young fellow. She did not like to run off, because the old man had money in the bank, and if she run off there wasn't no way for her to get the money. And the young fellow didn't want to leave town anyhow, because he owned a blacksmith shop and was doing a good business. Betsey figured it would be better if the old man was blind, so he couldn't see what was going on between her and the blacksmith.

She went to the town doctor and told him what she wanted, but the doctor says it is against the law to go around putting people's eyes out, and he didn't want no part of it. But finally

153

he give her some stuff in a little bottle. It wasn't nothing but marrow out of a beef bone, but Betsey thought it was poison that would make her old man blind. The doctor told the old man all about it the next night, because they both belonged to the same Lodge. The old man decided to let on like he was blind for a few days, so he got a little boy to lead him home. When Betsey run out and wanted to know what's the matter, he says, "I had a kind of a dizzy spell, and now I can't see very good."

When they got up next morning, the old man says he can't see nothing at all hardly. Betsey had to help get his clothes on, and lead him out to the privy. Things went on like that for pretty near a week, and every night the old man seen her put some of Doc's beef marrow into his supper.

So then one day he says, "Give me my walking stick, as I am going down by the river." Betsey says she will go along too, and when they come to the deep place above the riffle the old man stood right on the edge of the high bank. He seen Betsey step back a little, and he knowed she was going to push him off the bluff. But just as she went to push the old man he jumped to one side, and Betsey couldn't stop so she run right off into the deep water. There was a big splash, and he heard her holler twice, and that was all. The old man set down on a rock and rested awhile. Then he walked into town and told the folks that his wife has fell in the river and she can't swim a stroke and he is afraid she got drownded. So everybody run down there and dragged the river, and after while they found Betsey laying in the water, but she was dead.

The blacksmith begun to talk around how somebody has murdered Betsey, and maybe her husband done it. But the doctor says, "I have examined this woman's body, and the lungs are full of water, and there ain't a mark on her, and no sign of foul play." The sheriff went out to her house and the

154

place where she fell off the bluff, and he says it is either a acci-dent or else she drownded herself on purpose. And then the sheriff says, "Young man, if you have been holding back in-formation about this case, you better tell me right now. And if you *don't* know anything you had better shut up, because we don't want no goddam gossip unless you've got some evidence to back it up." The blacksmith thought about this awhile, and then he says he don't know nothing about the case, and that was the end of it.

After they got the inquest and the burying over, the old man stayed at the hotel for a few days, and then he bought a little house in the edge of town. Pretty soon he got himself a likely young widow woman for a housekeeper. Him and her got along fine, and everybody says the old man done right well the rest of his life.

SCRATCHES ON THE BEDSTEAD

ONE TIME there was an old bachelor named Zack that owned a little patch of ground, and he lived in a shanty built out of old boards. Zack raised his own garden truck, and run trotlines, and picked berries. He was a great hand to find bee-trees, and sometimes he would dig yellow root and sell it to the yarb doctors. In the winter time he done some trapping, and his credit was always good at the store. Zack never made no money to speak of, but he always had plenty to eat.

He was setting on the porch one evening, when here come a draggled old woman down the trail. She didn't have no place to go, and it was a-raining, so Zack let her stay all night. When he woke up, the sun was a-shining and the birds was a-singing.

155

The old woman was getting breakfast, and it sure did smell wonderful. There was coffee and eggs and bacon, and she made some pancakes besides. After breakfast the old woman scrubbed the floor and washed both windows, and then she hung the quilts out in the sunshine. They had catfish with hushpuppies for dinner. And when it come supper time there was fried meat and cornbread, besides a fine ginger cake and wild strawberries. The old woman never said nothing about leaving. Just before they went to bed Zack says, "What's your name?" and she told him her name was Sugar Finney.

Next morning they had fried sidemeat and biscuits with sorghum, and Zack drunk three cups of coffee. "Them victuals sure do taste good," says he. "A man gets tired of his own cooking." Sugar Finney just grinned, but she didn't return no answer. Pretty soon the old woman says she better be on her way, as she is going to get a job in the tomato cannery down at the crossroads. But Zack says there is a very low class of people hangs around that cannery. "You better stay right here at home," he says. Sugar Finney just looked at him. "I need a housekeeper awful bad," says Zack, "and I'll pay you three dollars a week, with board and lodging throwed in." The old woman grinned, and she says, "Well, I'll try it for a week or two, and see how we make out."

Him and her got along fine, and the victuals tasted better every day, and Zack sure did love to lay in bed while she was a-getting breakfast. But he bought a lot of groceries and stuff, so when Saturday night come he didn't have no money for her wages. "That's all right," says Sugar Finney, and she just made three little scratches on the foot of the bed. Then her and Zack turned in just like they always done, and he never thought no more about it.

Next week they needed a can of coal oil and some other things from the store, so when Saturday night come he didn't have no three dollars to pay Sugar. But she just says, "That's all right," and made three more little marks on the foot of the bed. So that's the way it went all summer and part of the winter, too. And then Zack took sick and couldn't do no work for two whole months. Sugar Finney nursed him like a regular granny woman, and fed him just as good as ever. But every Saturday night, just before they went to bed, she would make three more little marks on the bedstead.

After while it got so the whole foot of the bed was covered with them little scratches, and Zack counted up and found out he owed Sugar pretty near two hundred dollars. "That's just about what this here farm is worth," says he, "and it's all I got in the world. But God hates a welsher, and I always pay my debts." So he went to town and deeded the place to Sugar Finney, and then he begun to pack his stuff in a old satchel. He says he is going down to Little Rock and get a job on the public works. "Do they feed good?" says Sugar, but Zack never made no answer. Pretty soon she says, "Listen, Zack, I can't run no farm all by myself. You better stay right here at home." Zack thought about it awhile, and then he says, "You want me to be a hired man?" Sugar just grinned at him. "I don't aim to give no orders," she says. "You do just like you always done, and I will pay you three dollars a week, with board and lodging throwed in." When Saturday night come around Sugar didn't have no money, so Zack made three little scratches on the head of the bed. And he done the same thing every week from that time on.

Along about pawpaw time Zack counted up again, and there was just as many marks on the head of the bedstead as there was on the foot. Sugar Finney didn't have no money, so she deeded the place to Zack. "That makes us even," she says. "We're all out of debt, and we don't owe each other nothing." Pretty soon Zack says, "Listen, Sugar, this here scratching

on the bed and making out deeds ain't getting us nowhere."
The old woman just looked at him, but she didn't say nothing.
"Let's you and me go to town and get married," says he. "Then
we'll own the farm in cahoots, and be done with all this goddam book-keeping." Sugar just grinned at him, and she says it
sounds like a good idea. So that's what they done, and him and
her lived happy ever after.

THE PEA-GREEN JUG

ONE TIME there was a man that liked to sing songs
and tell stories, but he loved liquor better than anything else
in the world. He was a good fellow too, but he wouldn't work,
and so he never had no money. He just hung around places
where they was selling whiskey, and everybody liked to hear
him talk, so they would give him a drink every so often. But
it seemed like he never could get enough, and he was always
terrible thirsty in the morning.

It was one of these mornings he was walking down the road,
when a little old man come along. The little old man was dressed
kind of funny, and some boys was throwing dirt on his green
coat. So the thirsty fellow run the boys away and brushed the
dust off the little man's clothes. The little old man says, "Come
with me, as I have got something for you." They walked over
to a grove of trees, and the little old man pulled a pea-green
jug out of a stump. The thirsty fellow grabbed it and took a big
drink right now. It was the best whiskey he ever tasted. The
little old man says, "That ain't no common jug, and you better
take good care of it. You can drink all you want, and give your
friends a dram. But don't never sell a drop, or you'll be plumb
out of luck." The thirsty fellow took another big snort, and

158

he says a man would be crazy to sell whiskey like this, because what could he buy with the money? The little old man didn't return no answer, and he must have snuck off through the brush some way.

When he seen the little man was gone, the thirsty fellow took another drink and listened to the birds sing awhile. Then he went on back home, and stayed happy drunk all day, and took a few more drinks before bedtime. Next morning he woke up terrible dry, and he figured the pea-green jug must be empty, but it was plumb full. So he got along fine that day, and when he woke up the second morning the jug was still full. The thirsty fellow kind of sobered up then, and he put a good stout strap through the handle, so the jug couldn't be got off of him nohow. He went into town and give a lot of his friends a drink, but the pea-green jug still had whiskey in it. And it was full all the time after that, so he always had plenty no matter what happened. Lots of fellows got to coming out to his house, particular when they didn't have no money. He give pretty near everybody a drink, but the pea-green jug held out wonderful. The neighbors got so they would fetch in hams, and fried fish, and beans, and pies, and all kind of victuals. They give him some good clothes, too, and lots of tourists would offer to pay cash for a drink out of the jug. But the thirsty fellow just laughed and told them he didn't have no license to sell whiskey, so he wouldn't take their money.

One day he got drunker than common, and he come into town a-scratching where he didn't itch. When he woke up next morning there was two gold pieces in his pocket, but the jug was empty as a dead man's eyes. The boys fetched some store-boughten whiskey and poured in, like priming a pump, but it was just trouble throwed away. The pea-green jug had went dry, and there wasn't nothing anybody could do about it.

From then on the thirsty fellow was just like any other dram-drinker that didn't have no money. He hung around places where they was selling whiskey, and everybody liked to hear him talk, so they would give him a drink every now and then. He used to tell about the pea-green jug sometimes, but most people thought it was just one of them old-time fables. The thirsty fellow had got pretty old by that time, and everybody knows a man can't tell the truth very good after his hair turns white.

CONFEDERATES IN THE NEWS

ONE TIME the G.A.R. boys was having a reunion, and the whole town was littered with Yankee flags and blue uniforms. They put up a lot of black pennants too, because some fellow had killed President Garfield. The streets was full of gamblers and pimps and fancy women and thieves, and all the saloons was jammed with G.A.R. men a-bragging how they won the War. To hear them old windbags talk, you'd think they had whipped the Confederacy all by themselves, with one hand tied behind their back. The best people in town was mostly Southerners, but they wasn't looking for no trouble, so they all shut up their stores that day and stayed home.

Mighty few Yankees can carry their liquor, and by four o'clock they was all drunk and hollering like Indians at a peach-seed shaking. Some of 'em was running around singing black-guard songs like "Marching through Georgia" and "John Brown's Body" about how they was going to hang President Davis to a sour-apple tree. There was one old scoundrel that claimed he had been a captain, and he was making more noise than anybody. All of a sudden he stopped singing and begun to holler "Robbers! Stop thief!" and he says somebody has stole his wallet with forty-seven dollars in it.

Our town marshal seen three young fellows a-running, and he was a-horseback, so he caught them right quick and horsed them over to the calaboose. But when old Captain Blabbermouth got his wallet back, he kept right on a-hollering. He says the loyal veterans that saved the Union is being robbed on the street in broad daylight, and this is what comes of having our reunion in a bushwhacker town, and let's tear down the jailhouse and hang them son-of-a-bitches! The marshal and his deputies rode their horses right into the crowd, and it looked like touch-and-go for a minute, as you could hear people a-cocking pistols all over the place. But pretty soon the Yankees come to their senses, and went a-whooping back to the saloons and whorehouses where they belonged.

The home folks was pretty sore about all this, but they didn't say much, and most of the blue-bellies left town next morning. But the newspaper printed right on the front page how the fellows that stole the wallet was confederates! Before dark there was a big mob in front of the *Clarion* office, a-raging up and down looking for the editor, which they was going to run him out of the country or maybe hang him.

The town marshal and our mayor went over to the newspaper office. The crowd was milling around like steers, and they had broke out the window glass. They drug the editor out on the steps, and he kept saying it was all a mistake, but the mob didn't pay no attention. The mayor climbed up on the fence, and he says, "Listen to me, you goddam fools! I got this stiff leg at Pea Ridge. The Yanks hit me once and missed me a thousand times." Everybody laughed at that, and things eased up a little. "Do you know what *miss* means? Spell it with a big *m,* and it means a lady. But use a little *m,* and it just means you didn't hit the target." The crowd was quiet for a minute, and then they begun to holler this ain't no spelling bee, and what's little *m* and big *m* got to do with this goddam Yankee that has insulted the Stars and Bars? "I'm a-coming to that," says the mayor. "If you spell Confederate with a big *c*, it means men that fought for the South, like us. But spell it with a little *c*, and it just means anybody that's in cahoots, like them pickpockets." The crowd begun to growl and argue amongst themselves, and then old Doc Morris climbed up on the fence. "I rode with Jeb Stuart," says he, "and you all know I ain't no Republican. But I want to tell you that the mayor's right. This newspaper man spelled it with a little *c*, and he didn't mean no disrespect to the Southern Confederacy." The crowd was still a-grumbling, but it begun to thin out around the edges, and pretty soon there was nobody left but a few drunks and troublemakers. The marshal knowed how to handle them, all right.

The mayor took the newspaper man back into the office, and he says, "I'm sorry them damn fools raised such a disturbance. But you got to remember this is a Southern town, and we're still kind of touchy about the War." And the editor says, "Good Lord, sir, the War's been over for twenty years!" The mayor he laughed kind of weary like. "Twenty years ain't long enough to forget a war, especially for the folks that lost it," says he. "Another thing is, we ain't got much book-learning here, because most of us joined the army instead of going to college. Some of the best men in this county can't write their own names. It's no wonder so many of our people don't know the difference between big *c* and little *c*."

The editor brought out a bottle of whiskey, and him and the mayor took a drink. "You're a good citizen," the mayor says. "We need you here, and we need the *Clarion* too. I'll see that you get the county printing." The editor didn't say nothing. "If you'll just take note of our little prejudices, and be kind of careful, everything will turn out all right," says the mayor. "I'll be careful," says the editor, "I'll be careful from now on out." And then he grinned a little, and him and the mayor took another drink.

THREE BLACK CATS

ONE TIME there was a fellow come down the road in the middle of the night, and it begun to rain. He went into a old deserted house to get out of the wet. It was awful dark in the house, but there was some dry leaves and sticks scattered round, so he built him a fire in the chimney. Soon as the place warmed up a little, here come a black cat and set down on the hearth. It was a pretty good-sized cat. The fellow just set there and looked at it. He didn't like cats much, especially black ones, because he thought they was unlucky.

Pretty soon he heard a little noise, and when he looked round there was another black cat, twice as big as the first one. Them two cats warmed theirself by the fire, and the fellow just set there and looked at them. After while the big cat opened his mouth wide, and he says, "Let's do it now." But the little cat answered back, "We better wait till Martin comes."

The fellow just set there and looked at them two black cats, and he thought maybe he was dreaming. Pretty soon he heard a little noise, and in come another black cat. This one was big as a panther, and when he set down on the hearth his head reached plumb up to the fireboard. After while the biggest cat yawned, and he says, "Let's do it now." The biggest cat had a coarse voice, like a bull a-roaring down a rain barrel. But the little cat answered back, "We better wait till Martin comes."

163

The fellow just set there and looked at them three black cats, and he thought maybe he was going crazy. It was raining harder than ever by this time, and there was lots of thunder and lightning, with the wind blowing like a regular hurricane. Pretty soon the fellow heard a little noise behind him, but he did not wait to see whether Martin was a-coming or not. He just give one big jump out of the door and run down the road in the dark. He run plumb into town and waked up some of his kinfolks, but he was out of wind and couldn't tell them what was the matter. The folks seen he was wet as a drownded rat, so they give him a hot toddy and put him to bed.

Next morning he borrowed some dry clothes, and him and his brother-in-law went out to the old deserted house. There was the fresh ashes to show where he built the fire in the chimney. And there was some tracks on the floor, but they was just common cat tracks, no bigger than you'll see around any other old house. His brother-in-law says it must be you have been drinking a little too much here lately. So the fellow just wagged his head. He didn't have no more to say about the three black cats that was a-waiting for Martin to come.

THE WOMEN SUCKED HIS BLOOD

ONE TIME there was some little boys playing ball in the road, and one boy knocked the ball over a high stone fence. They could not climb over because the fence was too high, and they was afraid to go in anyhow, because there was a old witch lived in that house. They figured she might kill them, and it was better to let the ball go, and not take no

164

chances. So the little boys all run away, but there was one big boy there, and he walked right in the gate.

The old witch kept herself hid, but there was a pretty blond-headed girl come out to see if she could toll the big boy into the house. When the boy seen her he says, "Where is the old woman?" The girl says, "The old woman don't live here no more, and I am all by myself. I am lonesome, because there is nobody for me to play with, and if you come in the house I will give you a big red apple." He went in and eat the apple, and then she give him some fine red cherries and he eat them too.

Pretty soon the blond-headed girl says, "If you come in the other room, I will give you a gold ring, and then we will play games." So he went in, and she give him the gold ring. Pretty soon him and her got to tickling each other and rassling around like young folks do. And while they was a-romping on the floor, the blond-headed girl out with a little sharp knife and cut his throat. Then she began to suck blood like a mink, and the old witch come in, and she sucked some blood too. And while the boy was a-dying, they put a wash-basin under his head to catch the rest of the blood. Then after it got dark they took him down back of the house and throwed him in the river.

About a week after that the folks found him laying in the water with his throat cut and the blood all gone out of him. Everybody knowed who killed that boy, but they couldn't prove nothing. The old witch and her blond-headed girl had lots of money. They paid off the lawyers and took care of them courthouse rats, so nobody ever done anything about it.

165

HOW JACK GOT HIS BIG FARM

ONE TIME there was three brothers owned a big farm, because their parents died and left it to them. The youngest boy was named Jack, and they made him do all the hard work. Will and Tom just set around in the shade while Jack done the farming. He wanted them to buy his third of the place, but they wouldn't do it. Then Jack found out that Will and Tom was planning to kill him soon as he got the crop laid by, so they could get his share for nothing. He went to town and told the sheriff, but the sheriff just laughed and he says Jack must have dreamed it. The sheriff says Will and Tom are fine young fellows, and they sure ain't going to murder their own brother.

Jack started back home through the woods, and he seen a little man that had fell in a deep hole. Jack cut a pole and helped the little man out, and they set down under a tree to rest awhile. Pretty soon Jack told the little man what he was up against. The little man thought about it a long time, and then he advised Jack what to do.

Jack went home and told his brothers that the sheriff has give him a job, and that all he's got to do is to sleep in the sheriff's bed. He says the sheriff is going to arrest a couple of fellows that is up to some meanness in town. These fellows will look in the window, and when they see somebody in the bed, they'll think it is the sheriff. So they will go right ahead with their plans, and the sheriff can catch them easy because they won't be expecting him. Will says, "Is there anybody else in the sheriff's house?" Jack says no, as the sheriff's wife has gone to visit her kinfolks. So then Will and Tom figured this was their chance to kill Jack and blame it on somebody else.

When it come dark Jack was gone, so Will and Tom got two clubs and sneaked over to the sheriff's house. They seen somebody in bed, and they thought it was Jack, so they begun to club him. The sheriff was hurt bad at the first lick, but he grabbed his gun out from under the pillow and shot both of them. When he lit the lamp and seen Will and Tom laying there on the floor, the sheriff didn't know what to think.

He went out to the farm, and there was Jack in bed, sound asleep. Jack woke up and he says, "Sheriff, what are you doing here this time of night?" The sheriff says "Listen, Jack, did you tell your brothers how you come to see me yesterday?" And Jack says, "Yes, I did. I thought if they knowed I told you about it, they would be afraid to kill me." The sheriff he thought awhile, and then he says, "Well, Jack, you don't need to worry no more. Will and Tom is both dead as doornails."

Some folks thought there was something fishy about that killing. But the sheriff swore he always got along fine with Will and Tom, and he didn't have no idea it was them till he lit the lamp after the shooting. The judge grumbled a little about it, but the sheriff says, "Listen, Judge, what would *you* do if some fellows broke into your house in the middle of the night, and jumped onto you with big clubs?" And Jack himself says he feels mighty bad about his brothers getting killed, but they was doing something wrong, and he don't hold no grudge against the sheriff. So finally they turned the sheriff loose, and that was the end of it.

Jack owned the whole farm after his brothers was dead, and he had money in the bank besides. He got two hired men to do the heavy work, and they fixed up the place something wonderful. There was a pretty little schoolmarm come to the crossroads that winter, and it wasn't long till her and Jack got married and lived happy ever after.

HIRAM AIN'T HERE NO MORE

ONE TIME there was a boy named Hiram, and he wanted to be a fiddler. His folks got him the best fiddle that money could buy, and old fiddlers from miles around tried to learn him how to play, but it wasn't no use. Hiram was a smart fellow and he had book-learning too, but he was the sorriest fiddler that ever put rosin on a bow. There was a half-wit family lived down the road that couldn't write their own name, and didn't know enough to pour chamber-lye out of a boot, but they could make a fiddle just talk and sing. Hiram used to listen at them fools a-fiddling, and it made him so goddam mad he'd break right down and cry like a baby.

A silly old woman told him that fiddle-tunes was Hell's own music, and all the best fiddlers is a-working for the Devil. Hiram just laughed and says that's just the job he's looking for, only he can't play good enough to suit Old Scratch. So then Hiram started for home, but there was a stranger waiting at the crossroads. "Meet me right here at midnight," says he, "and bring your fiddle." And then the stranger walked on down the road. The sun was a-shining, but the stranger didn't throw no shadow. There was snow on the ground, but he didn't leave no tracks.

After that Hiram was out somewhere pretty near every night, and he got to be the damndest fiddler in the whole country. He could play "Nancy Rollins" and "Big Limber" till you'd think Hell was full of Presbyterians a-dancing, with the Devil calling the figures. Hiram could make a fiddle talk all right, but it sure talked dirty. Even the names of them reels and hornpipes ain't fit to be wrote down on paper. He could play tunes that would make an old man's hair stand up, and if a woman listened at him awhile she just went plumb crazy.

There was a gang of rich people from some big town had a camp back in the woods, and they always come and got Hiram to play for them. They was kind of a wild bunch, and lots of times they used to dance all night out there in the timber. Some folks say that the gals at them frolics didn't wear clothes enough to wad a shotgun, and carried on scandalous right before everybody. The home folks figured they must be witches, but probably they was just fancy women that them fellows brought down from Kansas City.

The rich people was having a big party one night, when the whole camp burnt up, and everybody says it must have been lightning-struck. The home folks went over next day and scratched around in the ashes of them fine cabins. They found some gold watches and a lot of other truck, but there wasn't no bones. Nobody ever did find out what went with all them people. Hiram never come home no more, neither, and his kinfolks was afraid something bad might have happened to him. But maybe Hiram just run off with one of them city gals. Maybe he's a-fiddling at a dance hall in one of them big towns right now, or even a-playing on the radio somewheres.

THE SHERIFF AND
THE GALLOWS

ONE TIME there was a fellow killed a peddler so he could steal his horse and wagon. He thought there was a sack of gold in the wagon too, but the peddler didn't have nothing but a pocketful of silver money to make change. They caught

169

the fellow that done the killing, and sentenced him to be hung. The sheriff was terrible upset, because he never hung nobody before, and he says it's against his religion to hang people. But when he found out that the state would pay him three hundred dollars, he begun to feel better.

The sheriff was going to hang the fellow to a tree down by the river, but the judge says that ain't legal, because you got to have a regular gallows. There wasn't no gallows in the county, so the sheriff has got to have one built and pay for it out of his own pocket. The sheriff begun to sweat blood and talk about his religion again, but it didn't do no good. He dickered with the carpenter a long time, and finally the carpenter says he will furnish the lumber and build the thing for seventy-five dollars. They built the scaffold right up against the courthouse, and the sheriff handed over the seventy-five dollars, but it pretty near killed him.

After he got the thing all built and the trap fixed and the rope tied, them lawyers begun to talk about how the governor would most likely call the whole thing off at the last minute and send the prisoner to the penitentiary instead. The sheriff was all broke up when he heard that, because if there wasn't no hanging he wouldn't get no three hundred dollars, and stood to lose seventy-five dollars of his own money. He wanted to hang the fellow right away, but the judge says they must wait till the regular day, because the papers was all made out and it would be against the law to have the hanging any sooner.

The sheriff got terrible nervous the last few days. Folks thought he was worried about his religion, but the truth is he was scared of losing the seventy-five dollars. When the time come, the prisoner walked out cheerful enough. He says he's done made his peace with God, and maybe the doctor had give him a shot of morphine. He grinned at all the people, and shook hands with the sheriff. "I'm prepared to die," says he, "and I don't hold nothing against you." The sheriff was shaking like holly in a high wind, but there wasn't no telegram from the governor, so he knocked the trigger. Pretty soon the doctor says the fellow is dead, and that was the end of it.

There was some boys run through the crowd selling pieces of the gallows for souvenirs, but mighty few people would pay ten cents for a little splinter of wood. Next day the sheriff and two jailbirds took the scaffold down careful, so as not to split them good boards, and they pulled all the nails out. The sheriff peddled the stuff all over town, and they do say he got pretty near thirty dollars for it. There's henhouses and privies around here yet that was built out of that gallows lumber.

SI BURTON'S LITTLE BLACK DOG

ONE TIME there was an old fellow and he had been in the Confederate army, so the folks called him Captain Billy. The neighbors all figured he was kind of crazy, because he thought there was a dog follering him around. He used to holler and cuss and throw rocks sometimes, just like anybody would do if they was trying to run off a stray dog. Only there wasn't no dog there.

The story goes that back in 1865, when Captain Billy come home from the War, the whole country was full of robbers and bushwhackers. Everybody carried guns all the time, and people was always fighting and killing each other. One day Captain Billy met up with a fellow named Si Burton and shot him. Si's horse run off and left him a-laying there with his back broke.

171

He hollered for Captain Billy not to kill him, but Captain Billy done it anyhow. Si's little black dog kept a-running round the corpse and whining kind of pitiful. Captain Billy was mad, so he killed the dog too, and left both of them a-laying right there in the road.

Captain Billy went to bed in the tavern, but all night long he could hear the little dog a-whining round outside. Next morning he *seen* it, and from then on the little black dog stuck mighty close to Captain Billy. Not a day went by without he seen it, or heard it, or smelled it. When he set in the shanty, the little black dog kept a-scratching outside the door. And every time he went to town, the little black dog follered him. Captain Billy was always finding dog hair in the bed, or even in his victuals, and every fence post on the place smelled like green cordwood. "It ain't no dream and it ain't no ghost," says he. "It ain't nothing only Si Burton's little black dog. What I say is, that dog is *there* for me, but it *ain't there* for nobody else. And I ain't no more crazy than them smart alecks in town, neither."

Things had went on like that for pretty near fifty years, and then one morning the neighbors didn't see no smoke coming out of Captain Billy's chimney. They went over there, and Jack Loomis found the body in a field out back of the house. At first it looked like maybe somebody had killed Captain Billy, but there wasn't a mark on him. He was laying in a little skift of snow, and there wasn't no footprints only what he made himself. "There wasn't no sign at all," says Jack Loomis, "only where a little dog had been a-sniffing round the corpse. You know how dogs do, sometimes. Well, I just wiped the stuff off Captain Billy's face with my handkerchief, and never said nothing to the folks about it."

The town doctor allowed that Captain Billy was pretty old, and probably his heart went back on him, or else he died of cold and exposure. But the old-timers didn't take no stock in such notions. Most of them figured maybe Si Burton's little black dog had something to do with it.

WHITE-BEAR WHITTINGTON

ONE TIME there were three sisters, all very beautiful and kind-hearted. A crippled old man come down the road, and he asked for something to eat. The oldest girl brought him a nice chair to set in. The second girl gave him some clean clothes. The youngest girl cooked him a good dinner. Next day the old man come back, carrying a funny-looking chair. He says it is a wishing chair, and each girl can set in it and make a wish. The oldest girl wished that the handsomest man in the world would come along and marry her. The second girl wished for the next handsomest man. So of course the youngest girl had to take third place.

173

The wishes all come true, just like the old man said. The youngest girl's husband was very good-looking, but he always wore a long white coat made of bearskin, so the folks called him White-Bear Whittington. Him and his wife got along fine for several years, and they had three children. But then a young witch come down the road, and she sung a wicked song and cast a strong spell on White-Bear. So pretty soon he run off to follow the witch. His wife and children felt very bad, but there was nothing they could do about it.

One day a man come to the house, and it was the same old man that brought the wishing chair. He give the girl a gold ring, a gold bracelet, and a gold comb. "Go to the shore of a red sea," he says. "Don't be afraid, but get in the boat and go right across. Then you'll come to a cliff on fire, but don't be afraid, as there are steps so you can climb up all right. Then just follow the path till you come to the witch's castle." And after that he told her how to break the spell so she could get her husband back.

The girl did just like the old man said, and when she got to the castle the witch wanted her fine gold ring. The girl says if they will give her five minutes alone with White-Bear Whittington, the witch can have the ring. When she got into the room, there was her husband in a deep sleep, but she says:

> Three children born to you,
> The red sea crossed for you,
> The fire cliff climbed for you,
> Old White-Bear, look at me!

White-Bear Whittington didn't wake up, because he was asleep from a magic drug, but that night he dreamed about his wife and children.

The next day the girl gave the witch her gold bracelet for five minutes alone with White-Bear Whittington, and she talked

174

to him again. White-Bear didn't wake up, but that night he had a vision of his wife and children.

The third day she gave the witch her gold comb, and this time when she says "Old White-Bear, look at me!" he woke up and looked right at her. The third time is a charm, and so the spell was broke for good. White-Bear and his wife went out of the castle, and along the path, and down the fire cliff, and across the red sea, till finally they got back home.

From that time on White-Bear Whittington stayed right there with his wife and children. He didn't pay no attention to women that come along the road, and witches could sing till they was black in the face for all he cared. And so they lived happy ever after.

THE MARE WITH
THE FALSE TAIL

ONE TIME there was a fellow up in Missouri owned a big fine-looking saddle mare, except she didn't have no tail, as it had got cut off some way. But there was a wigmaker in Kansas City that fixed a false tail so good you couldn't tell the difference, and it was fastened onto the stub with eelskin and rubber.

The trader that owned the mare got a fine saddle and bridle with silver on it, and he rode around to all the fairs. He would sell the mare for a good price, but he never sold the saddle and bridle. Soon as he got the money in his pocket, he always took off the saddle and bridle, and then he would pull the mare's tail off. She just had a little stub about six inches long, and it was shaved smooth and dyed yellow. It sure did look funny, so all the people would laugh, and the fellow that bought the mare begun to holler for his money back. But the horse trader says the tail does not belong to the mare, because it come off another animal. He says he bought the tail separate in Kansas City, and he has got a bill of sale to prove it. False tails is just like a woman's bustle, and if any gentleman wants a artificial tail, they can go to Kansas City and see the wigmaker, says he.

So then he would go set in the livery stable, and pretty soon the fellow that bought the mare would come around talking turkey. Then the horse trader would say, "I always try to do the right thing, and not work no hardship on the customers. So I will take the mare back, if you will give me twenty dollars for my trouble." That's the way it went all over the country, and sometimes he would sell the mare three or four times in one day. The horse trader was a-living the life of Riley, and putting money in the bank besides.

One day he rode into a little town in Arkansas, and right away an old man bought the mare for two hundred dollars. When the horse trader pulled the mare's tail off, the old man didn't bat an eye, and he just laughed like the rest of the boys. The horse trader hung around the livery stable all day, but the old man never showed up. The horse trader stayed at the hotel that night, and the next day he borrowed a pony and rode out to the old man's place. He says he don't feel right about the sale, so he will take the mare and give the old man his money back, and no hard feelings.

The old man just laughed, and says he hasn't got no complaint, as a bargain is a bargain. He says he likes the mare fine, and he is going to braid a new tail out of corn shucks, and paint it blue to match his wife's eyes. The horse trader figured the old man must be out of his head. But he had to get the snide mare back somehow, so he offered to pay the two hundred dollars and give the old man ten dollars besides. The old man just laughed louder than ever, and he says the mare is worth four hundred dollars easy, and she ain't for sale anyhow. So the horse trader come back to town. He set around the hotel mighty glum, and all the home boys was laughing about it.

Next morning he went out to see the old man again, and says he will give two hundred and twenty-five dollars for the snide mare. The old man says, "Don't talk foolish, because me and my wife has got attached to the mare now, and she is just like one of the family." And then he says he knowed that tail was a fake all the time, because he used to swap horses with the Indians when he was a young fellow.

The horse trader thought about it awhile, and then he says, "Listen, that snide's all I got to live on, and feed a big family. Do you want to take the bread out of my little children's mouth?" The old man he says, "No, I wouldn't do nothing like that. Give me three hundred dollars, and you can have your mare back." The horse trader started to write a check, but the old man wouldn't take no check, so they went to the bank, and the horse trader give him three hundred dollars in cash. All the loafers was a-laughing about it, and the banker laughed louder than anybody. So then the horse trader put the mare's tail where it belonged, and he rode out of that town. He never did come back, neither.

Lots of people up North think the folks that live down in Arkansas are all damn fools. But it ain't so, particular when it comes to swapping horses and things like that.

COMMENTS OF A FOLKLORIST

by Herbert Halpert

MR. RANDOLPH'S COLLECTION of tales, like all his folklore work, is important for its variety and completeness. He gives us an excellent picture of the Ozark storytelling tradition. Not only are there American versions of many of the standard European folktale types but also many kinds of local stories.

Practically all European folktale types except religious tales are found in this volume, although some, such as animal and formula tales, are sparsely represented. Nearly nine years ago, in an essay I wrote for Richard Chase's *The Jack Tales,* I predicted that other examples of the *Märchen*—the type of longer folktale dealing with magical occurrences—would be found in this country. There are at least eight of them in Mr. Randolph's collection—welcome additions in evidence that such stories exist in the United States.

This book demonstrates an important aspect of the American white storytelling tradition: the strong tendency to tell nearly all stories as "true" stories. They are so thoroughly localized in place and time, so completely Ozarkian in tone and coloring, that the unsuspecting reader might well accept them as local yarns, either based on fact, or legendary, that is, believed to be true. Yet parallels in Europe, as well as elsewhere in the United States, indicate that they are genuine folktales. Years ago E. S. Hartland commented on the same aspect of storytelling in England.

The primary justification for supplying notes for more than half these tales is to demonstrate that the stories are part of the

European-American culture area. I have concentrated chiefly on American, British, and Irish parallels, and the geographical distribution of the tales is noted. For other European parallels the reader is advised to follow up the references in Stith Thompson's *Motif-Index of Folk-Literature* and *The Types of the Folk-Tale* by Antti Aarne and Stith Thompson. In my notes "Motif" and "Type" refer to these two books, which contain keys to published European folklore collections, as well as to the indices of folktales in the European folklore archives. Especially valuable as supplements to the Thompson volumes are: *The Handbook of Irish Folklore,* which leads to materials in the great archives of the Irish Folklore Commission; Parsons, *Folk-Lore of the Antilles,* Part 3, a monument to the scholarship of the late Elsie Clews Parsons, America's most active collector of folktales from the American Negro. Her notes give references to American and African parallels of many tales.

My own notes make no pretense to completeness, for I have had to rely on the resources of my personal folklore library; furthermore, I felt guilty to be taking time generously given me for another project by a fellowship from the John Simon Guggenheim Foundation. I feel certain that by more effort I might have found European parallels to "Talking River" and "The Queen's White Glove." I could also have supplied Motif references to a few other tales; but I did not think that doing so would be sufficient justification for their inclusion, especially since I could not find folktale parallels.

Mr. Randolph has supplied the references to his own earlier collections and to other publications of Ozark material; in the latter field his knowledge is unrivaled. He demonstrates the probability that several other stories are folktales, for example, "Them Newcomers Ruined the Meat" and "Uncle Johnny's Bear," although I know of no parallels outside the Ozarks.

180

Probably some of the stories, such as those based on folk customs, and a few of the jests, are actually of local origin. Their inclusion in a folktale collection is amply justified by the fact that they are part of the story lore of the Ozarks. They demonstrate that the repertory of storytellers includes all yarns that interest them, not just "folktales." Similarly, folksingers unhesitatingly sing nineteenth-century popular songs with as much enjoyment as they do the older ballads, which delight the scholar.

I suspect, however, that the number of truly local stories in this collection is actually small. I have mentioned parallels from my unpublished collections to show that some of them are folktales in general circulation. I feel certain that other collectors will find variants of some tales for which I was unable to cite published references.

I hope that the publication of this first major collection of American-English white folktales for an adult audience will stimulate further collecting in other regions of the United States.

NOTES

WHO BLOWED UP THE CHURCH HOUSE?

Told by a gentleman in Reeds Spring, Mo., November, 1942. He prefers to remain anonymous. The practice of placing explosives in firewood to discourage thieves is rather common in the Ozarks. When I lived at Galena, Mo., in 1933, the Methodist Church was wrecked by an explosion. Nobody was in the building but a janitor named Mills, who escaped without injury. Had the explosion occurred an hour later, many children in the Sunday School would surely have been killed. The woodpile belonged to a friend of mine, one of the most popular men in southwest Missouri. I don't know who loaded that stick or why, but I'm sure nobody intended to blow up the church. (V.R.)

SHE ALWAYS ANSWERED NO

Told by Mrs. Marie Wilbur, Pineville, Mo., June, 1930. When I asked for more light on the third question, Mrs. Wilbur said she did not know what it was; she reported the tale exactly as told by Mrs. Lucinda Mosier, also of Pineville. This is a familiar ballad theme. Compare the "Oh, No, John" piece reported by Cecil Sharp (*Folk-Songs from Somerset,* 1904, pp. 46–47). For American texts see Wolford (*Play-Party in Indiana,* 1916, pp. 73–74) and Eddy (*Ballads and Songs from Ohio,* 1939, p. 146). Also my *Ozark Folksongs,* 1949, III, pp. 104–5. Homer Croy (*What Grandpa Laughed At,* 1948, pp. 219–20) has a modern prose version which he says was popular in 1917. (V.R.)

Motif K 1331, "No!" Also compare Type 853 (IV, *b* and *c*). The theme of the no's turned to favorable answers by the wooer's shifting the question is found in German "Singspiele" and English "jigs." See Baskervill, *The Elizabethan Jig,* pp. 266–72, where references are also given to Italian, German, and Alsatian folktale versions. Baskervill also discusses the long career of "the simple jest of the woman's no's turned to consent" in English ballads and folksongs, analyzing several types. To his folktale references add Parsons, *Folk-Lore from the Cape Verde Islands,* I, 139–40. Dr. Parsons refers to Portuguese and Jamaican texts. (H.H.)

A SLOW TRAIN THROUGH ARKANSAS

Told by H. A. Coverse, Little Rock, Ark., December, 1949. Thomas W. Jackson's pamphlet *On a Slow Train through Arkansaw* was first published in 1903, by the Thos. W. Jackson Pub. Co., Chicago. More than eight million copies have been printed, and it is still selling. For information about Jackson see the Springfield, Mo., *Leader & Press* (June 9, 1934), James R. Masterson's *Tall Tales of Arkansaw* (1943, pp. 276–78, 385), and my *We Always Lie to Strangers* (1951, pp. 281–82). The indignation aroused by Jackson's joke book lasted nearly half a century. As recently as 1948 Karr Shannon, veteran Arkansas newspaperman, issued a booklet *On a Fast Train through Arkansas* (Little Rock, 1948) with the subtitle "A Rebuke to Jackson's *Slow Train*." For a note on Governor McMath's reply to the Texan see Spider Rowland's column in the *Arkansas Gazette* (Little Rock, Ark., Sept. 24, 1949). (V.R.)

THE COOKSTOVE AND THE CIRCUS

Told by Mrs. May Kennedy McCord, Springfield, Mo., March, 1934. She heard it in Stone county, Mo., in the early 1900's. Mary Austin, *Earth Horizon,* p. 161, heard the story in 1885 from her uncle, who kept a little store on the Pomme de Terre River, in Missouri. He sold several cookstoves, but the customers brought them back "to trade in for a trifle of cash, when a circus was advertised in a nearby town." Eleanor Risley, *An Abandoned Orchard,* pp. 158–59, reports a similar tale about some Missourians who sold their stove to buy circus tickets. Cf. *Hoosier Folklore,* IX, 1950, 42–43. (V.R.)

THE DEPUTY'S WIFE

Told by a lady in Joplin, Mo., December, 1946. She had it from her boy friend, who grew up in Picher, Okla., just across the Missouri-Oklahoma line. I published this item in *Hoosier Folklore,* IX (1950), 43–44. (V.R.)

THE CHAMPION LIAR

Told by Reggie Courtney, Joplin, Mo., March, 1926. He had it from a resident of Jane, Mo., near the Arkansas border. A condensed version in *Funny Stories about Hillbillies,* p. 21, was reprinted in *Hoosier Folklore,* IX (1950), 46–47. Cf. a similar item in my *We Always Lie to Strangers,* pp. 269–70. A related story about a Dr. Titterington, of Marionville, Mo., is in the Centennial Edition of the Crane, Mo., *Chronicle,* May, 1951, p. 6. (V.R.)

Type 1920 B, The one says, *"I have not time to lie,"* and yet lies. For American versions see Halpert, *Journal of American Folklore,* LVIII, 133 (Pennsylvania); Brendle and Troxell, *Pennsylvania German Folk Tales,* pp. 192–93; Federal Writers' Project in Indiana, *Hoosier Tall Stories,* p. 9; Halpert, *Hoosier Folklore Bulletin,* I, 13, 54 (Indiana); Butler, *Hoosier Folklore,* VI, 151–52 (Indiana); Smith, in *ibid.,* V, 54 (Illinois); Boatright, *Publications of the Texas Folklore Society,* XX, 29–30 (American oilmen). (H.H.)

SNAKE IN THE BED!

Told by O. St. John, Pineville, Mo., July, 1921, who related it as the experience of a physician at Anderson, Mo. "I know for a fact," he added, "that snakes do get into people's beds sometimes." Cf. *Hoosier Folklore,* IX (1950), 45–46. (V.R.)

THE STRANGER AND THE BEANS

Told by Price Paine, Noel, Mo., October, 1923. He had it from farmers near Noel in the late 1890's. This must be old and widely known. I heard it about 1900 in a fish-camp on the Cowskin River, in McDonald county, Mo. George Milburn, of Pineville, Mo., published a literary version in his *Oklahoma Town,* pp. 158–62; it appeared as "Die Chance eines Jungen Mannes" in the German translation (*Die Stadt Oklahoma,* Berlin, 1932, pp. 168–71). See my discussion in "Aged in the Woods" (*University Review,* Kansas City, Mo., Spring, 1937, pp. 181–82). James R. Masterson, *Tall Tales of Arkansaw,* p. 392, has a similar item from oral tradition in Polk county, Ark. Cf. *Funny Stories from Arkansas,* pp. 23–24, and *Hoosier Folklore,* IX (1950), 47–48. (V.R.)

This story seems to have some relation to Type 1775, "The Hungry Parson," but I have been unable to check it. There is an unpublished text from New Hampshire in the Halpert collections. (H.H.)

FILL, BOWL, FILL!

Told by Lew Swigart, Lamar, Mo., June, 1927. Mr. Swigart has two versions, one for mixed company and another for male audiences. The text given here is the ladies' tale. Cf. *Western Folklore*, X (1951), 4–5. (V.R.)

This *cante fable* is Type 570, "The Rabbit-Herd." There is a North Carolina text with a tune in Chase, *Jack Tales,* pp. 89–95, for which I supplied some discussion, as well as American and British references (p. 193). See also *Handbook of Irish Folklore,* p. 568; and compare p. 619, No. 37; Parsons, *Folk-Lore from the Cape Verde Islands,* Vol. XV, Part 1, 251–56; Parsons, *Antilles,* III, 277–78. (H.H.)

HOW KATE GOT A HUSBAND

Told by Frank Payne, Galena, Mo., November, 1932. He says it was popular in his neighborhood about 1899. "Just an old fable," he explained, "there ain't no truth in it." The story appears also in a ballad, usually called "Kate and Her Horns." The song is reported by MacKenzie, *Ballads and Sea Songs from Nova Scotia,* pp. 325–27, with historical information in a headnote. See also Sharp, *English Folksongs from the Southern Appalachians,* I, 405–6, and Belden, *Ballads and Songs,* pp. 231–32. Cf. *Western Folklore,* X (1951), 5–6. (V.R.)

For a prose version of this story which is closely related to the broadside ballad form and a discussion see Gardner, *Folklore from the Schoharie Hills, New York,* pp. 194–96. (H.H.)

THE HERON AND THE EEL

Told by Lon Jordan, Farmington, Ark., October, 1941. He got it from the boys around Fayetteville, Ark., in 1905. The tale of herons swallowing the same eel several times is old and widely distributed. W. L. McAtee, *Nomina Abitera,* pp. 24–25, gives European versions from Charles Swainson, *The Folk Lore and Provincial Names of British Birds,* p. 145, and Bishop Erich Pontoppidan, *The Natural History of Norway,* II, p. 77. McAtee adds an American variant which he heard in Grant county, Indiana. See *Hoosier Folklore,* IX (1950), 38–39. (V.R.)

Parsons, *Antilles,* III, 167–68, gives an abstract of a Trinidad tale with a motif curiously similar. After the hero's dogs have eaten many little devils, the first dog swallows the old witch, but "she comes out behind. The next swallows her and the next. The fourth swallows her and sits down." There is an unpublished New Jersey text in the Halpert collections. (H.H.)

186

THE DUMB SUPPER

Told by Lew Beardon, Branson, Mo., December, 1938. He heard it at Forsyth, Mo., in the 1890's. Cf. Myrtle Lain's "Dummy Supper in the Ozarks," *Arcadian Magazine* (Caddo Gap, Ark.), August, 1931, pp. 9–10. Mary Elizabeth Mahnkey, of Mincy, Mo., tells a smiliar story in the *White River Leader* (Branson, Mo.), Jan. 4, 1934, except that the girl is murdered by her husband; the details about the missing knife are the same as in Mr. Beardon's version. There are many tales concerning dumb suppers; see a discussion of the subject in my *Ozark Superstitions*, pp. 178–81. Cf. *Hoosier Folklore*, IX (1950), 39–40. (V.R.)

American reports of the ritual performance of the dumb supper are common, but versions with the motif of the missing knife seem to be limited to the Ozark region. It is this motif which justifies classifying this story as a legend rather than merely a folk belief and custom. That this legend is probably international is demonstrated by a related story from Derbyshire, England, in Addy, *Household Tales*, pp. 75–76. A girl accidentally performed a compulsive-magic act which made the form of her future husband appear and leave his penknife. After their marriage he sees her using this knife, takes it from her, and kills her with it. (H.H.)

THE BOY THAT FOOLED HIS FOLKS

Told by Ed Wall, Pineville, Mo., July, 1925. He heard the tale about 1890 and thought it was a true story about a family in Arkansas. Cf. Dorrance, *We're from Missouri*, p. 13. A related narrative appears in the British ballad of "Young Edmond Dell," though here it is not the son, but a daughter's sweetheart who is murdered. For references to the song see Belden, *Ballads and Songs*, pp. 127–28, also my *Ozark Folksongs*, II, 59–64. (V.R.)

Motif N 321, "Son returning home after long absence unwittingly killed by parents." The theme is used in Robert Penn Warren's poem "The Ballad of Billie Potts." The tale, with some European notes by the editor, appears in *Western Folklore*, X (1951), 1n. (H.H.)

HOOT-OWL JESSUP

Told by Lon Jordan, Farmington, Ark., December, 1941. He said it was supposed to be a true story, about a politician "up in Missouri somewheres." Near Fulton, Mo., they used to tell it on a lawyer, alleging that he answered the owl: "I am William H. Russell, formerly of Kentucky, but now of Callaway county, Missouri, and I am a Member of the Legislature!" In Christian county, Mo., the hero was Billy Gideon, member of a prominent pioneer family, who made and sold hats. William was a common name in the clan and this man had several cousins who answered to it. When the owl first called "Whoo-oo are you?" the man said simply, "I'm Billy Gideon." When asked again, he replied more specifically, "I'm Billy Gideon, the hatter!" I published Mr. Jordan's version in *Hoosier Folklore,* IX (1950), 44–45. (V.R.)

This is a form of Motif J 1811.1, "Owl's hoot misunderstood by lost simpleton." An early North Carolina version is in Taliaferro, *Fisher's River (North Carolina) Scenes and Characters,* by "Skitt," pp. 227–28, reprinted in Boggs, *Journal of American Folklore,* XLVII, 271–72. For other American texts see Halpert, *ibid.,* LVIII, 133 (Pennsylvania); Dorson, *ibid.,* LXI, 149–50 and note 29 (Michigan); Halpert, *Hoosier Folklore Bulletin,* I, 68 (Kentucky). There is an unpublished text from New Jersey in the Halpert collections; from New York in the Folklore Archive in The Farmers Museum, Cooperstown, New York. For other misunderstandings of the owl's hoot see Parsons, *Folk-Lore of the Sea Islands, South Carolina,* p. 59 (Negro); Hyatt, *Folk-Lore from Adams County, Illinois,* p. 68, No. 1530; and from Cornwall, England, Hunt, *Popular Romances of the West of England,* pp. 336–37. (H.H.)

THE DEVIL IN THE GRAVEYARD

Told by Lewis Kelley, Cyclone, Mo., May, 1927. He learned it from his parents near Cyclone in the late 1880's. Nearly all elderly hillfolk seem to know this tale. I have reported Missouri versions in *Ozark Ghost Stories,* pp. 3–4, *Ozark Superstitions,* pp. 211–12, and *Western Folklore,* X (1951), 2. (V.R.)

This is Type 1791, Motif X 424, "The devil in the cemetery." A version is in *A Hundred Mery Talys,* ed. by W. Carew Hazlitt, pp. 31–36. For the United States see: Halpert, *New York Folklore Quarterly,* II, 96 (New York); Bacon and Parsons, *Journal of American Folklore,* XXXV, 297–98 (Virginia; Negro); Boggs, *ibid.,* XLVII, 311–12 (North Carolina); Halpert, *Hoosier Folklore Bulletin,* I, 24 (Indiana); Halpert, *ibid.,* I, 55–56 (Indiana; learned in Illinois); Hartikka, *Hoosier Folklore,* V, 80–81 (Indiana); Neely and Spargo, *Tales and Songs of Southern Illinois,* pp. 124–25; also in *Journal of American Folklore,* XLVII, 263–

64. For Canada see Lanctot, *ibid.,* XLIV, 232–33 (French Canadian); Waugh, *ibid.,* XXXI, 80 (Ontario). For Great Britain and Ireland see Addy, *Household Tales,* pp. 4–5 (Derby, England); Campbell, *Clan Traditions and Popular Tales of the Western Highlands and Islands,* pp. 32–36 (Scotland); Curtin, *Tales of the Fairies and of the Ghost World,* pp. 54–57 (Ireland); *Handbook of Irish Folklore,* p. 586; *Béaloideas,* V, 269 (Ireland). The latter item also gives other Irish references. For a story in which a frightened lame man beats the dog home see: James W. Blakley, *Tall Tales,* pp. 62–63; Parsons, *Journal of American Folklore,* XXX, 184 (North Carolina, Negro); *Ibid.,* XXXII, 398 (Alabama; Negro); Fauset, *ibid.,* XL, 271–72 (Negro); Brewer, *Publications of the Texas Folklore Society,* X, 38–39 (Texas; Negro). (H.H.)

HOW BOOGER DONE HIS WIFE

Told by Joe Keithley, Day, Mo., August, 1940. He relates it as an actual occurrence, with names and addresses of people whom I know personally. But the old settlers say that the tale was told in the neighborhood as long ago as 1875, before any of these persons were born. This is substantially the story of the upholsterer of Tours, told in the *Heptameron of Margaret of Navarre* (5th day, novel XLV) published in the sixteenth century. There is a similar yarn in Nakshebi's *Tooti Nameh,* under the title "The Shopkeeper's Wife." Cf. Lafontaine's story "La Servante justifiée." William Allen White (*Autobiography,* 1946, p. 46) tells it for the truth, claiming that he saw the whole thing himself near El Dorado, Kan., in the late 1870's. I published Mr. Keithley's version in *Western Folklore,* X (1951), 3–4. (V.R.)

This tale belongs under Motifs J 1151, "Testimony of witness cleverly discredited," and K 1580, "Other deceits connected with adultery." For an English folksong version of this story see Williams, *Folk-Songs of the Upper Thames,* pp. 124–25. (H.H.)

THE PORTER AND THE SQUIRE

Told by Mrs. Mary Burke, Springfield, Mo., December, 1935. She got it from an uncle in Christian county, Mo., about 1910. Cf. *Western Folklore,* X (1951), 2–3. This is the same theme as the "Love in the Tub" ballad, which Belden (*Ballads and Songs,* 1940, pp. 233–35) found in Howell county, Mo. There is a printed broadside of the song in the Harvard Library, No. 1976. (V.R.)

THE JENKINS BOYS

Told by John Turner White, Jefferson City, Mo., February, 1935. Judge White heard it in Greene county, Mo., related by a farm laborer about 1885. This story has much in common with Chaucer's "The Reeve's Tale." Cf. *Western Folklore,* X (1951), 6–7. (V.R.)

Type 1363, Motif K 1345, "Tale of the cradle." See F. N. Robinson's note on "The Reeve's Tale" in his edition of *The Complete Works of Geoffrey Chaucer* (Boston, 1933), p. 790; *Sources and Analogues of Chaucer's "Canterbury Tales,"* ed. by W. F. Bryan and Germaine Dempster (Chicago, 1941). (H.H.)

HOGEYE AND THE BLACKSNAKE

Told by an elderly man in Neosho, Mo., February, 1928. He learned it from his parents, not far from Neosho, about 1889. Mrs. Marie Wilbur, Pineville, Mo., June, 1930, says that an almost identical tale was told by people who had lived in Searcy, Ark. She thought that the story was not intended to be taken literally and that the blacksnake represented a Negro woman. Herbert Ravenel Sass (*Saturday Evening Post,* Dec. 21, 1946, p. 66) has a related item about "an alligator in human form" who slipped out at night "to visit his saurian sweetheart in the fens." Sass heard the tale when he was a boy in South Carolina. (V.R.)

THE BOOT THAT KILLED PEOPLE

Told by Jeff Strong, at Roaring River near Cassville, Mo., April, 1941. He heard the yarn in southwest Missouri about 1900, but always described it as "one of them Oklahoma stories." Thomas Hart Benton (*An Artist in America,* 1937, pp. 210–11) devotes a paragraph to "this crazy, farfetched tale." Masterson (*Tall Tales of Arkansaw,* 1943, pp. 390–91) prints a variant from Polk county, Ark., adding that he found a similar item in a manuscript dated 1714, in the British Museum. The story is reduced to one sentence in my *We Always Lie to Strangers,* p. 142. I have heard it at least a dozen times, in Missouri and Arkansas. (V.R.)

See James R. Masterson's amusing study, "The Tale of the Living Fang," *American Literature,* XI (March, 1939), 66–73, for an

190

examination of several early versions of this story. On p. 73, note 13, Dr. Masterson reports that the acting curator of the New York Zoological Park has often had the story brought to his attention in letters of inquiry. See also Boatright, *Tall Tales from Texas,* pp. 2–6. (H.H.)

THIRTY PIECES OF SILVER

Told by Mrs. Ethel Barnes, Hot Springs, Ark., April, 1938. She had it from relatives in Garland county, Ark. This tale is sometimes attributed to Jeff Davis, who was governor of Arkansas from 1901 to 1907, and later represented Arkansas in the United States Senate. But I have so far been unable to find it in print. (V.R.)

THE TOURIST THAT WENT TOO FAR

Told by Frank Payne, Galena, Mo., November, 1932. Payne placed the action at the village of Protem, Mo., which he said was the toughest little town in the Ozarks. The old-timers whom I interviewed at Protem disclaimed all knowledge of the story. (V.R.)

For an amusing reversal of the Ozark story see Bradley, William O., *Stories and Speeches,* Lexington, Ky., 1916, pp. 113–14. Drunk stranger brags successively that he can whip any man living in town, in the county, and finally in Kentucky. First two brags are ignored; on third he is beaten up. Whereupon he exclaims: "Gentlemen, excuse me, but in that last remark, I kivered too d—d much territory." (H.H.)

OLD KITTY ROLLINS

Told by J. H. McGee, Joplin, Mo., July, 1934. He had it from some children near Sparta, Mo., about the turn of the century. Martha Emmons (*Publications of the Texas Folklore Society,* XI [1933], 99–100) has a related tale, reprinted by Botkin (*Treasury of Southern Folklore,* 1949, pp. 540–41). I published a shorter version of this item in *Ozark Superstitions,* pp. 236–37. Cf. *Southern Folklore Quarterly,* XIV (1950), 80–81. (V.R.)

Motif F 241.2.3, "King of Cats"; but compare Motif F 442.1, "Mysterious voice announces death of Pan." Archer Taylor has studied the widespread legend of the King of the Cats in his "Northern Parallels to the Death of Pan," *Washington University Studies, Humanistic Series,* X (1922), 3–102. Versions which feature the cat are given on pp. 60 ff. I added some references in my notes to the Virginia Negro text (collected in Indiana) published by W. H. Jansen in *Hoosier Folklore Bulletin,* I (1942), 79–80. Compare *Handbook of Irish Folklore,* p. 622, No. 53. (H.H.)

THE SNIPE HUNTERS

Told by Frank Payne, Galena, Mo., November, 1932. He got it from W. D. Mathes, also of Galena. The snipe-hunt joke was popular throughout the Middle West in the 1880's and 1890's. I saw it pulled in eastern Kansas about 1912. Floyd A. Yates (*Chimney Corner Chats,* Springfield, Mo., 1944, pp. 5–6) prints a similar tale of a snipe-hunt that backfired. In Yates' version the chump throws a fit and feigns unconsciousness, so the jokers have to carry him all the way home. (V.R.)

Snipe-hunting is a widespread custom not only in the United States but also in France. See Jo Chartois, and others, "Hunting the Dahut: a French Folk Custom," *Journal of American Folklore,* LVIII, 21–24. (H.H.)

UNCLE ADAM'S COW

Told by a citizen of Eureka Springs, Ark., who wishes to remain anonymous, May, 1950. This individual says that the story is true and dates to the late 1880's. Otto Ernest Rayburn told me in June, 1950, that he heard similar tales from John Jennings and Sam Leath, old residents of Eureka Springs, Ark. Other people in Eureka Springs intimated that such exchanges were not unknown in pioneer days. Rayburn printed the story in *Ozark Guide* (Eureka Springs, Ark., Spring, 1951, p. 44) under the title "Ozark Swap." (V.R.)

In 1800 a Kentuckian whose wife left home with a preacher pursued the couple. The preacher offered his saddle mare with its bridle and saddle for the wife. The Kentuckian, an admirer of good horses, swapped. Cited in Clark, *The Rampaging Frontier,* pp. 293–94. (H.H.)

DEACON SPURLOCK AND THE LEGISLATURE

Told by Mrs. Mary Burke, Springfield, Mo., December, 1935. She had it from her relatives in Christian county, Mo., and thought that it might be a true story. I told this tale to Jack Short, long-time political boss of Stone county, Mo., in 1940. He said he had heard it years before, and believed that something of the sort actually happened in the Missouri legislature. (V.R.)

192

GRAVELS FOR A GOOSE

Told by Ed Wall, Pineville, Mo., April, 1922. He had the story from a trapper who lived on the Cowskin River, near Noel, Mo., in the 1890's. According to one version of this tale, the strangers returned a bit battered, but triumphant. "She sure put up a hell of a fight," they told the farmer, "but we finally wrastled her down." Cf. my *Funny Stories about Hillbillies,* pp. 22–23; also *Hoosier Folklore,* IX (1950), 41–42. (V.R.)

THE GREAT BADGER FIGHT

Told by Farwell Gould, Pittsburg, Kan., June, 1929. He said it was a true story which he heard in Greene county, Mo., about 1895. The badger-fight joke was common in Missouri and Arkansas in the 1880's and 1890's. According to the Springfield, Mo., *News & Leader* (Dec. 7, 1936), such a fight was staged by the Elks Lodge in Springfield about 1906. As recently as Dec. 1, 1936, the American Legion at St. Charles, Mo., put on a badger-pulling after an elaborate newspaper build-up. A schoolteacher tried to stop the affair, which he said would be "void of all qualities of sport, as a dog would not have a chance with a ferocious badger." Eric A. Hansen, director of the Humane Society of Missouri, denounced the whole business as a "brutal, un-American spectacle," but the Legion went right ahead and persuaded a St. Charles newspaperman to pull the badger out of the box. For a detailed account of this, see the St. Louis *Star-Times* (Dec. 2, 1936). Edmund Wilson (*Memoirs of Hecate County,* 1946, p. 92) tells the story of "pulling the badger" in a club at Oklahoma City, Okla., with a great deal of colorful detail. (V.R.)

THE BIG OLD GIANT

Told by A. L. Cline, Joplin, Mo., July, 1922. He heard the tale as a child in Benton county, Ark., about 1895, and said that he had never seen it in print. Charles Morrow Wilson (*Backwoods America,* 1934, pp. 56–58) reports a related "Jack and the Beanstalk" yarn from "an isolated village in the Arkansas hills." Bob Wyrick, Eureka Springs, Ark., May, 1951, told me a similar tale, in which Jack kills the giant by a trick, but it is the giant's *wife* who pursues him and falls to her death. (V.R.)

Despite the cornstalk, which here has replaced the more familiar "beanstalk," this tale is obviously a version of "Jack and the Beanstalk." Chase, *Jack Tales,* pp. 31–39, has a composite text; in my

193

notes, which appear on pp. 190–91 of the same book, I have discussed the American, British, and Irish texts of this form of Type 328, "The Boy Steals the Giant's Treasure." See also Wilson's Ozark version; a New England text, Johnson, *What They Say in New England,* pp. 205–7; and one from the Antilles, Parsons, *Antilles,* III, 288. (H.H.)

NO RESPECT FOR THE DEAD

Told by Mrs. May Kennedy McCord, Springfield, Mo., April, 1947. She got the story from a minister in Springfield, who had it from an old-time rural preacher. Variants of this tale are common in southern Missouri and north Arkansas. Jack Short, Galena, Mo., told me in 1940 that something of the sort actually happened near Galena in the 1880's. Mrs. McCord repeated a shorter version in her "Hillbilly Heartbeats" broadcast over KWTO, Springfield, Mo., Dec. 14, 1947. (V.R.)

LITTLE AB AND THE SCALDING BARREL

Told by Ed Wall, Pineville, Mo., August, 1924. Mr. Wall believes it to be true, because Little Ab lived nearby and was related to one of the prominent families in Pineville. When Mr. Wall told me this tale, I remarked that there was something like it in Boccaccio's *Decameron* (seventh day, second tale). But on learning that Boccaccio was an Italian, Mr. Wall said that no European could have heard about the incident, because Ab never set foot outside his native state and "didn't have no truck with foreigners." The old-timers around Pineville say that Little Ab's real name was Bill Matney and that he was shot to death near Noel, Mo. See a reference to this in an article by Floyd Sullivan (Springfield, Mo., *Press,* July 5, 1930). I printed one version in *From an Ozark Holler* (1933, pp. 156–59). Cf. *Western Folklore,* X (1951), 7. (V.R.)

This belongs to Type 1419, "The Returning Husband Hoodwinked," and is a variant of Motif K 1517.1.1, "One lover disguised and carried out of house by other." In this form of the tale the lover is hidden in a jar (barrel) and either thrown out or carried out by another lover. See Boggs, *Journal of American Folklore,* XLVII, 307 (North Carolina); Parsons, *Folk-Lore of the Sea Islands, South Carolina,* p. 89 (Negro); Smiley, *Journal of American Folklore,* XXXII, 372 (Georgia; Negro); Botkin, *A Treasury of American Folklore,* pp. 504–5 (Ozarks; quoted from Vance Randolph); Parsons, *Journal of American Folklore,* XLI,

514 (Bahamas; Negro); Beckwith, *Jamaica Anansi Stories,* XVII, 163–64 (Negro); Parsons, *Antilles,* III, 303 (Negro); and see headnote to No. 307 for some African references. Compare Hazlitt, *Tales and Legends of National Origin,* pp. 150–53. (H.H.)

PENNYWINKLE! PENNYWINKLE!

Told by Lon Kelley, Pineville, Mo., July, 1930. He had it from his parents, who were pioneer settlers in McDonald county, Mo. It is undoubtedly related to Grimm's tale of "The Juniper Tree." See Goethe's *Faust* for a rhymed version, which Marguerite sings in the dungeon scene. A shorter text, from the same informant, appears in my *Ozark Ghost Stories* (Girard, Kan., 1944, p. 23), and *Ozark Superstitions* (1947, p. 236). See *Southern Folklore Quarterly,* XIV (1950), 83. (V.R.)

Type 720, "My Mother Slew Me; My Father Ate Me," and compare Type 780. A Devonshire text given in the "Appendix: Household Tales" by S. Baring-Gould in the first edition of W. Henderson, *Notes on the Folklore of the Northern Counties of England and the Borders* (London, 1866), pp. 314–17, was reprinted, somewhat revised, in Jacobs, *English Fairy Tales,* pp. 15–19, No. 3. Mr. Jacobs noted that he had heard this *cante fable* in Australia and that a friend had heard it in Co. Meath, Ireland. I have not seen the English text in *Notes and Queries,* 4th Series, VI, 496. A version from Lowland Scotland is given in Chambers, *Popular Rhymes of Scotland,* pp. 49–50. Only the text of the song is given in Montgomerie, *Scottish Nursery Rhymes* (London, 1947), p. 28. A text with tune learned from Liverpool children was given by Frank Kidson in *Journal of the Folk-Song Society,* II (1906), 295–96, with notes by A. G. Gilchrist. Mr. Jacobs and Miss Gilchrist note that this *cante fable* was known as "Orange and Lemon" to London street children. There is some connection between this story and the ending of the English singing game "Oranges and Lemons." Most versions of the game conclude with some form of this couplet:

> "Here comes a light to light you to bed;
> Here comes a chopper to chop off your head."

See Gomme, *The Traditional Games of England, Scotland and Ireland,* II, 25–35. From North Carolina, Boggs, *Journal of American Folklore,* XLVII, 297–98, published a version from a White informant. For versions collected from Negroes see Parsons, *Antilles,* III, 118, and the references in the headnote to No. 126. (H.H.)

JAY CAUGHT THE DEVIL

Told by Lon Kelley, Pineville, Mo., July, 1930. He heard it as a boy, in the early 1900's. "Just an old fairy tale," said Mr. Kelley. "Maybe it's in the Bible, for all I know," he added. About 1940 I saw a movie version of a related tale, with Sir Cedric Hardwicke as the Devil. It was doubtless adapted from the play "On Borrowed Time," listed by Dr. Halpert in the notes which follow. (V.R.)

This is one of the forms of Type 330, "The Smith Outwits the Devil," in which Death replaces the Devil. It is interesting that the magic knapsack that forces persons into it or holds anyone who enters it has been rationalized so that Jack gets Death into his towsack by strength rather than by magic. Death trapped up a tree is used in the play "On Borrowed Time" by Paul Osborne. It is also one of the elements in the Virginia version in Chase, *Jack Tales,* pp. 172–79, which combines Type 330 with Type 332, "Godfather Death." The mixture of the two types (including Death stuck to a tree and later tricked into a bottle) is found in the Illinois version published by David S. McIntosh, "Blacksmith and Death," *Midwest Folklore,* I, 51–53. To my notes for Type 330 in Chase, *Jack Tales,* p. 200, add Chase, *Grandfather Tales,* pp. 29–39 (Virginia); Parsons, *Antilles,* III, 317–19 (see headnote for further references); Curtin, *Irish Folk-Tales,* pp. 45–49, and p. 160n; MacManus, *In Chimney Corners,* pp. 85–104; *Handbook of Irish Folklore,* p. 561. To the references for Type 332 add: Davidson, *California Folklore Quarterly,* II, 182–83 (Colorado); Sweeney, *Hoosier Folklore Bulletin,* III, 43–44 (Indiana); *Handbook of Irish Folklore,* p. 561. (H.H.)

TALKING RIVER

Told by William Hatton, Columbia, Mo., July, 1929. He heard it in Lawrence county, Mo., about 1905. "There are some dirty words in this story," he said, "but I'll leave them out if you're going to write it down on paper." Otto Ernest Rayburn (*Ozark Life,* Kingston, Ark., Feb. 9, 1929, p. 5) published a similar tale, crediting it to the Billings, Mo., *Times* (no date). Allsopp (*Folklore of Romantic Arkansas,* 1931, I, 287–89) prints an almost identical tale. Rayburn used it again in the *Arcadian Magazine* (April, 1932, p. 4). I published another version in my book *Ozark Mountain Folks* (1932, pp. 152–58). Collins (*Folk Tales of Missouri,* 1935, pp. 83–88) prints a text much like Rayburn's; he says the boys' name was Conley and that the action took place at Terrill Spring, south of Billings, Mo. There are other stories in this region about men turned into frogs by some supernatural malignancy. Will Rice (*Arkansas Democrat,* April 11, 1948) tells of a fellow who was transformed into a bullfrog because he didn't do right by his childhood sweetheart. Cf. *Western Folklore,* X (1951), 8–10. (V.R.)

THE LITTLE BLUE BALL

Told by Mrs. Mary Burke, Springfield, Mo., December, 1935. She had it from an uncle near Ozark, in Christian county, Mo., about 1910. Cf. *Western Folklore,* X (1951), 8. (V.R.)

Obviously this tale belongs to the Bluebeard, or "forbidden chamber," group and fits most nearly with Type 311, "Rescue by their sister." The versions of this story listed below resemble each other and are sufficiently distinct from the standard type to suggest the need for setting up a separate type number for them when the Aarne-Thompson Index is revised. Here is a generalized outline. Three sisters in turn chase an animal (bull, ox, or horse) from the garden. Often her stick or some other object clings to the animal. Each girl is carried to a castle or great house and is well-treated, but forbidden to enter one room. She enters and finds it filled with corpses, and gets blood on her person (shoes or keys) which she cannot remove. The animal (in one case he has turned into a man) then kills her. The youngest sister avoids the fate of the first two because she feeds a cat (sometimes also a robin), and the blood is either licked off or otherwise removed. Since no stain is found on her, she is not killed, but instead marries the disenchanted animal, which has turned into a prince. Usually the older sisters are restored to life. In the New York text they are buried. See Gardner, *Folklore from the Schoharie Hills, New York,* pp. 109–10 and discussion pp. 110–12; Fauset, *Folklore from Nova Scotia,* pp. 12–13 (variant text); MacManus, *In Chimney Corners,* pp. 107–23 (Ireland); *Handbook of Irish Folklore,* pp. 618–19, No. 33. In Mr. Randolph's version the enchanted animal-prince is missing, and it is the pursuit of a blue ball which leads each girl to the stranger's house. The cat is replaced by a dog. The ending ignores the corpses. Nonetheless, I think it unquestionable that his tale is a modernized version of the story type described. (H.H.)

197

JACK COULDN'T MAKE NO CHANGE

Told by an elderly gentleman at Springfield, Mo., December, 1941. He got it from a saloon-keeper named Max Brooks, also of Springfield. It appears that variants of this tale were known throughout southern Missouri in the 1880's and 1890's. Circus followers and "carnies" were using the twenty-dollar-bill routine in small-town liquor stores as recently as 1949. (V.R.)

For versions of the first story compare: Brown, *Wit and Humor,* pp. 287–88; Landon, *Wit and Humor of the Age,* p. 109; Davis, *Vermont Historical Society Proceedings,* n.s. VII, No. 1 (1939), 10; Dorson, *Jonathan Draws the Long Bow,* p. 21. A New York text is in the Halpert collections. (H.H.)

THE WOMAN AND THE ROBBER

Told by Jeff Strong, at Roaring River near Cassville, Mo., April, 1941. He got it from "Watermelon Charley" Smith, of Aurora, Mo. Cf. *Southern Folklore Quarterly,* XIV (1950), 79–80. A similar story appears in the ballad "Lady Isabel and the Elf-Knight." For Missouri and Arkansas versions of this song see Belden (*Ballads and Songs,* 1940, pp. 5–16); also, my *Ozark Folksongs* (I, 1947, pp. 41–47). (V.R.)

As Mr. Randolph points out, this story parallels that of the ballad of "Lady Isabel and the Elf Knight" (Child 4). Professor F. J. Child gives an exhaustive discussion of both ballad and tale versions of European forms of the story in his headnote to the ballad. See Child, *The English and Scottish Popular Ballads* (1882–98), I, 22–55. Add Rotunda, *Motif-Index of the Italian Novella,* Motif K 551.4.2*, "Making Modesty Pay." For tales which parallel the ballad form in that the lady shoves the robber over a cliff (or into a deep pit), see Lady Wilde, *Ancient Legends, Mystic Charms, and Superstitions of Ireland,* pp. 270–71; Carter, *Journal of American Folklore,* XXXVIII, 373 (Tennessee). A Negro text in *cante fable* form, i.e., tale with song, is close to the ballad story. A man has pushed a succession of wives into a deep well after making them strip; his last wife pushes him in. See Parsons, *Folk-Lore of the Sea Islands, South Carolina,* pp. 128–29. Compare also Parsons, *Antilles,* III, 261–62 (Martinique; Negro). (H.H.)

THEM NEWCOMERS RUINED THE MEAT

Told by Lew Beardon, Branson, Mo., December, 1938. He heard it near Walnut Shade, Mo., in the 1890's. "Some folks used to tell it for the truth," said he. This tale is widely known in the Ozarks. Mrs. C. P. Mahnkey, Mincy, Mo., says that "a certain family" in her neighborhood "boiled the meat with whippoorwill peas and ruint it, so that it had to be thrown away." Mr. Marcus Brewer of Baxter, Mo., contended that the Taylor-Perkins feud began when the Taylors borrowed a squirrel-head from the house of Perkins and cooked it in a pot of blackeyed peas. Floyd A. Yates (*Chimney Corner Chats,* Springfield, Mo., 1944, p. 28) tells how some folks borrowed a piece of fat-back and used it to season cabbage, which "danged nigh ruined the flavor of it." The owner of the meat sued for damages, and the court awarded him eighty-five cents. I published a variant (*Funny Stories about Hillbillies,* Girard, Kan., 1944, p. 23). Cf. *Southern Folklore Quarterly,* XIV (1950), 84–85. (V.R.)

THE BANJO-PICKING GIRL

Told by an elderly lady in Joplin, Mo., August, 1935. Insisting that her name must not be published, she said that the story was true and that she had been associated with the Keene family in the early 1900's. Pete Woolsey, Pineville, Mo., September, 1924, recalled a similar case in northwest Arkansas. A man named Burns was commanded by an Angel of the Lord to leave his wife and marry the female evangelist, a virgin with child by the Holy Ghost. Wayman Hogue (*Back Yonder,* 1932, pp. 44–53) tells the story of Everet Howard, of Van Buren county, Ark., who said that the Lord told him to divorce his wife and marry a younger woman. The members of Everet's church decided that this was a genuine revelation of God's holy will, so they granted the divorce. Compare the "Cedar Brake Miracle," reported by Harold Preece and Celia Kraft (*Dew on Jordan,* 1946, pp. 63–79); this project was a disappointment, because the "Messiah" turned out to be a girl baby. Related tales are told in connection with James Sharp, an Arkansas preacher who called himself "Adam God, the Father of Jesus Christ." Sharp died in Joplin, Mo., March 9, 1946, and there were many accounts of his misadventures in the newspapers. (V.R.)

Compare Motif J 1264.6, "Nun claims her child is by the Holy Ghost." (H.H.)

LITTLE WEED MARSHALL

Told by a newspaperman in Kansas City, Mo., July, 1932. Weed Marshall ran the hotel at Mayview, Mo., from 1888 to 1917, and many stories are told of his eccentricities. Several such tales and a picture of Mr. Marshall were printed in the Kansas City *Star* (Nov. 11, 1917). The article is unsigned, but I believe it was written by A. B. Macdonald. Marshall rode with Joe Shelby in the 1860's, and his name is mentioned in *Shelby and His Men*, by Major John N. Edwards. I knew Mr. Marshall about 1920, when he lived with relatives in McDonald county, Mo. He was a dapper little man, almost blind, with a neatly trimmed white beard. He told me that the stories about him were "exaggerated some." Mr. Marshall chuckled. "But I did throw my gun on that fellow in the hotel, when he lied about Shelby's men," the old gentleman added. (V.R.)

THE VINEGAR JUG

Told by A. W. Marshall, Pineville, Mo., January, 1920. He heard it at Mayview, Mo., in the early 1900's. Isaac Stapleton (*Moonshiners in Arkansas*, Independence, Mo., 1948, pp. 76–77) tells the same tale, except that his bootlegger had the stuff in a cardboard box, which he said contained new shoes. Mr. Stapleton relates it as his own experience. (V.R.)

UNCLE JOHNNY'S BEAR

Told by a resident of Carroll county, Ark., March, 1934. This individual credited it to Louis Hanecke, who used to run the Allred Hotel in Eureka Springs, Ark. Sam Leath, secretary of the Chamber of Commerce at Eureka Springs, told an almost identical story in 1948, and showed me the remains of a shotgun which he said was used in killing the bear. Mr. Leath thought the incident occurred in 1881 or 1882. Otto Ernest Rayburn wrote a story based on Leath's account. It was published in the Eureka Springs *Times-Echo* (April 20, 1950) and reprinted in *Ozark Guide* (Spring, 1951, p. 53). Rayburn says that "the twisted barrels of the old gun may be seen at the Ozark Museum," which is on Highway 62, west of Eureka Springs. Both Leath and Rayburn give the name of the hunter as Johnny Gaskins, who killed more than two hundred bears and wrote a book (*Life and Adventures of John Gaskins*, Eureka Springs, Ark., 1893, pp. 113) describing his hunts in great detail. But Gaskins does not mention this adventure. Some old residents think it was Johnny Sexton who killed the bear at the bawdy-house. Cora Pinkley Call (*Pioneer Tales of Eureka Springs*,

200

Arkansas, 1930, p. 24) prints a photograph of Sexton with a shot-gun in one hand and a wildcat in the other, but without any reference to the White Elephant. Constance Wagner tells the story in her novel *Sycamore* (1950, pp. 151–52), but doesn't mention the bear-slayer's name. (V.R.)

THE NEWFANGLED CAPSULES

Told by Frank Payne, Galena, Mo., November, 1932. He attributes it to Dr. Fate Henson, who came to Stone county, Mo., in the late 1880's. The anecdote seems to be widely known. John Dunckel (*The Mollyjoggers,* Springfield, Mo., n.d., pp. 31–32) tells a similar tale about an old woman who quit smoking after taking some capsules. A daughter filled her pipe and set a live coal on top of the tobacco. "Git away from me with that fire," cried the old lady. "Don't you know I've got ten of them cattridges in me?" Hal L. Norwood (*Just a Book,* Mena, Ark., 1938, p. 6) recalls his boyhood near Mena. "I remember when the first capsules were brought into our section," he writes. "The doctor gave a fellow named Simon Dollarhide some calomel in capsules. When he asked his patient if the medicine had done any good, Simon said the medicine had a good effect, but he had not 'got rid of them dinged hulls.'" I quoted Norwood's version in *Funny Stories from Arkansas* (Girard, Kan., 1943, p. 12). (V.R.)

HIGH WATER AT TURKEY FORD

Told by Lon Jordan, Farmington, Ark., October, 1948. He heard it near Fayetteville, Ark., and believed that the tale was based on an actual occurrence. See a reference to the subject of rain dances and prayers for rain in my *Ozark Superstitions,* p. 30. (V.R.)

THE ABOLITION OF SCOTT COUNTY

Told by Lon Jordan, Farmington, Ark., August, 1942. He thought it was probably a lie. "You can't tell, though," he added thoughtfully, "some mighty funny things have happened in the Arkansas legislature." This tale is almost as widely known as the famous "Change the Name of Arkansas" speech attributed to Senator Cassius M. Johnson. Hal L. Norwood (*Just a Book,* Mena, Ark., 1938, pp. 25–26), sometime Attorney General of Arkansas, says he got it from Senator James P. Clark. Judge John Turner White, of Jefferson City, Mo., told me that there was a related story about

201

two Missouri counties, but he believed it was just an adaptation of the Arkansas yarn. Cf. my *Funny Stories about Hillbillies* (Girard, Kan., 1944, p. 23). (V.R.)

HUNTING THE OLD IRON

Told by Miss Marion Neville, Chesterton, Ind., November, 1950. She had it from her father at Springfield, Mo., in the early 1900's. "Don't ask me what an *old iron* is," she says. "It's some kind of an animal. I always pictured it as a giant flatiron, with head and feet like a cat." She adds that her grandfather, Kentucky-born in 1816, heard the tale as a boy. When a child pestered his elders by demanding a story, they sometimes responded with one of these repetitive yarns, known as "teaser tales." Such stories are told in a slow, monotonous, sing-song fashion, and go droning on and on until the child falls asleep. (V.R.)

This belongs under Type 2300, "Endless Tales." In Archer Taylor's "A Classification of Formula Tales," *Journal of American Folklore*, XLVI, 77–88, a revision of one section of Aarne-Thompson's *The Types of the Folk-Tale*, this Ozark tale would be classified more specifically under Type 2350, "Rounds: stories which begin over again and repeat." All too few "formula" tales have been published in this country. (H.H.)

THE DEAF MAN'S ANSWERS

Told by Hawk Gentry, Galena, Mo., April, 1938. He heard it near Galena about 1910. Simon Hanna, a fiddler from Joplin, Mo., repeated a similar yarn in Springfield, Mo., April, 1934; he said it was at least fifty years old then. Booth Campbell, Cane Hill, Ark., told the same story, placing the deaf man in the woods near Pineville, Mo. He thought the tale was known in the 1880's, perhaps much earlier. (V.R.)

This belongs under Type 1698, Motif X 111, "Deaf persons and their foolish answers." It is most closely related to Type 1698 H, Motif X 111.8, "The deaf man with the bird in the tree." (H.H.)

A PALLET ON THE FLOOR

Told by Hawk Gentry, Galena, Mo., May, 1933. He heard it about 1910, credited to "Sugarheel" Hodge, a lawyer who lived at Galena in the 1890's. Raymond Weeks (*The Hound-Tuner of Callaway,* 1927, pp. 236–40) tells the story as the adventure of two pioneer preachers in Callaway county, Mo. Hal. L. Norwood

(*Just a Book,* 1938, p. 60) claims it as his own experience when he was campaigning for Attorney General in 1908. "The next morning when I woke up," he writes, "the man and his wife were in the bed, and I was on the pallet with the three boys. I do not know at what time of night they transferred me from the bed to the pallet." Fred High (*Forty-Three Years for Uncle Sam,* Berryville, Ark., 1949, p. 108) says it happened to a man and woman who traveled through Carroll county, Ark., in the early days. Cf. *Southern Folklore Quarterly,* XIV (1950), 80. (V.R.)

THE RAIL-SPLITTER

Told by Pete Woolsey, Pineville, Mo., September, 1924. He believed that the story came from Benton county, Ark. Earl A. Collins (*Folk Tales of Missouri,* 1935, p. 43) makes an early settler named McCool the hero of this tale. "In McDonald county, in south Missouri," he writes, "lies a huge petrified log with an Indian statue beside it, in the position that McCool left them when he made his escape." I lived in McDonald county for more than a decade, and the story is well known there. But I heard no mention of McCool, or the petrified log, or the Indian statue described by Collins. My mother knew this tale in the 1880's, as told by people who had lived in southern Illinois. She thought it had been printed in some old schoolbook, perhaps one of the McGuffey readers. Cf. *Southern Folklore Quarterly,* XIV (1950), 81. (V.R.)

Compare Motif K 1111, "Dupe puts hand (paws) into cleft of tree (wedge, vise)." Thompson, *Body, Boots and Britches,* says (p. 51): "The same story is related about Tim Murphy and other heroes of our New York frontier; it is even told of Daniel Boone in Kentucky and has claim to being the classic trickster story of the American frontier." Botkin, *A Treasury of New England Folklore,* p. 511*n,* says the "ruse is attributed to many [New England] Indian-fighters," and names two of them: Ford and Weare (or Wyer). For other American versions see: Dorson, *Southern Folklore Quarterly,* X, 122 (New England); New Hampshire's Daughters, Folk-Lore Committee, *Folklore Sketches and Reminiscences of New Hampshire Life,* p. 14 (New Hampshire); Skinner, *Myths and Legends of Our Own Land,* I, 207–8 (New Hampshire); Gardner, *Folklore from the Schoharie Hills, New York,* pp. 26–27; Thompson, *Body, Boots and Britches,* pp. 51, 60 (New York); Hayeslip, *New York Folklore Quarterly,* I, 84–85 (New York). An unpublished New Jersey text is in the Halpert collections. Compare catching the Devil's hands by knocking a wedge out of a tree stump: Dasent, *Tales from the Fjeld,* pp. 57–58 (Norway). Compare also the catching of a witch's hand in a split tree: Conway, *Demonology and Devil-Lore,* I, 312. (H.H.)

DIVIDING UP THE DEAD

Told by Mrs. Marie Wilbur, Pineville, Mo., June, 1930. She had it from Mrs. Lucinda Mosier, also of Pineville, who heard the story about 1885. This is, perhaps, the commonest of all the Ozark tales, and I know at least fifty persons who can tell it. See my *Ozark Ghost Stories* (Girard, Kan., 1944, p. 4); also *Ozark Superstitions* (1947, pp. 212–13) and *Southern Folklore Quarterly,* XIV (1950), 82–83. (V.R.)

This is another form of Type 1719, Motif X 424, "The devil in the cemetery (compare No. 14, "The Devil in the Graveyard.") Nuts or fish are most frequently divided in the cemetery. The usual punch line is, "You take this one and I'll take that one," or, "One for you and one for me." See Schermerhorn, *Schermerhorn's Stories,* pp. 111–12; Bacon and Parsons, *Journal of American Folklore,* XXXV, 296–97 (Virginia; Negro); Parsons, *Journal of American Folklore,* XXX, 215 (Negro; told in Pennsylvania); Boggs, *Journal of American Folklore,* XLVII, 312 (North Carolina); Parsons, *Journal of American Folklore,* XXX, 177 (Negro); Parsons, *Folk-Lore of the Sea Islands, South Carolina,* p. 68 (Negro); Writers' Program of the Work Projects Administration in South Carolina, "South Carolina Folk Tales," *Bulletin of University of South Carolina,* October, 1941, pp. 104–6 (South Carolina; Negro); Hurston, *Mules and Men,* pp. 117–19 (Florida; Negro), reprinted in Botkin, *A Treasury of American Folklore,* pp. 444–45; Halpert, *Southern Folklore Quarterly,* VIII, 113–14 (Mississippi); Brewer, *Publications of the Texas Folklore Society,* X, 39–40 (Texas; Negro); Brewster, *Folk-Lore,* L, 299–300 (Indiana); Halpert, *Hoosier Folklore Bulletin,* I, 25, 56–57 (Indiana); Halpert, Mitchell and Dickason, *Hoosier Folklore Bulletin,* I, 88 (Indiana). There are unpublished versions from New York, New Jersey, South Carolina, Tennessee, and Newfoundland in the Halpert collections. For Canada see Fauset, *Folklore from Nova Scotia,* pp. 104–5 (2 Negro, 1 White); Waugh, *Journal of American Folklore,* XXXI, 81 (Ontario); Halpert, *California Folklore Quarterly,* IV, 48–49 (Alberta); for other versions in English see: Parsons, *Journal of American Folklore,* XXXVIII, 241–42 (Bermuda; Negro); Parsons, *ibid.,* XLI, 513–14

(Bahamas; Negro). For England see: *Folk-Lore,* LIV (1943), 368 (Huntingdonshire); Wilson, *ibid.,* LIV, 260 (Westmorland). For Wales: Halpert, *Journal of American Folklore,* LVIII, 51 (Gwent). Also compare a related Scottish-Gaelic story: Mac-Dougall and Calder, *Folk Tales and Fairy Lore in Gaelic and English,* p. 305. (H.H.)

THREE LITTLE PIGS

Told by Mrs. Elizabeth Maddocks, Joplin, Mo., June, 1937. She heard it near Chadwick, Mo., about 1900. "We didn't have any story-books," she said. "I was a grown woman, and married, before I ever saw this tale in print." It is evidently an Ozark version of the old story found in many children's books. Compare Walt Disney's splendid animated cartoon which featured "The Big Bad Wolf" song in the 1930's. (V.R.)

This tale combines a form of Type 124, Motif Z 81, "Blowing the house in," with Motif K 714.2, "Victim tricked into entering box." See Bacon and Parsons, *Journal of American Folklore,* XXXV, 267–69 (Virginia; Negro); Chase, *Grandfather Tales,* pp. 81–87 (North Carolina). A Negro text collected in New Jersey is in the Halpert collections. For "Blowing the house in" as an independent story (with occasional variation of the animals) told by white storytellers in the United States see: Gardner, *Folklore from the Schoharie Hills, New York,* pp. 100–101 (with discussion on pp. 101–3); Boggs, *Journal of American Folklore,* XLVII, 293–94 (North Carolina). Other versions (all Negro) are in: Owens, *Lippincott's Magazine,* XX, 753–54; Parsons, *ibid.,* XXX, 186–87 (North Carolina); Parsons, *ibid.,* XXXIV, 17–18 (South Carolina); Harris, *Nights with Uncle Remus,* pp. 37–43 (Georgia; No. 8); Jekyll, *Publications of the Folk-Lore Society,* LV, pp. 79–83 (Jamaica); Parsons, *Antilles,* III, 314 (Antigua). Other white versions are: Lanctot, *Journal of American Folklore,* XXXIX, 141 (French Canadian); Jacobs, *English Fairy Tales,* pp. 68–72 (England; No. 14); Campbell, *Popular Tales of the West Highlands,* I, lxxxvi (Scotland). For a different form compare the following Negro versions: Backus, *Journal of American Folklore,* XI, 290–91 (North Carolina); Fauset, *ibid.,* XL, 240 (Louisiana); Parsons, *ibid.,* XXXVIII, 272 (Barbados). For American Negro texts of "Victim tricked into entering box" see "Story of a Fox and a Pig," *Southern Workman,* XXVII (1898), 125; Cox, *Journal of American Folklore,* XLVII, 351–52 (West Virginia); Parsons, *ibid.*, XXX, 175–76 (North Carolina); Harris, *Uncle Remus; His Songs and His Sayings,* pp. 63–67 (Georgia; No. 13); White and others, *The Frank C. Brown Collection of North Carolina Folklore,* I, 704. (H.H.)

THE PIN IN THE GATEPOST

Told by A. W. Marshall, Pineville, Mo., January, 1920. He said he heard it in southwest Missouri during the War between the States. This tale is known all through the Ozark country. Mrs. C. P. Mahnkey, Mincy, Mo., recalls that the children in Taney county, Mo., used to tell it in the late 1890's. Clarence Sharp, Pittsburg, Kan., gave me a slightly different version which he heard many years ago at Dutch Mills, Ark. Cf. *Southern Folklore Quarterly,* XIV (1950), pp. 85–86. (V.R.)

Type 1456, Motif K 1984.5, "Blind fiancée betrays self." In a South Carolina Negro text it is an old woman who wants to marry a young man. See Smiley, *Journal of American Folklore,* XXXII, 365. (H.H.)

THE LITTLE BOY AND THE SNAKE

Told by Pete Woolsey, Pineville, Mo., September, 1924. He got it from people who had lived in Benton county, Ark. See a reference to this child-and-serpent theme in my *Ozark Superstitions,* p. 257. Compare *Southern Folklore Quarterly,* XIV (1950), 84. (V.R.)

Type 285, "The Child and the Snake." Child shares milk (food) with (poisonous) snake. If the snake is killed, the child often pines away. For American versions see: Masterson, *Journal of American Folklore,* LIX, 177; Milling, *Southern Folklore Quarterly,* I, No. 1, p. 51; Johnson, *What They Say in New England,* pp. 102–3 (New England); Witthoft, *New York Folklore Quarterly,* III (1947), 134–37 (2 New York texts and 1 from the Objibwa Indians of Ontario); Bayard, *Journal of American Folklore,* LI, 56 (Pennsylvania); Bacon and Parsons, *ibid.,* XXXV, 281–82 (Virginia; Negro); Parsons, *ibid.,* XXX, 185 (North Carolina; Negro); Musick, *Hoosier Folklore,* VI (1947), 47 (West Virginia); Adams, *Congaree Sketches,* pp. 10–11 (South Carolina; Negro); Milling, *Southern Folklore Quarterly,* I, No. 1, pp. 50–51 (Negro text from Georgia); Smiley, *Journal of American Folklore,* XXXII, 373 (Alabama; Negro); Roberts, *ibid.,* XL, 203 (Louisiana); Parsons, *Antilles,* III, 302 (Martinique). An unpublished New York text is in the Folklore Archive at The Farmers Museum, Cooperstown, New York. See also Hunt, *Popular Romances of the West of England,* p. 420 (Cornwall, England); White and others, *The Frank C. Brown Collection of North Carolina Folklore,* I, 638. (H.H.)

BELLE STARR AND JIM REED

Told by Farmer Goodwin, Joplin, Mo., February, 1930. This is a garbled fragment of pioneer history. Jim Reed was shot to death by John Morris, near McKinney, Tex., in the summer of 1875. For information about Belle Starr see S. W. Harmon (*Hell on the Border,* Ft. Smith, Ark., 1899, pp. 557–616), Duncan Aikman (*Calamity Jane and the Lady Wildcats,* 1927, pp. 158–206), Burton Rascoe (*Belle Starr,* 1941, p. 340), and William Yancey Shackleford (*Belle Starr, the Bandit Queen,* Girard, Kan., 1943, pp. 9–10). Belle's refusal to identify Reed's body is mentioned by nearly all her biographers. Stanley Vestal wrote an eleven-stanza ballad about the incident (*American Mercury,* April, 1926, p. 402). George Milburn published a similar story, "Honey Boy" (*Collier's,* March 10, 1934), with reference to a later Oklahoma bandit. Milburn told me that he got the idea from the old tale of Belle Starr and Jim Reed. (V.R.)

THE MAN FROM HOCKEY MOUNTAIN

Told by Mrs. Marie Wilbur, Pineville, Mo., March 1931. She had it from her father, about 1910. Lorna Ball published a similar story (*Arcadian Magazine,* Eminence, Mo., April, 1932, pp. 7, 38). Otto Ernest Rayburn reprinted Ball's tale (*Ozark Country,* 1941, pp. 292–96) under the title "The Fighting Parson." (V.R.)

See the version in Botkin, *A Treasury of American Folklore,* pp. 411–12, quoted from *Echoes, Centennial and Other Notable Speeches, Lectures & Stories* by Governor Robert L. Taylor (Nashville, Tenn., 1899). (H.H.)

SHIRTTAIL BOYS

Told November, 1948, by a lady in Greene county, Mo., who does not want her name mentioned here. The tale is often attributed to a local gambler named Horine. In the early days, small boys wore only one garment, a long shirt that reached below the knees. "As late as 1888," writes May Kennedy McCord (Springfield, Mo., *News,* Jan. 12, 1939), "boys wore those tail-shirts to school and everywhere, without pants, in south Missouri and the northern part of the Arkansas Ozarks. The shirts were made of homespun and came down long something like a girl's dress. Boys wore them until about ten or twelve years old, but were humiliated if they had to wear them longer. When a boy began to get into adolescence he was put into trousers, and my, how grand and big he felt!" Stories about shirttail boys are common in the Ozark country today, but many of the best ones are unprintable. (V.R.)

THE WOOL ON PAPPY'S FILLY

Told by Pete Woolsey, Pineville, Mo., January, 1924. He had it from people who lived in Benton county, Ark. I used a slightly different version of this tale in *Ozark Mountain Folks* (1932, pp. 162–63), and referred to it in *We Always Lie to Strangers* (1951, p. 255). Botkin (*Treasury of Southern Folklore*, 1949, pp. 453–54) reprinted the text from *Ozark Mountain Folks*. (V.R.)

Skin of horse (donkey) removed while it is still alive; sheep skin is pinned on (with blackberry thorns). Skin adheres and yearly grows wool (and blackberries). See Dorson, *California Folklore Quarterly*, V, 81; Dorson, *Jonathan Draws the Long Bow*, p. 102 (Vermont); Chase, *Grandfather Tales*, pp. 195–204 (Virginia); *Rayburn's Ozark Guide*, IX, No. 28 (Spring, 1951), 46–48 (Missouri); Federal Writers' Project of the Work Projects Administration, *Idaho Lore*, pp. 139–40; Davidson, *Tall Tales They Tell in the Services*, p. 11 (American Soldiers). A New York state text is in the Halpert collections. For Ireland see *Handbook of Irish Folklore*, p. 641, No. 18, where twigs for baskets replace the annual crop of blackberries. Compare moose hide put on skinned horse; it develops mooselike characteristics. New York: Cutting, *Lore of an Adirondack County*, p. 27; also in Thompson, *Body, Boots and Britches*, pp. 307–8. Compare the saint's legend in which a flayed animal is brought to life with its skin restored: Loomis, *California Folklore Quarterly*, IV, 126–27. There is popular Irish tale worth mentioning in connection with this story. When Conan, follower of Finn MacCool, is torn away from a bench on which he has been magically fixed, the fresh hide of a sheep is slapped on his skinless thighs, or back, and grows there. Enough wool is shorn from him yearly to make stockings, or greatcoats, for the Fiana. Occasionally this is told without naming Conan as the victim. See Joyce, *Old Celtic Romances*, p. 379; *Béaloideas*, II, 226; III, 399, 455; VI, 30, 107; Jacobs, *Celtic Fairy Tales*, p. 139; Lady Wilde, *Ancient Legends, Mystic Charms, and Superstitions of Ireland*, p. 85; Kennedy,

Legendary Fictions of the Irish Celts, p. 208; Curtin, *Myths and Folk-Lore of Ireland,* pp. 231, 303; *Handbook of Irish Folklore,* p. 595. See also Curtin, *op. cit.,* pp. 123, 257–58, for stories of the Gruagach Gaire, who has the skin of a sheep or goat growing on his back. Without the sheepskin motif the tale is given in Campbell, *The Fians,* p. 74; Curtin, *Irish Folk-Tales,* pp. 122–23. Compare the whopper of the man scalped by Indians, healed by having a piece of dog's hide fixed over the wound: Botkin, *A Treasury of American Folklore,* pp. 567–68. (H.H.)

THE FELLOW THAT STOLE CORN

Told by Bob Wyrick, Eureka Springs, Ark., March, 1950. He heard it in the late 1890's, near Green Forest, Ark. This tale seems to be common in many parts of the South. It is told as true in Bryan and Rose's *Pioneer Families of Missouri* (St. Louis, 1876, p. 514). Compare "The Corn Thief, a Folk Anecdote," reported from Texas (*Publications of the Texas Folklore Society,* VII [1928], 78). A similar yarn which I found near Pineville, Mo., in the 1920's (*Funny Stories about Hillbillies,* Girard, Kan., 1944, p. 12) includes the spelling-bee wisecrack. (V.R.)

Botkin, *A Treasury of American Folklore,* pp. 413–14, gives the story of the corn thief from *Beyond Dark Hills,* by Jesse Stuart. A version from Warren county, Kentucky, appeared in Allan M. Trout's column, "Greetings," Louisville *Courier-Journal,* March 13, 1951. (H.H.)

JASPER ACTED KIND OF FOOLISH

Told by Jack Short, Galena, Mo., February, 1940. He said that a whole cycle of such "fool boy" stories went the rounds in the 1880's and 1890's. The bear-trap tale is repeated by a radio entertainer known as "Mirandy" (*Breezes from Persimmon Holler,* Hollywood, Calif., 1943, p. 89). "Mirandy" used to live near Galena, and it may be that she heard the story there, perhaps from Jack Short himself. (V.R.)

For the yarn about plowing to the cow or hog see Hudson, *Humor of the Old Deep South,* p. 452; Brendle and Troxell, *Pennsylvania German Folk Tales,* pp. 164–65, told as an Eileschpijjel (Eulenspiegel) story. Several unpublished texts of the story, told about the New York raftsman and trickster "Boney" Quillan, are in the Halpert collections. For the jest about covering a man's ears while he reads a letter so that he cannot hear it see C. Bancroft, "Cousin

Jack Stories from Central City," *Colorado Magazine,* XXI (1944), 53. (H.H.)

THE POPPET CAUGHT A THIEF

Told by Price Paine, Noel, Mo., October, 1923. He heard it in McDonald county, Mo., in the 1890's. The story was based, he said, upon something that happened near Fort Smith, Ark., in pioneer days. Fred High (*Forty-Three Years for Uncle Sam,* Berryville, Ark., 1949, p. 31) tells one about a preacher who put a rooster under a wash kettle, then made the suspects tap on the kettle. When the guilty man tapped, the rooster was supposed to crow three times. The rooster didn't crow, and all but one of the crowd had soot on their fingers. The man with clean hands was the culprit. (V.R.)

The variant form of the story—in which a rooster placed under a pot is used to catch the guilty man—is reported from Newfoundland, *Journal of American Folklore,* IX (1896), 147. It is also known in Mississippi, but as a Negro story. See Puckett, *Folk Beliefs of the Southern Negro,* pp. 281–82. (H.H.)

THE QUEEN'S WHITE GLOVE

Told by Franklin Allen, Eureka Springs, Ark., June, 1950. He got it from an old man in a mining camp near Joplin, Mo. I believe there is a parallel to this tale in some European collection, but have been unable to find it. (V.R.)

STRAWBERRIES ARE EASY WITCHED

Told by Rose O'Neill, Day, Mo., September, 1941. She had it from a neighbor. Miss O'Neill dictated the tale into my recorder and then revised the transcription, the better to reproduce her informant's way of speaking. Many elderly folk still believe that witches can put a spell upon growing crops, particularly strawberries and tomatoes; see my *Ozark Superstitions,* 1947, p. 271. The practice of killing strawberry plants with salt is well known. In May, 1933, Roy Williams of Goodman, Mo., was arrested "on a charge of salting an acre and a half of strawberries belonging to W. H. Anding." According to the Pineville, Mo., *Democrat,* "it appears that several hundred pounds of salt had been scattered over the patch, which not only destroyed the present crop but the plants as well." The Springfield, Mo., *Leader & Press* (May 20, 1936) carries a story about the scoundrel who sprayed Dr. L. L. Bryan's strawberry patch on Delaware Avenue with a salt solution, killing all the plants in a single day. (V.R.)

NAKED ABOVE THE WAIST

Told by a gentleman in southwest Missouri, near the Arkansas border, September, 1937. He wishes to remain anonymous. It may be that something like this really happened in one of the resort towns. Many old-timers have peculiar notions about what constitutes modest summer attire. It is said that a judge at Hardy, Ark., announced in 1935 that he would fine "any man who appears in public naked from the waist up." In the summer of 1936, on the door of the Adams Pharmacy in Noel, Mo., I saw and photographed a sign: MEN NAKED ABOVE WAIST NOT SERVED HERE. Tourists have told me of similar protests against swimming costumes and play suits in other Ozark villages. (V.R.)

THE STUPID SCHOOLMASTER

Told by Elbert Short, Crane, Mo., June, 1933. Mr. Short gave names and dates and said that he believed it to be true. County officials in Missouri and Arkansas assured me that such shenanigans were not uncommon a few years ago. I have known rural teachers who could scarcely read the headlines of an ordinary newspaper. (V.R.)

JOHNNY APPLESEED

Told by Wiley Burns, Joplin, Mo., May, 1931. He heard this version of the Appleseed story near Bentonville, Ark., in the early 1890's. Whether Jonathan Chapman ever visited the Ozark country is uncertain, but Allsopp (*Folklore of Romantic Arkansas,* 1931, II, 271–74) repeats a tradition that Appleseed wandered through both Missouri and Arkansas. See the "Folk Tale of Johnny Appleseed" in the *Missouri Historical Review,* XIX (1925), pp. 622–29. Collins (*Folk Tales of Missouri,* 1935, pp. 47–51) says that Johnny married an Indian woman and lived on Turkey Creek, in Ralls county, Mo. Compare the "Johnny Appleseed" story in *Arcadian Life* (Caddo Gap, Ark., Jan., 1936, p. 11). Otto Ernest Rayburn told me of a local belief that Johnny Appleseed came up White River and planted trees at Beaver, Ark.; he got the story from an Indian woman who said that Johnny slept in Counterfeiter's Cave, near Eureka Springs, Ark. Cf. *Ozark Guide,* Eureka Springs, Ark., Winter, 1949, p. 22. Many persons in Arkansas believe that the well-known "Jonathan" apple is named for Jonathan Chapman (*Arkansas Gazette,* Oct. 12, 1950). (V.R.)

THE SINGING TEACHER AND THE BEAR

Told by a farmer near Cyclone, Mo., November, 1930. He said the tale was widely known in the 1890's and often repeated by one of the Kelley boys, who used to run a store at Powell, Mo. Boys in the Ozarks throw stones with a force and accuracy astounding to city dwellers. There are many tall stories about it, of course. I reduced this one to a single paragraph in *We Always Lie to Strangers,* pp. 110–11. (V.R.)

This tale occurs in Chapter 4 of *The Travels of Baron Munchausen* (Broadway Translations). It is reported from oral tradition in New York and Wisconsin, and the Ozarks version demonstrates how widely the tale has spread. See Cutting, *Lore of an Adirondack County,* p. 26; Brown, *Bear Tales,* p. 3. (H.H.)

GEOMETRY IS WHAT DONE IT

Told by Ern Long, Joplin, Mo., August, 1931. Mr. Long thought that the story originated in one of the northwest Arkansas resort towns. The character of Tandy Simpson is perhaps related to Titanic Slim, a well-known gambler who flourished in the 1920's. His name was Alvin Clarence Thomas, and he grew up near Monett, Mo. Titanic Slim spent some time in Kansas City, Little Rock, Hot Springs, and Joplin, where he was famous for his freak bets. He once wagered that he could throw a pumpkin onto the roof of the Connor Hotel in Joplin, and won the bet by using a pumpkin about the size of a baseball. Newspaper files of the 1920's and 1930's are full of stories about him. He was held as a material witness in the Arnold Rothstein murder case in New York, about 1928. I last heard of Titanic Slim in 1936, when he returned to Monett, Mo., and told reporters he had decided to settle down and go into the oil business. (V.R.)

THE BROWN MARE

Told by Mrs. Rose Spaulding, Eureka Springs, Ark., July, 1950. She learned the song in Carroll county, Ark., about 1890, and heard the story told by relatives. The race was run in Newton county, Ark., in 1859, and the boy who rode the mare was Mrs. Spaulding's father. Mrs. Spaulding says that John Cecil became a

212

colonel in the Confederate Army, and his name was sometimes spelled Cecille. (V.R.)

SHE WOULDN'T BE A WITCH

Told by Mrs. Rose Spaulding, Eureka Springs, Ark., November, 1947. She had it from her neighbors in Newton county, Ark., about 1889. Mrs. Spaulding said that many people regarded it as a true story. The tale is known in Missouri, as well as Arkansas. Cf. W. L. Webb, "Burning Witches in Missouri," Kansas City *Post,* Kansas City, Mo., Jan. 16, 1916. (V.R.)

THE HEIRLOOM

Told by Franklin Allen, Eureka Springs, Ark., July, 1950. He heard the tale near Joplin, Mo., about 1915. (V.R.)

HOW THE STILL GOT BUSTED

Told by a gentleman in Bear Hollow, near Jane, Mo., August, 1929. He asked me not to publish his name. Explosions of stills, particularly those operated by amateurs in the Volstead era, were not uncommon. There is a brief description of this episode in my *The Ozarks* (1931, p. 230). I am personally acquainted with the central figure in this story, and I believe it is true in every essential detail. (V.R.)

THE LITTLE MAN AND THE GRANNY WOMAN

Told by Mrs. Rose Spaulding, Eureka Springs, Ark., August, 1950. She learned it from her grandfather in Carroll county, Ark., about 1890. (V.R.)

Motif F 372.1, "Fairies take human midwife to attend fairy woman." See also F 235.4.1, "Fairies made visible through use of ointment" (and following motifs in which magic soap, magic water, saliva, etc., replace "ointment"); F 361.3, "Fairies take revenge on person who spies on them." This legend is widespread in northern and western Europe. See the discussion in Hartland, *The Science of Fairy Tales,* Chapters 3–4. In most versions the midwife (sometimes just a nurse) does not see the fairies in their own shape until by accident or theft she gets some magic ointment (or salve or water, etc.) on one eye. She continues to have the power of seeing the fairies until she sees the fairy husband (usually) stealing in the market place. When she greets him, he finds out which eye has the power of seeing him and often blinds that eye completely. See Hunt, *Popular Romances of the West of England,* pp. 83–85; Curtin, *Tales of the Fairies and of the Ghost World,* pp. 42–45. (H.H.)

THE HORSELESS CARRIAGE

Told by Mrs. Mary Burke, Springfield, Mo., December, 1935. She had it from relatives in the backwoods of Christian county, Mo. The motor car came late to Missouri. In 1901, according to the State Historical Society, there were only two "horseless carriages" in Kansas City, and it was 1905 before one appeared at Columbia, the seat of the University of Missouri. Rufe Scott, of Galena, Mo., told me that he heard business men say seriously, about 1910, that the automobile would never be practical for this region "because there's too many stumps in the road." The possibility of hard-surface highways was not even considered in those days. Compare my *Funny Stories about Hillbillies,* p. 6. (V.R.)

OOLAH! OOLAH!

Told by Otto Ernest Rayburn, Eureka Springs, Ark., August, 1950. He had it from a judge in Jasper county, Mo. In my boyhood this story was always connected with the Populist agitators of Kansas, but later became attached to other politicians, such as Theodore Roosevelt. Now Bennett Cerf (*Saturday Review of Literature,* Oct. 28, 1950, p. 6) tells it as "the political anecdote of the year," with President Harry S. Truman as the central figure. Cerf credits the tale to Walter Richards, of Burbank, Calif. (V.R.)

THE FOOTLOOSE FAMILY

Told by Jack Short, Galena, Mo., February, 1940. He said that there were several such families near Hurley, Mo., in the 1890's, and recalled many similar stories. The yarn about chickens holding up their feet is widely distributed. I once told the tale to Frederick Simpich, who came down to write an article about the Ozarks for the *National Geographic.* He said the story had been known for centuries in Middle Europe, where it was attributed to certain tribes of Gypsies. Cf. my *Funny Stories from Arkansas,* Girard, Kan., 1943, p. 23. (V.R.)

For the jest of the chickens which expedite moving by lying down and putting up their feet to be tied see: Sandburg, *Abraham Lincoln; the Prairie Years,* I, 103, 288; Hertz, *Lincoln Talks,* p. 280;

Hulett, *Now I'll Tell One,* p. 96; Selby, *100 Goofy Lies,* p. 11; Botkin, *A Treasury of New England Folklore,* p. 735; Brewer, *Humorous Folk Tales of the South Carolina Negro,* p. 14. There is an unpublished New York text in the Halpert collections. (H.H.)

SHOES FOR THE KING

Told by Rose O'Neill, Day, Mo., February, 1941. She had it from an old gentleman named Cummins, who lived nearby. Miss O'Neill spoke into my recorder, but subsequently revised the transcript to reproduce Mr. Cummins' manner of speech. This story is evidently related to Hans Christian Andersen's familiar tale, a form of "The Luck-Bringing Shirt" mentioned by Stith Thompson (*The Folktale,* 1946, p. 143), who traces it through an Italian *novella* to a Greek legend about Alexander. Compare a modern literary version in Edwin Markham's poem "The Shoes of Happiness." (V.R.)

This is a version of Type 844, Motif N 135.3, "The luck-bringing shirt." See *Handbook of Irish Folklore,* p. 575. (H.H.)

JACK AND THE LITTLE BULL

Told by Mrs. Rose Spaulding, Eureka Springs, Ark., August, 1950. She heard her grandfather tell it in Carroll county, Ark., about 1890. (V.R.)

This tale is a curious combination of elements, chiefly Type 530, "The Princess on the Glass Mountain," plus a bull helper. The princess, with a gilded ball in her lap, sailing around in "some kind of an airship" is a delightful modern touch. This combination of elements, i.e., Type 530 plus the bull helper, is apparently also known in Virginia. Chase, *Jack Tales,* p. 190, mentions a fragmentary episode in which the king sets up "a greased plank beside a pole on top of which was a golden ball." He has omitted this episode from the composite text he published, pp. 21–30, in which the bull helper is combined with Type 511, "One-Eye, Two-Eyes, Three-Eyes." The latter combination (which I thought rare) is also found in Ireland: *Handbook of Irish Folklore,* pp. 614–15, No. 14. In my notes to the Chase version (pp. 189–90), I give some references to the animal helper found with various other tale types. To these add: MacManus, *In Chimney Corners,* pp. 1–19 (bull helper, ear "cornucopia," and belt of bull skin); MacManus, *The Donegal Wonder Book,* pp. 95–118 (sheep helper with ear "cornucopia"); Parsons, *Antilles,* III, 229 (which has a belt and key that obey orders and tie and choke a devil.) Although this tale seems "irregular" when checked against the Aarne-Thompson Type-Index, it suggests that the latter should be revised to incorporate as distinct types many tales found in the British-Irish-American tradition. This may be confirmed by checking, for example, the collections of Chase and Jacobs. (H.H.)

A COONBONE FOR LUCK

Told by a lady in Carroll county, Ark., July, 1950. I believe it is a wildly exaggerated account of a local man's experience. A coonbone is the dried *baculum* from the genitals of an adult male raccoon. Many old settlers carry coonbones as luck charms, believing that they somehow fortify the sexual powers. I have seen elderly sportsmen wearing gold-mounted coonbones on their watch chains. The best specimens look like polished ivory, and the oldtime jewelers call them "bone toothpicks." Dealers in Indian relics buy coonbones from trappers, drill a hole near the larger end, and sell them to the tourists as "Indian darning needles." (V.R.)

THE END OF THE BENDERS

Told by Farwell Gould, Pittsburg, Kan., April, 1930. He had this version of the Bender story from friends who lived near South Coffeyville, Okla., in the 1880's. Mr. Gould was personally acquainted with men who rode in pursuit of the Benders, and he was inclined to accept this tale as true. The Bender family ran a roadside tavern near Cherryvale, Kan., where they robbed and murdered a lot of people in the early 1870's. Eleven bodies were unearthed behind the tavern in 1873, but the Benders escaped into the Indian Territory. Rewards totaling $5,000 were posted, but the officers who pursued them returned empty-handed. Newspapers in Kansas City, St. Louis, and Chicago carried stories about the Benders in the spring of 1873, and much has been written about the case in later years. See a full-page Bender story, with many photographs, in the Kansas City *Journal-Post* (Jan. 24, 1932), also an article and letter in *Pic* magazine (Dec. 12, 1939, pp. 42–45; March 19, 1940, p. 52). Compare Allison Hardy's pamphlet *Kate Bender* (Girard, Kan., 1944), also Manley Wade Wellman's semi-fiction piece "The House by the Side of the Road" in *Short Stories,* Mar. 25, 1945, pp. 114–29. (V.R.)

For a discussion of facts and legends concerning the Benders

216

see Robert F. Scott, "What Happened to the Benders?" *Western Folklore,* IX (1950), 327–37. (H.H.)

THE THREE WISHES

Told by Lon Jordan, Farmington, Ark., December, 1941. "I changed this one a little," he said. "The ham was really stuck in the old woman's arse, but I put it down her throat instead. I know you don't want no vulgar talk on them phonograph records." (V.R.)

Type 750 A, Motif J 2074, "The transferred wish." Jacobs, *More English Fairy Tales,* No. 65; Harland and Wilkinson, *Lancashire Legends,* pp. 15–16; *Handbook of Irish Folklore,* p. 573. The tale was published in an undated Glasgow chap-book entitled: *Storys [sic] of Prince Lupin, Yellow Dwarf and The Three Wishes,* pp. 22–24, reprinted in Vol. III of John Cheap, *The Chapman's Library* (Glasgow, 1877–78). (H.H.)

TWO SEEDS IN THE SPIRIT

Told by Mrs. Ethel Barnes, Hot Springs, Ark., April, 1938. She had it from a relative who lived in Garland county, Ark., in the 1890's. This man had known several families of Two-Seed Baptists, and attended many of their meetings. Very few of the rural Baptists whom I interviewed would admit that they ever heard of the Two-Seeds-in-the-Spirit sect. But Harold Preece and Celia Kraft (*Dew on Jordan,* 1946, p. 108) say that the Two-Seeders had churches in Missouri shortly after the turn of the century and that there were "one or more congregations in the mountains of Arkansas" as recently as the early 1940's. I have no first-hand knowledge of Two-Seeder groups in the Ozark country, but men who should know say that the cult was still flourishing in the backwoods of Missouri, Arkansas, and Oklahoma about 1925. (V.R.)

The belief that Cain was the Devil's son was part of Hebrew rabbinical tradition. "All good souls are derived from Abel and all bad souls from Cain." See Baring-Gould, *Legends of the Patriarchs and Prophets,* chap. vi (various editions); O. F. Emerson, "Legends of Cain," *Publications of the Modern Language Association,* XXI (1906), 832–37. Emerson notes: "The devil origin of Cain was also a Manichaean heresy." Medieval legend also had the Devil as the father of evil children by an earthly mother. My unfamiliarity with the "folklore of the Bible" prevents me from stating whether or not the belief that each woman has two kinds of seed within her is old or not. (H.H.)

UNDER GRAVEL I DO TRAVEL

Told by Bob Wyrick, Eureka Springs, Ark., June, 1948. He heard it near Green Forest, Ark., about 1910. The rhyme in this story is an example of what Archer Taylor calls "neck-riddles." For information about this type of riddle see Halpert, "The Cante Fable in Decay," *Southern Folklore Quarterly,* V (1941), 197–200. (V.R.)

THE MARE'S NEST

Told by Lon Jordan, Farmington, Ark., December, 1941. Compare a Negro version in Allsopp's *Folklore of Romantic Arkansas* (1931, II, p. 173). See also my *Funny Stories about Hillbillies,* Girard, Kan., 1944, p. 12. (V.R.)

This is Type 1319, Motif J 1772.1, "Pumpkin thought to be an ass's egg," a tale well known both in Europe and the United States. See: Clouston, *The Book of Noodles,* pp. 37–38; Meier, *The Joke Tellers Joke Book,* p. 201. For versions collected in America see: Brendle and Troxell, *Pennsylvania German Folk Tales,* pp. 169–70; Harris, *Uncle Remus, His Songs and His Sayings,* pp. 10–11 (Southern Negro); *Southern Workman,* XXVIII, 192–93 and reprinted in *Journal of American Folklore,* XII, 226; Bacon and Parsons, *ibid.,* XXXV, 303 (Virginia; Negro); Boggs, *ibid.,* XLVII, 303 (North Carolina); Boggs, *ibid.,* XLVII, 303n (Mississippi); Fauset, *ibid.,* XL, 268 (Mississippi; Negro); Halpert, *Hoosier Folklore,* VII, 71 (Ohio); Brewster, *Folk-Lore,* L, 298 (Indiana); Federal Writers Project of the WPA, *Idaho Lore,* p. 131; Kirwan, *California Folklore Quarterly,* II, 29 (California; Armenian); Boatright, Publications of the Texas Folklore Society, XX, 11 (American Oilmen); Parsons, *Antilles,* III, 314 (Trinidad; Negro). See also: Waugh, *Journal of American Folklore,* XXXI, 78 (Ontario, Canada); Barbeau, *ibid.,* XXVIII, 94–95 (Wyandot Indians); *Béaloideas,* VII, 177 (Wales; mentioned); *Handbook of Irish Folklore,* p. 581; Jacobs, *More Celtic Fairy Tales,* pp. 111–12 (from the United States). (H.H.)

A NOTCH MARKS THE SPOT

Told by Mrs. Pearl Spurlock, Branson, Mo., who used to conduct parties of tourists through the Lake Taneycomo area. The date is missing from my record, but it must have been in the winter of 1934 or the spring of 1935. It is a very old "numbskull" story and

218

the basis of Til Eulenspiegel's famous joke on the men of Schoppen-stadt who hid their new bell in the sea. I published an Ozark version in *Funny Stories about Hillbillies* (Girard, Kan., 1944, pp. 20–21). As Brewster points out in the *Southern Folklore Quarterly,* XIV (1950), 100–2, the tale was featured in a Chicago *Tribune* comic strip as recently as Oct. 9, 1949. (V.R.)

This is Type 1278, Motif J 1922.1, "Marking the place on the boat." See: Clouston, *The Book of Noodles,* p. 99; Munchausen, *The Travels of Baron Münchausen,* p. 14; Moulton, *2500 Jokes for All Occasions,* No. 1938. For versions collected on this continent see: Boggs, *Journal of American Folklore,* XLVII, 302 (North Carolina); Parsons, *Folk-Lore of the Sea Islands, South Carolina,* p. 148 (Negro); Halpert, Mitchell, and Dickason, *Hoosier Folklore Bulletin,* I, 89 (Indiana); Waugh, *Journal of American Folklore,* XXXI, 78–79 (American Sailors); Waugh, *ibid.,* XXXI, 78 (Ontario, Canada). It is also told as a "little moron" story in: Brewster, *Hoosier Folklore Bulletin,* III, 17; Davidson, *Southern Folklore Quarterly,* VII, 101. (H.H.)

HE THROWED DOWN HIS GUN

Told by J. A. Sturges, Pineville, Mo., September, 1925. Judge Sturges heard the story in Newton county, Mo., about 1885. Some Oklahomans tell of frontier gunmen who could drop a six-shooter on the ground so that the impact would fire the weapon and the bullet would strike an enemy. The only printed reference to this that I have seen is in Dolph Shaner's *The Story of Joplin* (New York, 1948, p. 63). Shaner mentions a desperado from Granby, Mo., who "practiced throwing his gun down so the hammer would strike and discharge the gun. When in action the barrel would be pointed toward the intended victim." Shaner intimates that he saw the Granby man do this trick once, but the bullet missed its target. (V.R.)

JACK AND OLD TUSH

Told by Mrs. Rose Spaulding, Eureka Springs, Ark., September, 1950. She had it from her grandparents in Carroll county, Ark., about 1890. (V.R.)

This is the A form of Type 301, "The Three Stolen Princesses." It lacks the motif of the hero's betrayal by his treacherous companions, which is frequently found in this story. A North Carolina

219

version is in Chase, *Jack Tales,* pp. 106–13, for which I supplied chiefly British and Irish references (p. 194). To these add: Mac-Manus, *The Donegal Wonder Book,* pp. 207–30; Curtin, *Irish Folk-Tales,* pp. 14–24, and p. 159n; *Handbook of Irish Folklore,* p. 559; Claudel, *Journal of American Folklore,* LVIII, 210–12 (Louisiana; a version from a Spanish-speaking informant); Parsons, *Antilles,* III, 292–95, and see headnote for other references. (H.H.)

THE FIDDLER'S WIFE

Told by Farmer Goodwin, Joplin, Mo., February, 1930. He heard it in Little Rock, Ark., about 1895. Several persons have told me that a related piece was recited by a man named "Babe" Kerr, who used to run a saloon in Springfield, Mo. I have a similar story and song from Lewis Kelley, Cyclone, Mo., but parts of Mr. Kelley's version are unprintable. It appears that the tale was well known near Cyclone in the late 1880's. (V.R.)

Two North Carolina texts of this *cante* fable are given by Boggs, *Journal of American Folklore,* XLVII, 305, Version B. For two New Jersey variants with a tune, a fragmentary text from Brooklyn, N.Y., and some discussion see Halpert, *ibid.,* LV, 140–42. After my article appeared I received by mail three versions of the tale from different parts of the United States and Canada. Mr. Randolph's text demonstrates conclusively the wide distribution of the *cante fable* on this continent. Oddly enough, I have been unable to locate European parallels. (H.H.)

RICK TYLER AND THE LAWYER

Told by Jim Tooley, Grove, Okla., December, 1945. He mentioned it as something that happened recently in Newton county, Mo. I heard a slightly different version at Rolla, Mo., in 1934. An old gentleman at Mena, Ark., told a similar tale in 1937; he said it was regarded as a "new story" about 1898. (V.R.)

This is Type 1585, Motif K 1655, "The lawyer's mad client" (Pierre Pathelin). The story has been studied by T. E. Oliver, "Some Analogues of Maistre Pierre Pathelin," *Journal of American Folklore,* XXII (1909), 395–430. Some versions published in America are in: Brown, *Wit and Humor,* pp. 67–68; Landon, *Wit and Humor of the Age,* pp. 405–6; Botkin, *A Treasury of American Folklore,* p. 366 (from American sheepmen). Add: Parsons, *Antilles,* III, 329; *Handbook of Irish Folklore,* p. 584. (H.H.)

220

HOW BETSEY GOT DROWNDED

Told by Wythe Bishop, Fayetteville, Ark., December, 1941. Mr. Bishop had it from "a fellow that died drunk on a ten-pin alley in Eureka Springs" about 1900. Mr. Bishop knew many old songs, and I asked if there was a ballad about Betsey's death. He said that "circus clowns" used to feature such a song, but he had never bothered to learn it. The story is very close to the "Johnny Sands" ballad, common in the British Isles, as well as the United States. For Ozark versions of the song see Belden (*Ballads and Songs,* 1940, pp. 237–39); also my *Ozark Folksongs* (1950, IV, 246–49). (V.R.)

For tale versions see: Stewart, *Journal of American Folklore,* XXXII, 395–96 (South Carolina; Negro); Parsons, *Folk-Lore of the Sea Islands, South Carolina,* p. 88 (Negro); *Handbook of Irish Folklore,* p. 645, No. 72. (H.H.)

SCRATCHES ON THE BEDSTEAD

Told by Farwell Gould, Pittsburg, Kan., April, 1930. He had it from an Arkansawyer who moved to South Coffeyville, Okla., in 1902. James R. Masterson (*Tall Tales of Arkansaw,* 1943, pp. 235, 373) spins a similar yarn which he heard in 1931. He thinks that it is related to an item in the "Arkansaw Traveler" dialogue about the whiskey barrel with a spigot at both ends; the Squatter and his wife could sell each other drinks and pay cash every time, though they had but one coin between them. Dr. Masterson points out that the whiskey-barrel story was known in New York as early as 1753. Jack Carlisle (*Northwest Arkansas Times,* Fayetteville, Ark., Jan. 2, 1951) tells the story of John Turner and his son Walter, who alternately hired each other on a farm near Springdale, Ark. They took turns as landlord, and paid high wages, and both had a good living. "This has been going on for several years," writes Carlisle. "There must be a flaw somewhere, but it sounds like a good arrangement to me." During the Volstead era it was said that the citizens of a certain Missouri town were all bootleggers, whose only occupation was selling liquor to their fellow townsmen. I was told at the time that this crack derives from an old Irish wheeze about a village where the people supported themselves by doing each other's washing, but I have not seen the tale in print. (V.R.)

John Winthrop, in his *Journal* for April 13, 1645, notes the following: A master who had to sell a pair of oxen to pay his servant's wages, told him he could not afford to keep him. "The servant answered, he would serve him for more of his cattle. But how shall

221

I do (saith the master) when all my cattle are gone? The servant replied, you shall then serve me, and so you may have your cattle again." Quoted in Miller and Johnson, *The Puritans,* pp. 140–41. In the same vein, but even more exaggerated, Boatright cites in *Folk Laughter on the American Frontier,* p. 121, a Texas story of an old man and his sons who went to the barn on rainy days and traded coats with each other. They "often in this way made ten dollars each during the day." (H.H.)

THE PEA-GREEN JUG

Told by Mrs. Ethel Barnes, Hot Springs, Ark., March, 1938. She had it from people who lived in rural Garland county, Ark., about 1893. Mrs. Barnes said that her informants did not regard it as a true story. Tales of bottles and chests and wine casks that never need to be refilled are common in Ozark folklore. As recently as the autumn of 1950 our newspapers carried long stories about a rain barrel near Simmons, in Texas county, Mo., which was always full, whether it rained or not. Thousands of people drove out to see this barrel; many believe there is something supernatural about it, and some declare that the water has miraculous healing properties. For detailed accounts of this "mystery barrel" see the files of Missouri newspapers and Associated Press dispatches through late August and September, 1950. (V.R.)

See Motif D 1472.1.17, "Magic bottle supplies drink." (H.H.)

CONFEDERATES IN THE NEWS

Told by Farwell Gould, Pittsburg, Kan., June, 1929. He heard it in Greene county, Mo., in the early 1890's. Mr. Gould was a Union veteran, but he always told this story as if he were a "fire-eatin' Secesh" with an exaggerated Southern accent. He once dictated the tale to a stenographer, and I have used several sentences from the stenographer's transcript to fill gaps in Mr. Gould's oral narrative. It may be that something rather like this happened at the Wilson's Creek reunion, held in Springfield, Mo., Aug. 10, 1884. An unidentified newspaper clipping about this reunion mentions the "misunderstanding" featured in Mr. Gould's tale: "A gang of swindlers and confidence men followed the reunion. An old soldier was standing at the Square and St. Louis street when a dapper youth snatched his pocketbook and started off. The fellow was caught and arrested, as were several others. One of the local papers said that the thieves were 'confederates.' There was but one meaning of the

222

word confederate then, and another paper bitterly denounced the 'insult to the men who wore the gray.' Then it was explained that the word had no connection with the army of the South, but merely meant that the pickpockets were working together." As recently as 1930 I interviewed men in Springfield who remembered the incident. (V.R.)

THREE BLACK CATS

Told by Mrs. Marie Wilbur, Pineville, Mo., April, 1930. Mrs. Wilbur had it from an old woman in Searcy county, Ark., about 1912. She did not regard it as a Negro story. An almost identical tale was featured years ago by the Negro comedian Bert Williams and by many of his imitators. (V.R.)

This is a special form of the widespread story of the man who runs from a ghost or from talking animals or objects. It has also been used by stage comedians and newspaper cartoonists as "Wait Till Caleb (Martin) Comes." See Schermerhorn, *Schermerhorn's Stories,* p. 347. It has been reported principally from American Negro storytellers. See: Botkin, *A Treasury of American Folklore,* pp. 710–11; Jansen, *Hoosier Folklore Bulletin,* I, 78–79 (Virginia; told in Indiana); Cox, *Journal of American Folklore,* XLVII, 352–54 (West Virginia); Fauset, *ibid.,* XL, 258–59 (Alabama); Puckett, *Folk Beliefs of the Southern Negro,* p. 132 (Mississippi). (H.H.)

THE WOMEN SUCKED HIS BLOOD

Told by Elbert Short, Crane, Mo., June, 1933. He got it from some children near Marionville, Mo., in the early 1900's. The tale is evidently related to the ballad of "Sir Hugh" (Child 155). For local versions of this song see Belden (*Ballads and Songs,* 1940, pp. 69–73); also my *Ozark Folksongs,* I (1946), 148–51. (V.R.)

HOW JACK GOT HIS BIG FARM

Told by Lon Jordan, Farmington, Ark., December, 1941. He heard the tale near Fayetteville, Ark., in the early 1900's. It was supposed to be a true account, he said, of something that happened in Tennessee long ago. I played the recording for Wythe Bishop, an old-timer who had lived in Fayetteville many years. He said it was well known in his youth. "It sounds more reasonable than what you hear on the radio nowadays," said Mr. Bishop. (V.R.)

223

This belongs with stories under Motif K 527, "Escape by substituting person" in place of the intended victim. (H.H.)

HIRAM AIN'T HERE NO MORE

Told by Curt Boren, Bentonville, Ark., July, 1936. He got the story from an old man in a roadside tavern near Caverna, Mo. The detail about the Devil who "threw no shadow and left no tracks" is common. Cf. my *Ozark Ghost Stories* (1944, p. 20), also *Ozark Superstitions* (1947, p. 276). (V.R.)

The belief that the fiddle is the Devil's instrument or that "the Devil's in the fiddle" is widely held in Northwestern Europe, as well as in the United States. He gives great skill in playing the fiddle or other instruments to anyone who asks, and a crossroads is a favorite rendezvous. All he demands in payment is the musician's soul, and great violinists of the past, such as Paganini and Ole Bull, were believed to have made such deals. Sometimes instead of giving skill directly he merely enchants the musician's instrument, but inevitably the owner's playing makes him the best musician in his community. See, for example, "Balaam Foster's Fiddle," Botkin, *A Treasury of American Folklore,* pp. 727–31. Certain musical pieces are believed to have been learned from the devil; in New Jersey the well-known American fiddle piece "The Devil's Dream" is said to have been learned in this way. Historically speaking, much of the Devil's power and interest in music is comparatively recent. He has been substituted for various local deities or supernatural figures, such as fairies, elves, and water spirits, about whom similar legends were told. They gave such power as a free gift or in return for a sacrifice. When Christianity became dominant, the priests called all local demons "devils" and attached the Christian belief of the Devil's interest in acquiring human souls for his kingdom to any dealings with these local supernatural figures. See Halpert, "The Devil and the Fiddle," *Hoosier Folklore Bulletin,* II, 39–43, for a discussion and references on this subject. Dancing was also an interest of local supernaturals, e.g., fairies and elves, and likewise acquired devilish connections. There are many stories of the Devil's appearance at dances; and the dancing of the Devil and his attendant witches and imps was a feature of the "Witches' Sabbath." Sometimes the Devil himself played the fiddle or other instrument at such functions. The Devil, if invoked, has also been known to play at a human party, especially if the dancing continued past midnight on Saturday. In other stories a fiddler would occasionally play while the devil did a solo dance. In a New York legend in the Halpert collections a fiddler is engaged by the Devil to play for a dance. After the dance the whole crew disappears, and the fiddler soon dies. (H.H.)

THE SHERIFF AND THE GALLOWS

Told by an old gentleman in Stone county, Mo., February, 1940. He had been intimately associated with some of the parties concerned. Legal executions in Missouri nowadays are carried out at Jefferson City, by a professional killer. But a few years ago criminals were hanged in the county where the crime was committed. In 1936 I was at Galena, Mo., when the sheriff hanged a murderer named "Red" Jackson, on a homemade gallows. (V.R.)

SI BURTON'S LITTLE BLACK DOG

Told by Mrs. Marie Wilbur, Pineville, Mo., November, 1929. She had it from Mrs. Lucinda Mosier, also of Pineville. I published a version of the story in *From an Ozark Holler* (1933, pp. 79–84). It was known to many old residents of southwest Missouri in the 1920's. (V.R.)

An unpublished Tennessee legend in the Halpert collections has a faithful dog which mourned at the side of its Negro master after the latter was killed by a Union soldier. Some time later the murderer was found dead, with the marks of a dog's teeth in his throat. After that the dog was occasionally seen, always in pursuit of a Union soldier. A Southern Appalachian legend mentions a goblin dog which hunted a man to death: *Journal of American Folklore,* VII, 110. This ghostly white dog had not been a live dog, but only appeared to revenge the murder of a Negro woman. We thus have three versions of the legend of a dog revenger: in Tennessee, the live dog; in the Ozarks, the ghost of a slain dog; in the Appalachians, a goblin dog that had never been alive. (H.H.)

WHITE-BEAR WHITTINGTON

Told by Mrs. Rose Spaulding, Eureka Springs, Ark., October, 1950. She had it from her grandparents about 1890. (V.R.)

This is Type 425 A, "The Monster (Animal) as Bridegroom," but the husband enchanted into animal form has here been rationalized into a husband who always wears a white bearskin coat. Even more curious is the North Carolina version given by Carter, *Journal of American Folklore,* XXXVIII, 357–59, where the husband is "Whiteberry Whittington" and no trace remains of his animal character. Other American versions include: Gardner, pp. 112–14 (New York; the husband is a wolf); Chase, *Grandfather Tales,* pp. 52–64 (a Virginia–North Carolina composite). Gardner, *Folklore from the Schoharie Hills, New York,* pp. 114–18, discusses British-Irish versions of the tale and gives several parallels. Her reference (p. 116) to Mabel Peacock's text "from County Leitrim" should read "from Lincolnshire." Add to her notes: *Handbook of Irish Folklore,* p. 562; Jacobs, *More English Fairy Tales,* pp. 20–27 (No. XLVIII), p. 243*n.* Mr. Jacobs' text is adapted from Chambers, *Popular Rhymes of Scotland,* pp. 95–99, who also gives another version, pp. 99–101. The latter text was reprinted in Halliwell, *Popular Rhymes and Nursery Tales,* pp. 52–55. In these Lowland Scottish texts, as in the Jamaica one in Beckwith, *Jamaica Anansi Stories,* pp. 130–31, the enchanted husband is a bull. He is a bluebird in Parsons, *Antilles,* III, 233. A confused New England story has several elements of this tale, e.g., the enchanted prince in the form of a bull, but the motivation has been lost. See Johnson, *What They Say in New England,* pp. 256–58. Most versions have kept the *cante fable* element, i.e., the song in the story. Only Beckwith gives the tune of the woman's song. (H.H.)

THE MARE WITH THE FALSE TAIL

Told by Martin Travis, Joplin, Mo., December, 1926. He says it was well known along the Missouri-Oklahoma border in the early days. Lucile Morris (Springfield, Mo., *News & Leader,* Aug. 5, 1945) prints a similar story, placing it at Springfield in the middle 1890's. Some traders had a mule, she writes, "and they cut off his tail and fastened it to the harness. They would sell the mule and then take off the harness, saying that the tail belonged with the harness. The victim would pay them a handsome sum to trade back." (V.R.)

BIBLIOGRAPHY OF WORKS CITED

Aarne, Antti, and Stith Thompson, The Types of the Folk-Tale. Helsinki, 1928. Folklore Fellows Communications, No. 74. Cited as: Type.

Adams, E. C. L., Congaree Sketches. Chapel Hill, 1927.

Addy, Sidney Oldall, Household Tales with Other Traditional Remains. London and Sheffield, 1895.

Aikman, Duncan, Calamity Jane and the Lady Wildcats, New York, 1927.

Allsopp, Fred W., Folklore of Romantic Arkansas. 2 vols. New York, 1931.

Austin, Mary, Earth Horizon. New York, 1932.

Baring-Gould, S., Legends of the Patriarchs and Prophets. New York, n.d.

Baskervill, Charles Read, The Elizabethan Jig. Chicago, 1929.

Beckwith, Martha Warren, Jamaica Anansi Stories. New York, 1924. Memoirs of the American Folklore Society, Vol. XVII.

Belden, H. M., Ballads and Songs. Columbia, Mo., 1940.

Benton, Thomas Hart, An Artist in America. New York, 1937.

Blakley, James W., Tall Tales. Franklin, Ohio, and Denver, Colo., 1936.

Boatright, Mody C., Folk Laughter on the American Frontier. New York, 1949.

—— Tall Tales from Texas. Dallas, Texas, 1934.

Botkin, B. A., A Treasury of American Folklore. New York, 1944.

—— A Treasury of New England Folklore. New York, 1947.

—— A Treasury of Southern Folklore. New York, 1949.

Brendle, Thomas R., and William S. Troxell, Pennsylvania German Folk Tales, Legends, Once-Upon-a-Time Stories, Maxims, and Sayings. Norristown, Pa., 1944.

Brewer, J. Mason, Humorous Folk Tales of the South Carolina Negro. Orangeburg, S.C., 1945.

Brown, Charles E., Bear Tales. Madison, Wis., 1944.

Brown, Marshall, Wit and Humor. Chicago, 1880.

Bryan, William S., and Robert Rose, Pioneer Families of Missouri. St. Louis, 1876.

227

Call, Cora Pinkley, Pioneer Tales of Eureka Springs, Arkansas. Eureka Springs, Ark., 1930.

Campbell, J. F., Popular Tales of the West Highlands. 4 vols. Paisley, 1890–93.

Campbell, John Gregorson, Clan Traditions and Popular Tales of the Western Highlands and Islands. London, 1895. Waifs and Strays of Celtic Tradition, Argyllshire Series, Vol. V.

—— The Fians. London, 1891. Waifs and Strays of Celtic Tradition, Argyllshire Series, Vol. IV.

Chambers, Robert, Popular Rhymes of Scotland. London and Edinburgh, 1870.

Chase, Richard, Grandfather Tales. Boston, 1948.

—— The Jack Tales; With an appendix compiled by Herbert Halpert. Cambridge, 1943.

Child, Francis James, The English and Scottish Popular Ballads. 5 vols. Boston and New York, 1882–98.

Clark, Thomas D., The Rampaging Frontier. Indianapolis and New York, 1939.

Clouston, W. A., The Book of Noodles. London, 1888.

Collins, Earl A., Folk Tales of Missouri. Boston, 1935.

Conway, Moncure, Demonology and Devil-Lore. New York, 1879.

Croy, Homer, What Grandpa Laughed At. New York, 1948.

Curtin, Jeremiah, Irish Folk-Tales; ed. by Séamus Ó Duilearga. Dublin, 1943.

—— Myths and Folk-Lore of Ireland. Boston, 1890.

—— Tales of the Fairies and the Ghost World. London, 1895.

Cutting, Edith E., Lore of an Adirondack County. Ithaca, N.Y., 1944.

Dasent, G., Tales from the Fjeld. New York, n.d.

Davidson, [Sgt.] Bill, Tall Tales They Tell in the Services. New York, 1943.

Dorrance, Ward Allison, We're from Missouri. Richmond, Mo., 1938.

Dorson, Richard M., Jonathan Draws the Long Bow. Cambridge, Mass., 1946.

Dunckel, John, The Mollyjoggers. Springfield, Mo., n.d.

Eddy, Mary O., Ballads and Songs from Ohio. New York, 1939.

Edwards, John N., Shelby and His Men; or, The War in the West. Cincinnati, 1867.

Fauset, Arthur Huff, Folklore from Nova Scotia. New York, 1931. Memoirs of the American Folklore Society, Vol. XXIV.

228

Gardner, Emelyn E., Folklore from the Schoharie Hills. New York. Ann Arbor, 1937.

Gaskins, John, Life and Adventures. Eureka Springs, Ark., 1893.

Gomme, Alice Bertha, The Traditional Games of England, Scotland and Ireland. 2 vols. London, 1894–98.

Halliwell, James Orchard, Popular Rhymes and Nursery Tales. London, 1849.

Handbook of Irish Folklore, see Ó Súilleabháin, Seán.

Hardy, Allison, Kate Bender, the Kansas Murderess. Girard, Kan., 1944.

Harland, John, and T. T. Wilkinson, Lancashire Legends, Traditions, Pageants, Sports &c. London, 1882.

Harmon, S. W., Hell on the Border. Ft. Smith, Ark., 1899.

Harris, Joel Chandler, Nights with Uncle Remus. Boston and New York, 1920.

—— Uncle Remus; His Songs and His Sayings. New York, 1885.

Hartland, Edwin Sidney, The Science of Fairy Tales. 2d ed. London, 1925.

Hazlitt, W. Carew, ed., A Hundred Mery Talys. London, 1864. Shakespeare Jest-Books, Vol. I.

—— Tales and Legends of National Origin. London and New York, 1892.

Hertz, Emanuel, Lincoln Talks. New York, 1939.

High, Fred, Forty-Three Years for Uncle Sam. Berryville, Ark., 1949.

Hogue, Wayman, Back Yonder. New York, 1932.

Hudson, Arthur Palmer, Humor of the Old Deep South. New York, 1936.

Hulett, O. C., Now I'll Tell One. Chicago, 1935.

Hunt, Robert, Popular Romances of the West of England. London, 1881.

Hurston, Zora Neale, Mules and Men. Philadelphia and London, 1935.

Hyatt, Harry Middleton, Folk-Lore from Adams County, Illinois. New York, 1935.

Jacobs, Joseph, Celtic Fairy Tales. New York and London, n.d.

—— English Fairy Tales. 2d ed. New York and London, 1893.

—— More Celtic Fairy Tales. New York and London, n.d.

—— More English Fairy Tales. New York and London, n.d.

Johnson, Clifton, What They Say in New England. Boston, 1896.

Joyce, P. W., Old Celtic Romances. London, 1879.

Kennedy, Patrick, Legendary Fictions of the Irish Celts. London, 1866.

Landon, Melville D., Wit and Humor of the Age. Chicago, 1901.

McAtee, W. L., Nomina Abitera. Chicago, 1945.

MacDougall, James, and George Calder, Folk Tales and Fairy Lore in Gaelic and English. Edinburgh, 1910.

MacKenzie, W. R., Ballads and Sea Songs from Nova Scotia. Cambridge, Mass., 1928.

MacManus, Seumas, The Donegal Wonder Book. Philadelphia and New York, 1926.

—— In Chimney Corners. New York, 1899.

Masterson, James R., Tall Tales of Arkansaw. Boston, 1943.

Meier, Frederick, The Joke Tellers Joke Book. Philadelphia, 1944.

Milburn, George, Oklahoma Town. New York, 1931.

—— Die Stadt Oklahoma. Berlin, 1932.

Miller, Perry, and Thomas H. Johnson, The Puritans. New York, etc., 1938.

Mirandy (pseud.), Breezes from Persimmon Holler. Hollywood, Calif., 1943.

Montgomerie, Norah, and William Montgomerie, Scottish Nursery Rhymes. London, 1947.

Motif, see Thompson, Stith, Motif-Index of Folk-Literature.

Moulton, Powers, 2500 Jokes for All Occasions. Philadelphia, 1942.

Münchausen, Baron, The Travels of Baron Münchausen; ed. by William Rose. London and New York, n.d. Broadway Translations.

Neely, Charles, and John Webster Spargo, Tales and Songs of Southern Illinois. Menasha, Wis., 1938.

New Hampshire's Daughters, Folk-Lore Committee, Folklore Sketches and Reminiscences of New Hampshire Life. Boston, 1910.

Norwood, Hal L., Just a Book. Mena, Ark., 1938.

Ó Súilleabháin, Seán, A Handbook of Irish Folklore. Dublin, 1942. Cited as Handbook of Irish Folklore.

Ozark Guide. Eureka Springs, Ark. Several issues of this quarterly magazine are cited in the notes.

Parsons, Antilles, see Parsons, Elsie Clews, Folk-Lore of the Antilles.

Parsons, Elsie Clews, Folk-Lore from the Cape Verde Islands. 2 vols. Cambridge, Mass., and New York, 1923. Memoirs of the American Folklore Society, Vol. XV.

—— Folk-Lore of the Antilles, French and English. 3 vols. New

York, 1933, 1936, 1943. Memoirs of the American Folklore Society, Vol. XXVI. Cited as Parsons, *Antilles.*

—— Folk-Lore of the Sea Islands, South Carolina. Cambridge, Mass., and New York, 1923. Memoirs of the American Folklore Society, Vol. XVI.

Pontoppidan, Erich, The Natural History of Norway. 2 vols. 1755.

Preece, Harold, and Celia Kraft, Dew on Jordan. New York, 1946.

Puckett, Newbell Niles, Folk Beliefs of the Southern Negro. Chapel Hill, 1926.

Randolph, Vance, From an Ozark Holler. New York, 1933.

—— Funny Stories about Hillbillies. Girard, Kan., 1944.

—— Funny Stories from Arkansas. Girard, Kan., 1943.

—— Ozark Folksongs. 4 vols., Columbia, Mo., 1946–50.

—— Ozark Ghost Stories. Girard, Kan., 1944.

—— Ozark Mountain Folks. New York, 1932.

—— The Ozarks. New York, 1931.

—— Ozark Superstitions. New York, 1947.

—— We Always Lie to Strangers. New York, 1951.

Rascoe, Burton, Belle Starr. New York, 1941.

Rayburn, Otto Ernest, Ozark Country. New York, 1941.

Rayburn, Otto Ernest, ed., *Ozark Life* (Kingston, Ark.), Feb. 9, 1929.

Risley, Eleanor, An Abandoned Orchard. Boston, 1932.

Rotunda, D. P., Motif-Index of the Italian Novella in Prose. Bloomington, 1942.

Sandburg, Carl, Abraham Lincoln: the Prairie Years. New York, 1926.

Schermerhorn, James, Schermerhorn's Stories. New York, 1928.

Selby, E. E., 100 Goofy Lies. Decatur, Ill., c. 1939.

Shackleford, William Yancey, Belle Starr, the Bandit Queen. Girard, Kan., 1943.

Shaner, Dolph, The Story of Joplin. New York, 1948.

Sharp, Cecil, English Folksongs from the Southern Appalachians. 2 vols. London, 1932.

—— Folk-Songs from Somerset. London, 1904.

Skinner, Charles M., Myths and Legends of Our Own Land. 2 vols. Philadelphia and London, 1896.

Stapleton, Isaac, Moonshiners in Arkansas. Independence, Mo., 1948.

Swainson, Charles, The Folk Lore and Provincial Names of British Birds. London, 1866.

Taliaferro, H. E., Fisher's River Scenes and Characters. New York, 1859.

Thompson, Harold W., Body, Boots and Britches. Philadelphia, 1940.

Thompson, Stith, The Folktale. New York, 1946.

—— Motif-Index of Folk-Literature. 6 vols. Bloomington, Ind., 1932–36. Cited as Motif.

Type, *see* Aarne and Thompson.

United States, Work Projects Administration, Federal Writers' Project. Idaho Lore. Caldwell, Idaho, 1939.

United States, Works Progress Administration, Federal Writers' Project in Indiana. Hoosier Tall Stories. N.p., 1937.

Wagner, Constance, Sycamore. New York, 1950.

Weeks, Raymond, The Hound-Tuner of Callaway. New York, 1927.

White, Newman Ivey, and others, "The Frank C. Brown Collection of North Carolina Folklore," in "Folktales and Legends," ed. by Stith Thompson, Durham, North Carolina, 1952, I, 619–707.

White, William Allen, Autobiography. New York, 1946.

Wilde, Lady, Ancient Legends, Mystic Charms, and Superstitions of Ireland. Boston, 1888.

Williams, Alfred, Folk-Songs of the Upper Thames. London, 1923.

Wilson, Charles Morrow, Backwoods America. Chapel Hill, N.C., 1934.

Wilson, Edmund, Memoirs of Hecate County. New York, 1946.

Wolford, Leah Jackson, Play-Party in Indiana. Indianapolis, Ind., 1916.

Yates, Floyd, Chimney Corner Chats. Springfield, Mo., 1944.